Christa didn't want to feel for Ryder...

She didn't want to empathize with a man who was turning her world upside down. But she was drawn to him in spite of trying to hold back. "We should talk about the project after I've asked my father a few things," she said. "Though he probably won't change my mind about this new highway. Or keep me from fighting it."

"I'm happy to discuss it with you anytime." His eyes met hers, and she read a kaleidoscope of emotions in their depths–determination, sympathy and maybe even affection. She had to look away. She was afraid of what he might read in her eyes.

"Just remember, Christa. I'm not out to hurt you, or your family, or anyone in this town. I really do want to make this work for everyone's benefit."

His words sent a shiver of apprehension up her spine. Wasn't there a saying about guilty people who protested too much?

Dear Reader,

My family moved around fairly often when I was a child, which is maybe why I'm drawn to stories of families who have deep roots in a place. How wonderful to know that, no matter how far afield you roamed, you could always come back to a place where almost everything you looked at reminded you of beloved family members and family history. When everything else in life is in upheaval, that kind of home is one thing you can depend on.

But of course, things change, and home doesn't always stay the same. My heroine, Christa, has to cope with some big changes in this story. To me, big changes can be the perfect catalyst for romance. The right person comes along and helps you to be a stronger, better person. Ryder helps Christa, but she teaches him a lot, too, about taking risks and holding on to the things that really matter. Together, they're going to write their own definition of the perfect home.

I hope you enjoy Ryder and Christa's story. I'd love to hear your own stories of home. You can contact me online at www.cindimyers.com, on Facebook at facebook.com/authorcindimyers or on Twitter @ CMyersTex. Or write to me in care of Harlequin Books.

All the best,

Cindi Myers

HARLEQUIN HEARTWARMING

Cindi Myers

What She'd Do for Love

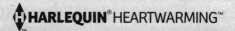

Recycling programs
for this product may
not exist in your area.

ISBN-13: 978-0-373-36680-4

WHAT SHE'D DO FOR LOVE

Copyright © 2014 by Cynthia Myers

Printed in U.S.A.

CINDI MYERS

is an author of more than fifty novels. When she's not crafting new romance plots, she enjoys skiing, gardening, cooking, crafting and daydreaming. A lover of small-town life, she lives with her husband and two spoiled dogs in the Colorado mountains.

Books by Cindi Myers

HARLEQUIN HEARTWARMING

4–HER COWBOY SOLDIER

HARLEQUIN INTRIGUE

1475–ROCKY MOUNTAIN REVENGE
1482–ROCKY MOUNTAIN RESCUE

HARLEQUIN SUPERROMANCE

1498–A SOLDIER COMES HOME
1530–A MAN TO RELY ON
1548–CHILD'S PLAY
1612–THE FATHER FOR HER SON
1643–HER MOUNTAIN MAN
1667–DANCE WITH THE DOCTOR

HARLEQUIN AMERICAN ROMANCE

1182–MARRIAGE ON HER MIND
1199–THE RIGHT MR. WRONG
1259–THE MAN MOST LIKELY
1268–THE DADDY AUDITION
1287–HER CHRISTMAS WISH

For Katie

CHAPTER ONE

THE CLOSER SHE drove to her hometown of Cedar Grove, Texas, the more anxious Christa Montgomery was to be home. She'd fought the idea of moving back to the family ranch, even temporarily, but losing a job she'd loved hadn't left her with many options. With only a few more miles to go, she had a hard time keeping to the speed limit. All she wanted was a hug from her father, homemade cookies from her mother, and the comfort of her parents' love and faith in her. With all the upheaval in her life of late, she needed the stability of home. Surrounded by their love and a familiar landscape, she'd regroup and find her feet again.

Her heartbeat sped up as she approached the sign for Cedar Grove town limits. She gripped the steering wheel more tightly and leaned forward, anxious for the first glimpse of the place where she'd grown up. The demands of working at one of the top marketing firms in Houston had kept her away except for brief holiday visits, which she mostly spent at the family ranch.

Elation turned to dismay, however, as she guided her car down the town's main street. What had once been a lively hub of activity was now almost deserted. She counted three For Sale signs in the first block. The grocery store was empty, as was the office supply store, Mavis Butler's dress shop, and the bookstore.

She knew, of course, that the economic recession and continued drought had hit the area hard, but she'd never expected this. The town where she'd gone to school, sat through movies with her friends and whiled away hours at the diner was practically a ghost town. The businesses that were left looked forlorn, windows dusty, the signs faded.

She drove on, out of town and onto the farm-to-market road that led to her family's ranch, the Rocking M. She relaxed when she spotted the white fencing that marked the beginning of her father's property, the paint fresh and crisp. A row of survey stakes topped with orange plastic streamers that snapped in the warm spring wind traced a line just inside the fence. Was her father planning to move the fence line?

A few minutes later she turned the car into the gravel drive beneath the welded iron archway with the Rocking M brand at its center. In the pasture beside the drive a few Black Angus cattle crowded around a metal stock tank beneath the gently turning blades of the windmill that pumped water to keep the tank filled. She looked for, but didn't see Duncan and Rodrigo, the two cowboys who helped her father.

When she reached the house, she parked the car in the shade of the tall oak that had once held her tire swing. She sat for a moment and studied the house, with its low, sprawling profile and front and side porches. Compared to the trendy, modern townhomes and mansions of the city suburbs, the house was sadly out of date, and much smaller than she remembered from her childhood. But none of that mattered. This was still her favorite place in the world. No matter how far away her life took her, no matter how many changes she experienced, she'd always feel grounded here, in this place that always remained the same.

She waited, but the front door didn't

spring open, and her parents didn't rush to greet her. She didn't even hear the dog barking. Maybe she should have called ahead, but she'd wanted to surprise them—and to avoid all the uncomfortable explanations about why she was here. Those would come later, when she was with them and talking came easier.

Her father's truck sat beneath a cottonwood her grandfather had planted, her mother's SUV nosed in beside it. Maybe Mom and Dad were riding on another part of the ranch. They'd return soon and Christa would be there—unexpectedly—to greet them. She collected her suitcase from the trunk of her sedan, leaving the boxes of books and other items for later. At the front door she hesitated, wondering if she should knock, then decided that was silly and let herself in. "Dad! Mom! It's me, Christa!"

The frantic scramble of toenails on the hardwood floor signaled the arrival of Jet, her parents' elderly Jack Russell terrier. Though he was growing deaf and slowing down, he still greeted her enthusiastically, jumping up and down on stiff legs and letting out excited yips. She rubbed his ears and patted his back. "Oh, Jet, it's good to see you, too."

"Christa? Is that you?" Her father, his voice hoarse from years of shouting at cows and cowboys over the howl of wind or the drone of machinery, emerged from the back of the house. Dressed in faded jeans and a gray snap-button shirt with a patch on one elbow, he looked more like a down-on-his-heels ranch hand than a prosperous ranch owner. His hair, which had more silver in it than she remembered, curled up at his frayed shirt collar, and needed combing. She stared. Had she woke him from a nap? In the middle of the day?

Her father's gaze dropped to the suitcase in her hand, then back to her face. "What are you doing here, honey?" he asked.

Not the enthusiastic welcome she'd expected. Her stomach tightened. Yes, she should have called ahead. She should have thought this out more. But she'd given up her apartment in Houston and put her furniture in storage. Only the thought of coming home, of being taken care of for a little while so she could regain her strength, had kept her from falling apart. "I've come home, Dad," she said. "Just for a little while."

His eyes narrowed and his expression hardened. "Who have you been talking to?"

"No one." She felt like a kid again, caught joy-riding on the tractor, or staying out past curfew. She half-way expected her dad to tell her how disappointed he was in her and to sentence her to mucking out horse stalls every Saturday for the next month. "I lost my job. Pemberton Professionals laid off one-quarter of their employees and I was one of them. I thought...I thought I could stay here a while, until I decided what to do next."

"Aw, honey." Dad rubbed his jaw, his hand scraping against a day's growth of beard. "You know your mom and I are always glad to see you."

Except he didn't sound very glad. "Where is Mom?" Christa asked. Suddenly, she wanted nothing in the world as much as a hug from her mother.

"She's resting. You can see her later."

"Bud?" Her mother's voice, sounding old and tired, interrupted them. "Who's there?"

Not waiting for her dad to intervene, Christa abandoned the suitcase and, with Jet on her heels, headed down the hallway that led to her old room on one side, with her parents' room at the end. The flowered carpet runner that stretched down the hall muffled her footsteps. When she reached the partially open door to her parents' room, she forced a cheerful smile to her face and took a deep breath. Her mother would be glad to see her, and Mom would have some reasonable explanation for Dad's behavior. Then again, what was Mom doing in bed in the middle of the day? Maybe they had been up all night with a sick calf, or any of the other chores that could distract a rancher.

Her mother sat propped in bed, looking a little pale, but otherwise okay. Jet hopped onto the bed and curled up beside his mistress. "Mom, is something wrong?" Christa asked.

"I'm just resting my eyes." Mom sat up straighter against the piled pillows and fixed Christa with the same look with which she'd questioned bad grades or poor choices in boyfriends. "What are you doing here in the middle of a work week?"

Christa sat on the edge of the bed. Though she'd rehearsed this conversation over and over on the drive up from Houston, and in the days before that, now that the moment was here her carefully prepared words deserted her. "I got laid off and between my student loan payments and my car payments things are really tight right now. I was hoping I could stay here a few months—just until I can get my life back together."

Mom's gaze darted to Dad, who had followed Christa into the room and stood in the doorway, his still-broad shoulders filling the frame. "Of course you can stay," Mom said. "Your old room is just like you left it."

"Are you sure everything is okay?" Christa asked. "You and Dad don't seem very happy to see me."

"You just caught us by surprise," Mom said. "Of course we're very happy to have you home."

"Are you sure? I feel like I caught you at a bad time. Why are you in bed? Are you sick or something?"

"She'll be fine. She got too tired yesterday, helping me move cattle. That's all." Her father's tone was brusque, but the tenderness in his expression when he looked at his wife made Christa's eyes sting. Something was going on here—some silent message passing between husband and wife in a code she couldn't break.

"Then I'd better let you rest." She stood

and moved toward the door. Jet looked up and thumped his tail, as if to say "Don't worry, I'll look after her," then laid his head back on his paws and closed his eyes. Father and daughter tiptoed from the room, and he shut the door softly behind them.

But Christa couldn't as easily shut the door on her worries. Her mother was one of the most vibrant, active women she knew. Adele Montgomery had spent a lifetime riding horses, hauling hay, cooking for cowboys, and managing the Rocking M alongside her husband. To see her in bed in the middle of the day had been more unsettling than Christa could have imagined. "Are you sure she's okay?" she asked.

"That's enough now, Christa. She'll be fine." Dad sank into the leather recliner that over the years had formed itself to the shape of his body. Christa sat on the sofa across from him. "Tell me the truth about what's going on with you," Dad said. "Are you broke? Do you need money?"

"I still have a little left in savings. Staying here will allow me to stretch that out."

"So Pemberton just let you go?"

"They let a lot of people go." She struggled not to squirm under her father's hard gaze. "I didn't have a lot of seniority, so I got the ax." Even though she knew losing her job wasn't her fault, the loss hurt.

He nodded. "Times are hard all over. They say the economy's picking up, but I think it's like one of those big cruise ships—takes a while to turn it around. You'll find another job."

Absolutely she would—as soon as she worked up enough nerve to send out some applications. The layoff had been such a paralyzing blow all she could think to do was to come home. Here, she was sure she'd find the strength to recover and get on with her life. She just hadn't expected things to feel so different in a place that had always been familiar. "Speaking of the economy, what's going on in town?" she asked. "I was shocked when I drove through—so many closed businesses."

"People would rather shop in the city these days," Dad said. "Between the drought and folks having a tough time financially, it's been a real challenge for some to hang on."

"Maybe some new businesses will come in," she said.

He shook his head. "I doubt it. The state's going to build a new highway that bypasses

Cedar Grove and offers a more direct route into Dallas."

Why hadn't Dad mentioned this in one of her weekly calls home? "When did this happen?" she asked.

"Oh, they decided it months ago," he said.

"You never said anything."

"I didn't think it would interest you. After all, you don't live here anymore."

"But this will always be my home. Of course it matters to me. How can they just decide to divert traffic that way? They must know how much it will hurt the town."

He shrugged. "It's the state. They can do what they want."

"Without even asking the people what *they* want? Didn't anyone in town object— *protest?*"

"Oh, a few people wrote letters to the editor and to their congressmen. But it didn't make any difference in the end. Now we've accepted it and are focused on getting on with things the best we can."

"But you can't…let the town die." She felt like crying all over again. Cedar Grove was home as much as the ranch was. She'd bought her first prom dress at Mavis Butler's dress shop, with money she'd made working part time at the grocery store. Her first date with Jordan Ledbetter had been to the movies at the Bijou Theatre, and her high school band had marched down Main Street every Fourth of July in the parade.

"The town won't die," Dad said. "It will simply change. Everything changes."

"But not every change is good." Her home wasn't supposed to change that drastically—home was supposed to be the one constant in her life that she could count on. "Someone should do something to stop this."

"I don't know what to tell you," he said. "But I have more important things to worry about than a highway project."

She waited for him to elaborate on what those things might be, but he'd fallen silent, staring off into the middle distance. She wondered if he even remembered she was here. With his graying hair and hunched back, he looked so much older than she remembered—her father wasn't supposed to get old. He was always supposed to be the tough cowboy, sitting tall in the saddle, master of his domain. The man who could fix anything and solve any problem for his little girl.

But she wasn't little anymore, and even

though she'd run back home, she couldn't expect her parents to solve all her problems. "Thanks for letting me stay for a while," she said. "I promise I'll do my share around here, and I'll leave before I wear out my welcome."

She expected him to say she was always welcome here, but that part of the familiar script had changed, too. He hefted himself out of the recliner. "Come on. Let's get the rest of your things out of your car and get you settled. You'll need to put sheets on the bed."

"Don't worry about it, Dad. I'm here to help, not to make more work."

He surprised her then, by slipping his arm around her and pulling her close in a hug so hard she feared her ribs might crack. "It's good to see you, Pumpkin," he said. "You caught us by surprise, but now that you're here, we're glad."

She blinked back stinging tears and laid her head on his shoulder. How many times over the years had he held her while she cried about everything from a lost dog to a boy who'd hurt her feelings? At least he hadn't changed; he was still the strong cowboy she could always rely on to be there

for her. "Thanks, Dad. I'm glad to be here."
Really glad. Now she could start her life
heading in the right direction again, with
home as the unchanging, fixed anchor point
from which she could launch herself into the
world once more.

The next morning Christa was surprised
to find her mother seated at the breakfast
table, sipping coffee and reading the paper,
Jet curled at her feet, while her father scram-
bled eggs and made toast. "You're making
breakfast?" Christa asked, unable to hide
her surprise. Her mother was the one who
cooked, while her father read the paper.

"I can do a lot of things you don't know
about. Coffee's over there." He nodded to
the current generation of the drip coffee-
maker that had been a fixture in that corner
of the kitchen for as long as Christa could
remember.

She poured a cup of coffee and sat at her
familiar place at the round wooden table in
the corner of the kitchen. Her father slid a
plate of eggs and toast in front of her, and Jet
moved over to sit by her chair, hoping for a
handout. She slipped him a bite of egg. "This
looks good," she said, noting the fluffy pile
of eggs and just-brown toast with twin yel-

low pools of butter. "Good for you, Mom, letting Dad wait on you for a change."

Her mother winced and set down her coffee cup. "Did you get everything sorted in your room?" she asked.

"Pretty much. I didn't bring a lot." She paused for a bite of egg and toast—not as good as her mom's, but not bad. "I only plan to stay a few weeks—a couple of months at most. Just until I can regroup and find a new job."

"It's a shame about Pemberton," Mom said. "You always sounded so happy when you talked about your work there."

"It was the perfect job," Christa said. "I got along great with everyone, and I loved the creative challenge of designing new marketing programs. We did everything from single print ads to lengthy television campaigns. My clients were a nice mix of private companies and nonprofits. My bosses were great, and the location was ideal." She got a little choked up, just thinking about how lucky she'd been to land such a great position right out of college. She'd planned to stay there until she retired.

"I'm sure you'll find something else you'll

love just as much," Mom said. "Where have you applied so far?"

"Um, I'm still considering my options." She enjoyed the last of the toast and egg. "I don't want to rush into anything I'll regret."

"You can stay here as long as you like," Mom said. "I'm sure it will be nice for you to touch base with your friends in town. What did you plan to do today?"

She pushed aside her empty plate. "I hadn't planned on doing much of anything. I thought it would be nice for the two of us to visit."

Mom and Dad tried to be subtle, but Christa would have had to be blind to miss the look they exchanged—as if they were two guilty crooks agreeing on a cover story. "I want you to run some errands in town for me," Mom said. "I need a few things."

"Why don't we go together?" Christa said. "We could have lunch at the Blue Bell." The Blue Bell Café was an institution in Cedar Grove. Christa and her mom had shared many confidences—from discussions of first bras and first boyfriends to the pros and cons of various colleges and career paths—over coffee and pie at the Blue Bell. Going there today would be like old times.

But Mom shook her head. "I'll be much too busy here at the ranch. I'd rather you went for me."

"All right. I can do that." Christa wanted to ask what her mother would be so busy with, but another evasive answer would hurt too much, so she pushed her curiosity aside.

After breakfast, Christa washed the dishes, then took the list her mother gave her and headed to Cedar Grove. The town seemed somewhat more lively this morning, with cars parked in front of most of the businesses. Her first stop was the library, where Mrs. Franklin manned the front desk, as she had for most of Christa's life. "I've got the books your mother requested right here," Mrs. Franklin said. She slid the stack of volumes toward Christa and studied her over the tops of her half glasses. "Are you home to stay, or is this another quick visit?"

"I'll be here for a few weeks. Maybe as long as a couple of months. I was laid off from my job in Houston." She might as well admit it up front; it wouldn't take long for the news to spread in a town the size of Cedar Grove.

"I'm sorry to hear that, dear. I can't say you'll find a lot of job opportunities in this neck of the woods, but if I learn of anyone hiring, I'll let you know."

Christa seriously doubted she'd find a position in town that would utilize her marketing degree, but she appreciated Mrs. Franklin's concern. "That's very thoughtful of you. I'm really here because I thought it would be nice to spend more time with my folks while I'm between jobs."

"That's good. I'm sure both your parents appreciate the help." Mrs. Franklin tapped a few keys on her computer and studied the screen. "Your old library card is still good, so feel free to use it while you're here. And we have a women's book club that meets the second Thursday evening of every month. You should come."

"Maybe I will. Thanks again."

Next on the list was the Blue Bell Café, for a jar of Etta Mae Cook's strawberry jam. "I thought Adele made all her own jam," Etta Mae said, after she'd given Christa a hug and slipped the jar of jam into a brown paper sack.

"Maybe she didn't have time this summer," Christa said. "She said she's been busy—too busy to even come to town with me today."

"Well, you tell her I'm flattered to know she likes my jam so much. She should stop by for coffee and a chat next time she's around."

"I'll tell her. Thank you."

"And you should come back Friday morning. The Chamber of Commerce eats breakfast here and everyone is invited. They're always looking for volunteers."

"Thanks, but I think I'm going to be pretty busy updating my résumé and applying for jobs."

"I hope you find one, honey. I wish Cedar Grove had more to offer young folks like you. Maybe this new highway will bring some new businesses and jobs with it."

"But I thought the highway was going to bypass the town," Christa said.

"Well, it is, dear. But there's talk of development out by the highway, so I guess businesses will gradually move out that way. I'm hoping for the best."

Christa wished she shared Etta Mae's optimism. The highway project might just as well be the death knell for the little town she loved. "I guess I'd better see to these other errands." She held up the list her mother had given her. "But I'll be back soon for a piece of your wonderful pie and a cup of coffee."

"I'll save one for you." Etta Mae winked, then turned to wait on the next customer.

By the time Christa walked into the Cedar Grove Bank an hour later, she was beginning to suspect that her mother had written her list with the goal of reacquainting Christa with as many familiar faces in town as possible, and luring her into all the clubs and activities. The teller, whose nameplate identified her as Traci, was a stranger to Christa, which was almost a relief. At least here, no one would feel obligated to invite her to join the gardening club or to volunteer with the 4H, as had happened at the Post Office and the Seed and Feed. "May I help you?" Traci asked.

"My mom sent me for paper coin sleeves," Christa said. "I guess she has a bunch of change to roll."

"Oh, sure." The teller opened a drawer and took out a fistful of coin wrappers for pennies, nickels, dimes and quarters, and slid them across the counter to Christa. "Here you go. Anything else?"

She glanced at the sign that offered free checking. "I'm going to be here a little while," she said. "Maybe a couple of months. Could I open an account for just that time? It would make banking easier."

"Sure you can." She looked past Christa to the young man who sat at the desk across from her. "Paul, can you help this customer with a new account?"

Christa recognized a boy who had been a couple grades ahead of her in school. So much for thinking she could come to the bank without seeing someone she knew. "Paul Raybourn, it's good to see you," she said.

"Christa. Great to see you." She sat in the chair across from his desk and they spent a few minutes catching up. She learned Paul had married a classmate of hers, Didi Moffat, and they had a baby boy, Alex. She told him about her job loss and her plans to spend the summer at the ranch.

"After living in the city, the ranch is going to seem dull as dirt," he said. "I predict in two weeks you'll be dying for any excuse to get out of town."

"Oh, I don't think so," she said. "I liked Houston, but I'm a small-town girl at heart. After so much upheaval in my life lately,

I'm looking forward to a stable, comfortable routine."

"If you say so. I could do with a bit more excitement, myself."

"I guess the new highway is going to bring a bit of excitement to town," she said.

"It already has, what with folks taking sides over whether or not this project is a good thing for Cedar Grove."

"And what do you think?" Christa asked.

"My view is, it's already a done deal, so we might as well make the best of it." He gave her the forms to complete to open a checking account and she was busy writing when Paul looked over her shoulder and said. "Hey, Ryder. There's someone I want you to meet."

She turned to see a good-looking, tall man striding across the bank. Dressed in pressed khakis and a sport coat, he stood out among the jeans and snap button shirts of most of the men. When he smiled, dimples formed on either side of his mouth. His sandy brown hair dipped low across his forehead, above a pair of deep blue eyes.

"Christa Montgomery, I'd like you to meet Ryder Oakes. Ryder's staying in town for the summer, too."

Christa rose and took Ryder's offered hand. "Hello, Mr. Oakes."

"Please, call me Ryder. It's a pleasure to meet you." His voice was soft and deep. A caressing kind of voice.

Where had that thought come from? She wasn't the type of woman who was easily bowled over by a handsome man — but she had to admit Ryder Oakes made her heart flutter a little. The thought almost made her laugh. Talk about bad timing. She needed to focus on finding a new job and getting her life back on track—the last thing she needed was the distraction of a romantic relationship.

"What brings you to town, Ryder?" she asked, determined to regain her composure.

"Work. My job takes me all over."

"Ryder's an engineer," Paul offered. "He's a University of Texas alum, like you."

Too bad she'd never run into him on campus. He looked a few years older than her, tiny lines fanning out from the corners of those gorgeous eyes. She searched for some remark to keep the conversation going. "Traveling all the time must get old."

"I grew up in a military family. My dad

was in the army, so I'm used to moving a lot."

"Christa's family owns the Rocking M, just south of town." Paul apparently felt his role was to fill in details, like a teacher coaxing two reluctant children together.

Or a matchmaker. She bit back a groan.

"It's a beautiful place," Ryder said.

So he knew the ranch. That wasn't so unusual. If he'd spent much time around Cedar Grove at all, he was bound to have driven by her parents' place. "We think so."

"I'm sure Bud and Adele are happy to have you home."

His use of her parents' first names surprised her. "How long have you been in Cedar Grove?" she asked.

"Not quite a month. I've really been trying to get to know people though."

He'd covered a lot of ground in that month—odd for someone who was only going to be here temporarily.

"Christa could introduce you to a lot of people," Paul said. "She was Miss Cedar Grove her senior year of high school. And growing up here, she knows pretty much everybody."

Paul was definitely matchmaking—as if a

man like Ryder would be impressed with her brief stint as the local beauty queen. "You know more people than I do now," she said. "After all, I've been in Houston the past few years." She handed him her stack of papers. "I think that's everything."

Paul looked at the papers in his hands, as if he'd forgotten why they were all gathered around his desk. But he recovered quickly. "Great. Let me get you an account number and you'll be all set. We can transfer funds from your account in Houston and you'll have access right away."

"Are you moving back to town from Houston?" Ryder asked.

"Just staying here for a little while, visiting my parents." She wasn't about to explain her job and money woes to this handsome stranger. She might not be interested in dating Ryder, but she didn't want to come off like a loser in front of him, either.

Thankfully, he didn't ask for more details. His phone buzzed and he slipped it from his pocket. "I'd better get this. It was nice meeting you, Christa. I hope I'll see you again."

These last words sent another shiver of awareness through her. Oh, Ryder Oakes was something all right. Too bad it was impossible for her to get involved with anyone right now.

CHAPTER TWO

THE CALLER ID on Ryder's cell indicated that the call was from his mother. His mother who, as far as he could remember, had never called him in the middle of a work day. "Mom! Is everything all right?"

"I'm fine. Why would you think something is wrong?"

"You never call me during the day."

"I'm on my lunch break and I wanted to catch you while you were still in cell range. I know how it is on some of those ranches—no cell tower for miles."

"Okay." He relaxed a little. "So what's up?"

"I've been thinking—instead of you coming for dinner on Saturday, I'd like to come there and see you. We can go to lunch somewhere."

"Sure. If that's what you'd prefer." His mother lived in Dallas and since Ryder had relocated to Cedar Grove, she'd made it a point to have him over for a meal at least once a week. He hadn't spent so much time with a parent since he'd graduated high school, but he had to admit, it was nice having Mom close.

"I want to see where you live," she said.

"It's nothing fancy—just a furnished rental." He didn't need more, since his stay here wasn't going to be permanent.

"Humor me. Now give me your address."

He rattled off the details and the main cross streets. "My new car has GPS," she said. "I'm sure I can find it. I'll see you about noon Saturday, then."

"I'll look forward to it."

He pocketed the phone and added "Clean apartment" to his mental to-do list. He wondered if his mom wanted to see him so much because she was lonely. After all, she'd married Ryder's dad right out of high school. To be on her own at this point in her life had to be tough. Of course, she'd been the one to ask for a divorce—something that still shocked Ryder. He'd thought his parents were happy in their marriage, or as happy as any couple ever was.

He'd better pick up some soft drinks and snack stuff at the store this afternoon; his provisions were limited to coffee, a loaf of bread and some lunch meat and condiments. He ate out for most of his meals. He fully expected Mom to fuss about his lack of a proper diet, a proper home or even a steady girlfriend. She rarely pried into his personal life, but she had strongly hinted that she thought it was time for him to settle down.

Hard to do when his job kept him on the road. His stint in Cedar Grove was likely to be one of the longest of his career, but even though plenty of women had indicated they'd be interested in getting to know him better, so far he'd kept his distance. Relationships always complicated things, especially when it came time to leave town.

That didn't stop people from trying to match him up with eligible females, though. Christa Montgomery was beautiful, no doubt about that, with dark brown hair that fell just to her shoulders, and clear brown eyes that had met his gaze with no hint of coyness or flirtation. That air of confidence and calm assuredness made her all the more attractive. He'd like to get to know her better.

That wasn't a new feeling for him; he met women all the time who might interest him, as he traveled around the state, overseeing various highway and bridge projects. But he was always careful not to start what he couldn't finish. He'd told the truth when he'd said his job required a lot of travel. He didn't mind, but being away from a home base so much made it tough to form relationships. He might date a woman one week, then not see her again for six or eight weeks. Texting and e-mailing couldn't take the place of a physical connection. And he wasn't the type to have a girl in every town, like some of the other engineers in his group.

But he'd settle for friendship—or a summer romance. If Christa wasn't planning to stay in Cedar Grove, maybe she'd appreciate some company for a few months. It would be nice to have someone to hang out with, to take in a movie or dinner, without the worry that she'd expect a more lasting commitment.

He stepped back into the bank, but Christa was gone. Paul looked up from his desk. "Is there something I can help you with, Ryder?" he asked.

Ryder remembered why he'd come to the bank in the first place. "We're going to have a lot of workers in and out of Cedar Grove for the next couple of years as construction on the highway progresses," he said. "I wanted to make sure there won't be a problem cashing their checks."

"No problem at all." Paul laughed. "I mean, if the state isn't good for the money, we're all in trouble."

He scanned the lobby once more, wondering if Christa had slipped out the side door—to avoid him?

"If you're looking for Christa, she said she had more errands to run," Paul said. "I take it she just got back to town yesterday afternoon."

"I guess she's staying at the Rocking M, with her parents?" He regretted the question as soon as he saw Paul's eyes light up.

"She is," the banker said. "She's been living in Houston since she graduated a few years ago, working at some big marketing firm. I guess the economic slump hit them the way it has almost everyone else. They laid off a bunch of people and she was one of the casualties. But I'm sure another firm will snap her up. She was always sharp."

"So she's only here temporarily, until she finds a new job."

"I guess that's the plan. But we all know plans can change." He grinned. "The number at the ranch is in the local directory, if you want to give her a call."

He bit back the impulse to tell Paul that he didn't need anyone else to set him up with a woman. He already had to dodge the local women who went out of their way to flirt and even outright proposition him. Something about a new, single man in town sent some females into overdrive.

But Christa wasn't like that. She'd been friendly, but cool. Not the kind of woman to throw herself at any man.

Which, in the perverse nature of the human spirit, made her all that much more attractive. But he wasn't going to let Paul know that. For some reason, the banker had made it his mission to introduce Ryder to every eligible woman in the county.

Time to change the subject. "Are you going to be at the public forum tomorrow night?" he asked. This was the last in a series of community gatherings in the area to answer questions about the new highway project. Ryder's job was to persuade people that the project was a good and positive thing for the people around here.

"I wouldn't miss it." Worry lines formed on Paul's forehead. "Are you concerned about the reception you'll receive?"

"I know some people are unhappy with me, but I'm hoping when I explain the benefits, I can sway them to my side." He believed the highway was a good thing, though he understood people's fears about having traffic siphoned from an already dying town. But the new route meant new opportunity. He'd help people see that.

"The other meetings—with the other people the state sent to talk to us—didn't always go so well," Paul said.

"I'm not those other people." The state had chosen him because of his ability to interact with a variety of people. Another lesson he'd learned from life as a military nomad.

"There are some pretty tough old cowboys around here. Set in their ways."

"I was never one to back down from a battle." His father had taught him that much. Except his weapons of choice were logic and control, not firearms. Facts and figures beat raw emotion any day, though it took some people longer than others to see that.

PINK GERANIUMS BLOOMED in half barrels flanking the door to the Cedar Grove Salon, where Christa had received her very first permanent wave from her best friend Kelly Jepson's mother, Janet. Someone had added the words "and Day Spa" after "Salon" on the familiar sign, but when Christa stepped through the front door, the salon was just as she remembered it. Black padded chairs faced antique dressers that served as the stylists' stations, and the air smelled of peroxide, hair spray and fruity shampoos. An older woman sat under a dryer in the corner, and Janet was just finishing a cut on another woman at her station.

As the string of sleigh bells on the back of the door fell silent, Kelly hurried from the back of the shop. "Christa!" she cried, and ran forward to hug her friend. Short, with a halo of brown curls framing her face, Kelly had gone into business with her mother right after high school. She and Christa kept in touch via Facebook and too-infrequent visits. "Etta Mae stopped by a little while ago and told us you were in town. For a while, I hope."

"A few weeks. Maybe a few months. Did Etta Mae tell you I'd lost my job?"

"She didn't say—I'm so sorry. I know how much you loved your work."

"To tell you the truth, I'm still kind of in shock."

"So you had no idea the layoff was coming?" Kelly asked.

"None. No one did. Apparently, the company had been in trouble for a while and we never knew."

"That's tough, but you'll bounce back. In the meantime, I'm thrilled you're home. And your hair looks gorgeous." Kelly fingered the blunt-cut ends of Christa's hair with a proprietary air. "Come see me when you're ready for a trim."

"Of course." She waved at Janet, who nodded even as she wielded her blow-dryer and comb. "Stepping in here is just like coming home—everything so familiar."

"Not everything," Kelly protested. "Didn't you see the sign? We're a day spa now, too. We have a massage therapist who works three days a week, and I'm certified to do facials and waxing."

"I guess that's good," Christa said. "Just don't change too much."

"We've got to keep up with the times," Kelly said. "Do what we can to bring in new customers."

"Not that any of it's doing us much good." Janet joined them at the front counter as her customer left. "I guess you noticed how many businesses around town have closed or are for sale," she said.

"My dad said the drought and the economy have hit everyone hard," Christa said. "It's awful."

"And now that new highway is going to send everybody flying right by without even knowing Cedar Grove is here," Janet said.

"Some people are talking about moving out nearer the new highway," Kelly said. "A developer has plans for a big new shopping center there."

"Where the rent will be twice what we pay here," Janet said.

"Mom has been a little stressed out about all of this." Kelly frowned.

"Don't get me started." Janet waved her hand as if shooing a fly. "It's good to have you back, Christa. I've got to go see to Mrs.

Newsome." She turned and headed for the woman under the dryer.

"Are you really thinking of moving the salon?" Christa asked.

Kelly shrugged. "Maybe. Mama doesn't like change, but I think it could be a good thing. Along with the shopping center, there's talk of a new housing development going in. The new highway will shorten the commute to Dallas, so the theory is more people will want to move out to the country. We could have a whole bunch of new clients for the salon. If we don't move, some chain will set up shop and take all our business. I think Mama will come around—I just have to work on her."

"I always admired your ability to see the bright side of things," Christa said. "I guess I'm with your mother—I don't like change. Did anyone even try to persuade the state that the route they chose for the highway wasn't the best? It seems to me they didn't have to bypass Cedar Grove altogether."

"Some people raised a fuss at first, but you know how it is—the state always has an answer for every objection. They said this route was the only economical one. They held a series of meetings to present their plans. There's another one tomorrow night."

"Are you planning to attend?"

Kelly sighed. "I wish we didn't have to, but Mama insists on going, and I go to help keep her calm. Frankly, I'll be glad when they break ground. Once construction is under way, I think she'll see there's nothing we can do to stop it. Besides, I'm looking forward to another advantage of the construction project."

"What's that?" Christa asked.

"There'll be lots and lots of men working on the project and they'll be staying in town for up to two years. Some of them are bound to be young and single."

Christa thought of Ryder Oakes. He'd said he was an engineer. Was he connected with the new highway project? The idea left a bitter taste in her mouth. She couldn't be as optimistic as Kelly about the effect the highway would have on her hometown. "I think I'll go to the meeting, too," she said. "If Mom and Dad don't need me for anything. I want to hear what the state's representatives have to say."

If nothing else, focusing on this new highway would take her mind off her own problems, for a few hours, at least.

ERRANDS COMPLETED, CHRISTA drove back to the ranch, where everything was exactly as she'd expected to find it yesterday, but hadn't. Today her father, dressed in a crisp long-sleeved Western shirt, freshly shaved, his hair neatly cut and combed, waved at her as he rode across the front pasture on his favorite horse, a sorrel gelding named Peanut. Mom, looking fresh and rested in denim capris and a pink blouse, opened the door as soon as Christa stepped out of the car and greeted her with a hug. At her side, Jet barked happily and wagged his tail in greeting. As Christa followed her mother into the house, the smell of roasting meat and baking pies greeted her.

The events of the day before might have been a bad dream. "Thank you for running those errands for me," Mom said, relieving Christa of her packages. "It was a big help. How was your afternoon?"

"Fine. Etta Mae says hello. She wants to have coffee with you soon."

"I'll have to do that. Did you stop by the salon and see Kelly?"

"Yes." Christa trailed her mom and Jet into the kitchen, where a pair of peach pies—Christa's favorite—sat cooling on the counter. "She told me they might move the salon after the new highway is built."

"That sounds smart." Mom dumped the coin papers in the drawer beneath the phone—the repository for all the miscellaneous items no one knew what to do with.

The back door opened and Dad stepped inside, removing his Stetson as he did so, and setting it, crown down, on a shelf above the row of coat hooks. "How are things in town?" he asked Christa.

"Everyone's talking about the new highway," she said. "It's really disrupting everyone's life. Some of the businesses are talking about moving to a new shopping center near the new route. If they don't, they'll probably go out of business."

"They have to go where the customers are," Dad said.

"But they shouldn't have to move," Christa said. "The state should have kept the highway close to town, instead of bypassing Cedar Grove altogether."

"I'm sure they had their reasons for choosing the route they did." Dad washed his hands at the kitchen sink, then dried them on a dish towel. "Those pies look good, Adi." He kissed his wife's cheek.

"Behave yourself and I might let you have some," she said, her smile taking any sting out of the words. She turned to Christa. "While you were in town, did you happen to run into Ryder Oakes?"

So she hadn't imagined Ryder's familiarity with her parents. "I met him," she said. "How do you know him?"

"Oh, we met somewhere in town." Mom gave a vague wave. "Such a nice young man, and about your age."

Of course. Her mother saw Ryder Oakes as a potential match for her twenty-six-year-old-and-still-single daughter. "Paul Raybourn at the bank introduced me to Ryder," she said.

"What did you think? He's very handsome, isn't he?"

"He is." She couldn't very well lie; with that thick sandy hair, brilliant blue eyes, dimpled smile and broad shoulders, Ryder was classically handsome. And he seemed like a nice guy. "But I really don't have time to date anyone while I'm here. I have to focus on finding a new job, and a new place to live after that. Besides, Ryder is probably already involved with someone else." The great guys always were.

"I'm sure he isn't," Mom said. "I think he's been out with a few women, but Etta Mae says he's never come into the café with the same woman twice. And did you know he went to the University of Texas, too?"

"Paul mentioned it." As if graduating from the same university guaranteed they'd hit it off.

"Ryder has a good head on his shoulders. I like him."

Christa stared at her father. This assessment of a stranger was the equivalent of the Pope's blessing—at least in her house. Dad wasn't one to throw around praise, and over the years Christa couldn't remember him having much to say about any of the boys and men she'd dated. "How do you know Ryder?" she asked.

"Oh, we've talked a time or two." He turned away. "Call me when supper's ready."

"How does Dad know Ryder Oakes?" Christa asked after her father had left the room. The casual acquaintance her mom had alluded to didn't add up to the praise Dad had given the man.

Mom lifted the lid on the slow cooker and studied the roast. "I suppose they ran into each other in town. At Cattlemen's Club meetings and things like that." She reached for the salt shaker.

"But Ryder isn't a rancher," Christa said. "Why would he be at a Cattlemen's Club meeting?"

Mom replaced the lid on the cooker. "I don't know, dear. Why don't you go freshen up? I'll call you when supper's ready."

"I can help, Mom. Just tell me what to do."

"That's all right, dear. Go on." She made shooing motions with her hand.

Christa started to argue, but decided to give in, for tonight, at least. She drifted into the living room, where Dad had assumed his usual place in his recliner, Jet in his lap.

"Kelly told me there's a public meeting tonight about the new highway," Christa said as she settled onto the sofa. "I'm thinking of going."

"That's a good idea."

"Maybe you and Mom would like to go with me."

"I don't think so, honey." He stroked the dog, whose head was resting on her dad's knee.

"Aren't you curious to know what the state has to say? How they can justify destroying the town?"

"Cedar Grove was dying a slow death before the idea of this highway project ever came along," Dad said. "The new highway could actually be a good thing."

"I don't see how." Her father's easy acceptance of such a big change bothered her. He'd lived in Cedar Grove all his life; was he really content to let the town just fade away?

"Maybe going to the meeting tonight will help you see things in a different light," Dad said.

"Maybe." Though she doubted it. Her father's eyes were already closed. Was he really napping, or merely avoiding discussing this with her?

She stood. "I guess I'll go freshen up before dinner."

"Say hello to Ryder for me when you see him tonight."

She froze halfway to the door. "I'm going to the meeting with Kelly, Dad. I won't be seeing Ryder." Did he think the meeting was some kind of excuse for a secret rendezvous with Ryder Oakes? She hadn't done that kind of thing since she was in high school. Had

her dad forgotten she was a grown woman—
a woman who wasn't interested in dating
right now?

"Oh, I imagine you'll run into him."

She would never have used the word
'smug' to describe her father, but that's exactly how he looked right now. As if he
knew something she didn't.

Then again, both her parents had been
acting strange ever since she'd arrived home.
She couldn't help but feel they were hiding
something from her, but what?

RYDER LOOKED OUT over the school auditorium which, as he'd expected, was filled
with what must be ninety percent of the
people who lived in or near Cedar Grove.
From his position in the wings of the stage
he could see men in checked shirts and cowboy hats standing along the back wall and
children racing up and down the aisles.

A trio of women in summer dresses
moved down the front row and he couldn't
keep back a smile as he recognized Christa
Montgomery, in a sleeveless, flowered shift
that showed off tanned arms. She was just
as lovely as he remembered. Maybe after
the meeting he'd find her and exchange a

few words. He'd try to gauge her interest in a casual, dating relationship—no strings attached. Since she only planned to stay in town a little while, he didn't have to worry she'd expect any long-term commitment from him. Spending more time with her would certainly make his own stay in Cedar Grove more pleasant.

"You ready to get this show on the road?" The high school principal, who was serving as the night's master of ceremonies, asked.

Ryder nodded. "Let's not keep people waiting."

While the principal droned on about the need to listen quietly and then ask questions, Ryder studied Christa. She sat next to a younger woman who had curly hair. The curly-haired woman did all the talking, while Christa studied the large map showing the highway route that was projected onto a screen in front of the stage. She frowned at the map, looking more severe. Apparently, she wasn't pleased.

He understood people's objections, but he figured she'd feel differently once he'd made his case for the project.

"And now here's Ryder Oakes. Mr. Oakes is the chief engineer overseeing this project.

He's going to say a few words and answer your questions."

Ryder straightened his shoulders and strode onto the stage. He wore pressed khakis and a white shirt with the sleeves rolled up. Nothing too fancy. He was a working man, just like most of these people. A man working to make their lives better, though not all of them saw this yet.

"The new highway, to be known as Spur Eighty-seven, is going to bring a lot of changes to life in Cedar Grove," he began. "And change isn't always easy. As humans, most of us are programmed to not like change. But sometimes change is good. When we switched from using horses to cars for transportation, most people didn't like it at first. Yet how many of us would give up our cars now? We still have horses, but we use them for recreation, and to work in situations where cars don't make sense."

A few people nodded. Many of them still worked with horses every day.

"Some of you are worried that your town will die without the traffic a highway brings to it," he continued. "More people will use the new road and forgo the back way that runs through your town. But I don't think

Cedar Grove will die. New people will come to live near the highway, and they will want to shop and use the services in town, as well as a place to take their kids on Saturday afternoons. You'll have the opportunity to expand and add new businesses.

"You've probably had friends and family who have left town to live in the city, closer to jobs. The highway will make the commute to Dallas faster and easier, so some of those friends and family will move back home. Others won't have to leave to find work. The state is also offering grants to rural transportation districts to establish bus service between rural areas and the city. That's something that could make commuting even more affordable and easier."

He set aside his sheaf of notes. "That's all I have to say by way of introduction. Now I want to hear your comments and questions."

Christa was one of the first people to raise her hand. He pointed to her. "Ms. Montgomery?"

She stood. "You paint a rosy picture of happy families and the town growing. But isn't it just as likely—more likely, even—that those families will go to Dallas for recreation? They'll shop in the big box stores in the city, where they can get cheaper prices. They won't patronize a small town to which they feel no connection."

"That might happen," he conceded. "But while those families may not have the roots here that you and your family have, everyone craves connection. Towns like Cedar Grove hold a strong attraction for people who are looking to be a part of a community. If you reach out to those families and give them a reason to shop here—to be a part of your lives—I believe they will come."

She opened her mouth as if to say something else, but the older woman on the other side of the curly-haired woman rose to her feet. "It's all well and good to talk about what a great community we are now," she said. "That doesn't make up for the state coming in with the route for the highway already laid out and not even consulting us. You bought the land for the route at bargain prices, cutting ranches in two, even forcing families to move out of their homes altogether."

"Everyone who sold to the state did so voluntarily," Ryder said. "At a time when the real estate market is severely depressed, we have offered the best price possible."

Objections rose from several quarters of the room. The principal stepped forward. "Everybody settle down," he said. "This is supposed to be a calm discussion."

From there Ryder moved on to answering questions about the new shopping center and housing development. Could the town annex the land to add to their tax base? Would those families be in the Cedar Grove school district? "I'm not part of the local government or school district," he said. "But I believe the answer to both those questions is yes."

More murmurs rose as the possibility of more money in the town coffers and growth in local schools registered. "So when are you going to get started?" one man asked.

"We hope to break ground in a couple of weeks," Ryder said. "Though it may take a bit longer to close the deals for the last of the right of way. But we want to get started as soon as possible, while the weather is on our side."

Others asked questions about traffic, the effect on local wildlife, fencing along the highway, and even trash pickup. Ryder answered as best he could. Christa raised her hand again and he called on her. He liked that she was still engaged in the discussion. And he liked the way her expression became so passionate and intense as she confronted him. "Why was this route chosen for the highway?" she asked. "Why not something closer to town?"

"Good question," he said. He picked up a pointer and carried it to the projected map. "It's a matter of geography. There's a formation here, alongside the town." He pointed to an area that would bring the highway much nearer to Cedar Grove. "There's a granite uplift sitting over an underwater reservoir—an aquifer. Building here would require blasting through the granite—an expensive process. The probability of opening fissures to the aquifer is strong. At a minimum, that would cause problems with flooding of the project, requiring expensive dams, pumps and greatly increasing both the timeline and the cost of the project. At worst, it could have disastrous consequences for the local water supply."

Murmurs rose from the crowd. After three years of drought, water was more valuable than oil to these people. They wouldn't want to risk losing a drop, much less a whole aquifer.

"What about on the other side of town?" Christa asked. "Couldn't you have routed the highway there?"

"Taking the highway in that direction makes the route longer and adds to the expense," he said. "Our goal was to shorten the distance to the city and to do so as economically as possible."

"And we end up paying the cost." But she sat down, still frowning. Ryder's heart sank. So much for him winning her over.

The questions wound down. "I think that's all we have time for," the principal concluded.

"If you have any more questions, you can catch me around town," Ryder said. "If I don't know the answer, I'll find someone who does."

As people moved out of the auditorium, he left the stage and slipped past a pair of men who looked as if they wanted to waylay him. Christa stood with her back to him, talking with her curly-headed friend. "He doesn't care about the people here," she said. "It's all cold logic to him. Just the facts, ma'am."

The words stung. He could have argued that basing decisions on facts and logic was more sensible than following blind emotion, but she wouldn't have listened. He needed more time to win her over to his point of view. He intercepted her as she stepped into the aisle. "You asked good questions tonight," he said. "I wanted to talk to you more—maybe over coffee?"

"I don't know." Her gaze slid sideways, avoiding him. "My parents…"

"Your parents will be snug in bed, watching crime dramas," her curly haired friend said. "I know because they're just like my mom."

"Kelly, have you met Ryder? Ryder, this is Kelly Jepson." Christa made the introduction.

Ryder nodded to Kelly, but focused on Christa once more. "It's just coffee," he said, wanting to reassure her, in case she suspected him of ulterior moments. "I'm just trying to avoid going back to my empty apartment. I'm not a fan of crime dramas."

This admission earned him the hint of a smile. "All right. But where can we get coffee this time of night?"

"The Blue Bell stays open late on Thursdays," Kelly volunteered. "The Lions Club used to meet then, and after they changed their meeting time, Etta Mae just kept the same hours."

"The Blue Bell it is," he said. "Should I drive?"

"I'll meet you there," she said, and left before he could protest.

CHAPTER THREE

BEFORE EXITING THE school parking lot, Christa called home to check with her parents. As Kelly had predicted, they were watching TV. "I thought I'd stay and have coffee with a friend," she said. Though her parents knew Ryder, she didn't want them jumping to conclusions. This wasn't a date—they were merely continuing their discussion about the highway project.

"Have a good time," Dad said. "You have your key to let yourself in."

"Yes." Later, she'd give her dad a hard time about not warning her that Ryder was the highway engineer. At least that explained how Ryder knew so many people in town; he'd been schmoozing the locals, winning them over to his side. Her dad had probably thought it was a good joke to play on his daughter.

"All right then. Good night."

She ended the call, fighting a nervous

flutter in her stomach. Maybe agreeing to meet up with Ryder had been a bad idea. He'd been so warm and charming in the meeting, but were those emotions real, or merely a show to get what he wanted?

Ryder was waiting in front of the Blue Bell when she parked a few doors down. It looked as if a good number of people who had attended the highway forum had retired to the café for coffee and pie. "Just sit anywhere," the waitress said when they entered.

Ryder escorted her to a booth along one wall, his hand resting very lightly against her upper back, guiding her through the crowd. The warmth of his hand through her dress made her heart beat a little faster. What was it about him that affected her so?

Several people greeted him as they passed—more than said hello to Christa, even. "You seem to have made a lot of friends in town," she said, as she slid into the booth across from him.

"Acquaintances, anyway. You know how people are around here—welcoming."

"Where are you from?" she asked.

"All over. I'd lived in three different countries by the time I entered first grade. We went wherever the army told my father to go, wherever he was needed."

She couldn't imagine what such a nomadic life would be like. She'd been born and raised in Cedar Grove; no matter where she lived from now on, this would always be home. She wouldn't want to be like Ryder— rootless.

The waitress came to take their order. "Just coffee," Christa said. "With cream."

"I'll have black coffee," Ryder said. "And do you have any of that blackberry pie left?"

"For you, I might be able to find a couple of slices." The waitress smiled at him, clearly flirting.

He looked at Christa. "You sure you won't indulge? It's homemade."

Her mouth watered at the memory of Etta Mae's pies. "All right. Thanks."

When the waitress left, Christa continued their conversation. "And now you're in a job where you travel a lot. What's the longest you've ever stayed in one place?"

"I'm hoping this will be it. This is the biggest job I've been on and it should take over two years."

Something about the pride in his voice made her hazard a guess. "Is this your first time overseeing a job this big?" After all, he couldn't be much older than her.

"Yes. I was only recently promoted. Obviously, I want my bosses to feel they made the right decision to put me in charge."

"You certainly seem to be winning over people in the meeting tonight."

"Present company excepted?" The dimples showed on either side of his mouth.

"I don't dislike you." She shifted in her seat. The opposite, really. He was a very easy man to like. "But I don't like what you're doing. I don't think it's right."

"You don't like the route chosen for the highway."

"I think it should be closer to town, so that the town is the focus and not some new development ten miles away."

"What about the rest of the route, beyond the town?" His expression grew wary, though she couldn't imagine why.

"I didn't pay much attention to that," she admitted. "I've never been very good at reading maps or envisioning things in space. I had to take remedial geometry in school." She was an idea person, not a picture person.

"Paul Raybourn said you worked for a marketing firm."

"I did." She hesitated, tempted to gloss over her unemployment, or even outright lie. But she wasn't a dishonest person and besides, she hadn't done anything wrong. "My company laid off a bunch of people and I was one of them. It's why I came home— to regroup and save money while I look for another job."

"Traveling for my job, I've met a lot of people in the same boat, but that doesn't make it any easier. I hope you find a new job soon."

"I'm sure I will." The job hunting seminar she'd attended in Houston had emphasized remaining positive. Of course, finding a new job also meant sending out résumés, putting in applications and networking with contacts in her field—all things she hadn't gotten around to doing yet. But she'd start the job hunt soon. She'd just wanted a little time to lick her wounds and regain her equilibrium.

"Have you thought of going into business for yourself?" he asked. "That's an option a few people I know have taken."

"When I first graduated college, I thought of starting my own business," she said.

"After I'd gained some experience working for others. But I don't know what I'd do."

The waitress returned with their coffee and pie. "That looks great." He admired the pie, and then returned his attention to Christa. "What would you really like to do?"

"Something service oriented, I think." She added cream to her cup. "I want to help people and solve problems. I'd like to make a difference." At her old job, she'd had the opportunity to work on a couple of campaigns for nonprofits. She'd enjoyed that work most, though the majority of her time was spent on other, less-satisfying projects.

"Then we're not so far apart. I want to help folks, too—help them get to jobs and spend less time commuting and more time with their families."

"People could do that if they stayed here in Cedar Grove."

"Except there aren't many jobs here—not that pay what jobs in the city do."

That was another problem altogether, one neither of them was likely to solve. But she wasn't going to let him off so easily. "I don't buy your argument that you had to choose the shortest route," she said. "A route to the north of Cedar Grove would still be shorter than taking the current road. It would meet your goal of a faster commute and it would be more convenient. Travelers could stop in Cedar Grove and get gas or a bite to eat, or to use the restroom."

"The new shopping development will have gas stations and restaurants. But a rest area with comfort stations and picnic tables is a good idea. I'll have to look into that." He pulled out his smartphone and tapped in a note.

She took a bite of pie. The combination of sweet-tart berries and flaky pastry was better than anything she'd had in the city—the kind of treat tourists would line up to buy, if they only got to town and discovered it. "You talk as if the highway is a done deal," she said. "As if it's too late to change anything. But all I've seen is drawings. You admitted in the meeting that you don't even have all of the right of way."

"We have commitments from everyone we need, but we're not rushing people. Despite what people like to think, the state doesn't bully its citizens. We'll complete the negotiations soon. We're surveying and expect to break ground on schedule."

"Until you start pouring concrete, there's still time to rethink this."

She focused on her pie, aware of his gaze on her. She couldn't remember a man looking at her with such intensity. What did he see? He wasn't hostile—when she glanced up, she was surprised to find only sympathy in his expression. "I know this isn't what you want," he said, in the gentle voice that had first attracted her. "But not every change is bad."

"This one isn't good." She tried to keep her attention on the pie, but was aware of him still watching her.

"You've had too much change in your life lately, haven't you?" he said after a moment.

"What do you mean?" Her heart was racing again. She hated that he unsettled her so.

"It can't be easy, losing your job and moving back home. That's a lot to adjust to."

And she wasn't adjusting well—was it so obvious, even to a stranger? Was he so perceptive, or just making a lucky guess? "I'm looking at this as a much-needed break. A vacation."

"And this highway project is just one more thing to deal with. One more upheaval."

"Yes. I guess you could say that."

"Just remember, this isn't really that important. Not like your future."

His words confused her. "You don't think this highway is important? Then why are you so unwilling to consider altering the plans?"

"The highway is important to me. And it will be important to a lot of other people, some who don't even live here yet. But it's a road, not a person. Even cold, logical engineers know the difference."

Her cheeks grew hot as she remembered what she'd said to Kelly. "I didn't mean for you to hear that," she said. "I was frustrated."

"I've been called worse." He sipped his coffee, still watching her over the rim of his cup. "Have you talked to your parents about the highway project?" he asked.

Why was he asking about her parents? "Not really. We've had other things on our minds."

"Of course. But ask your dad what he thinks. You might be surprised."

"He said he knew you. He even said you had a good head on your shoulders."

"I'm flattered. I like him too."

"He talks as if you two are friends."

"I like to think we are. Bud was one of the first people I met with when I came to Cedar Grove. One of the best."

"He hasn't said much, but he doesn't seem very upset about the new highway."

"Talk to him. You might learn some things that surprise you."

"Neither one of my parents have talked to me all that much since I got here," she said. "Not about anything important. They seem, I don't know, distracted."

"But they're happy to have you home, I'm sure."

"I don't know about that either." Despite their attempts at enthusiasm this afternoon, dinner had been quiet, conversation strained. Neither parent had asked more about Christa's job, though she would have thought they would have wanted to know the details of her layoff. "Sometimes I think they'd be happier if I wasn't here. Mom seemed anxious to get me out of the house this afternoon, and she keeps urging me to get involved with clubs and things in town. She has a whole calendar of activities planned for me, as if she doesn't want me around the house any more than necessary." Telling Ryder these things was like letting air out of an over-inflated balloon. Tension eased from her shoulders and she felt better than she had in days.

"It's a big adjustment for all of you," he said. "It's something I've never had to deal with."

"Where do your parents live?" she asked, ready to change the subject.

"My dad is in Wyoming. We lived there when I was small, but I don't remember much about it. My mom is in Dallas. She teaches at a private school."

"They're divorced?"

"It only happened last year. I'm still trying to get used to the idea."

Maybe he knew more than she'd given him credit for about unsettling changes. "Were you surprised they split up?"

"Very. I thought they had a good marriage."

"I think divorce is hard on everyone involved, but sometimes people are happier after the split."

He rubbed the back of his neck, as if trying to massage away a cramp. "I have mixed feelings about it. Part of me wishes they'd found a way to work things out and stay together. But Mom says she was unhappy for years. She wanted to stay in one place—make friends, have a job, join clubs. I thought she could have done all those things and stayed married to my dad, but she says no."

"What does your dad say?"

"Not much. He's always been pretty stoic."

"Your mom must like having you close to her."

"She does. And she does seem very happy with her new life. So maybe you're right, and this is for the best." He waited while the server refilled their coffee. "She's coming for lunch on Saturday. She says she wants to see where I live. I'm afraid she's going to be disappointed."

Christa stiffened. "Does she have something against small towns?"

"No. She'll love Cedar Grove, I'm sure. But my apartment is just a furnished rental, nothing fancy. I know she'll expect better, but it doesn't make sense for me to spend money on a house when I'm not going to be here that long."

Such logical practicality seemed so cold to her. How could he feel at home when even his furniture wasn't his own? "Where do you think of as home?" she asked.

"I don't really think about it." He pressed the back of his fork into a few stray crumbs on his plate. "I've learned to be content wherever I am."

"Do you think you'll ever want to settle down? I mean, if you have a family…" She let the words trail away. Maybe she was getting too personal.

"Maybe then I would want to find one place and grow roots," he said. "Moving so often was tough when I was a little kid. I was always the new guy, always trying to catch up. On the other hand, it taught me to relate to a lot of different kinds of people. I grew used to the moves, even learned to like them."

He sounded so matter of fact and upbeat. But she remembered his comment about not wanting to go back to an empty apartment. Having no deep connections to other people implied a loneliness she couldn't begin to imagine.

She didn't want to feel sorry for Ryder. She didn't want to empathize with a man who was turning her world—her connections—upside down. But she was drawn to him in spite of wanting to hold back. "We should talk again, after I've had a chat with my father," she said. "Though I don't think he's going to change my mind about this project. Or keep me from fighting it."

"I'm happy to talk with you anytime." His eyes met hers, and she read a kaleidoscope of emotions in their depths—sadness, determination, sympathy, and maybe even affection. She had to look away, afraid of what he might read in her own eyes. "Just remember, Christa. I'm not out to hurt you or your family or anyone in this town. I really do want to help."

The words sent a shiver of apprehension up her spine. Wasn't there a saying about people who were guilty protesting too much? Ryder was hiding something from her, she was sure. But she couldn't imagine what that might be.

THOUGH RYDER LINGERED over coffee with Christa as long as possible, by 8:30 the crowd at the café had thinned and Etta Mae was starting to wipe down tables and stack chairs. "I guess we'd better go," Christa said, pushing out of the booth.

"I guess so." Admittedly he was reluctant to end the evening. Though he'd learned over the years to talk to almost anyone about anything, seldom did those conversations delve as deep as his discussion with Christa tonight. He hadn't talked about his parents' divorce with anyone before. Knowing that she understood his mixed emotions about the situation made him feel closer to her.

The parking lot alongside the café was almost empty when he walked Christa to her car. She stopped beside the sedan and looked up at the sky. "Living in the city, I'd forgotten how bright the stars could be," she said.

He joined her in admiring the night sky, spangled with glittering stars. A memory of another night, standing under a similarly bright sky, hit him like a physical pain. "When I was six, we moved from Virginia to Kyoto," he said. "I caught the flu on the transport over and was pretty miserable by the time we got there. I had a meltdown, crying and screaming that I wanted to go home. To calm me down, my mom took me outside and told me to look up at the stars. She'd been teaching me the names of the constellations, and she pointed out that I could see some of the same ones in the sky over Japan as I could in the United States. It was like seeing old friends who'd be there wherever I lived."

"Your mom sounds like a pretty smart woman."

"I guess she is." He shook his head. "Funny—I hadn't thought of that in years."

"It's a good memory to have." She touched his arm—the briefest brush of her fingers, yet the sensation lingered, a warm acknowledgment of the connection they'd shared. "Good night, Ryder. Thank you for the coffee."

"Thanks for the talk."

He waited until she'd driven away before he climbed into his truck and started the engine. He didn't want to go back to his apartment, but he could think of nowhere else to go, so he took the long way home, down a back road that skirted the edge of town. He'd rented rooms above the garage of what once must have been one of the finest homes in town, a large Greek Revival home with stately columns and rows of tall windows. The garage sat to the side and a little behind the house, accessible from a side street. Ryder parked beneath the large live oak out front and made his way up the stairs to the suite of rooms that had been furnished in the 1970s, judging by the plaid upholstery and dark wood furniture.

He'd lived in half a dozen similar apartments since his college days. The outdated décor never bothered him. All he needed was a bed to sleep in and a comfortable chair in which to watch TV. But now he saw the rooms as his mother or Christa might see them: worn and sparse and devoid of personality.

He sank onto the sofa and studied the scarred coffee table and thought of the base housing they'd lived in over the years, which had ranged from cinder-block barracks in Mississippi to a neat, nearly new bungalow in Germany. His mother had transformed every one of those rooms into a home, hanging pictures and slip-covering furniture. Within a week of their arrival even the most foreign of places would seem familiar. What a gift she'd given them, with this ability to ease the transition from one place to another. He'd have to remember to thank her.

What would his dad do, now that he didn't have Mom to work her magic at each new posting? Maybe, like Ryder, he wouldn't notice at first. He wouldn't consider furniture or pictures important. But a man who had

had his family around him for years was bound to be lonely now.

Ryder pulled out his phone and punched in his dad's number. It was only a little after eight in Wyoming, not too late to call.

"Hello." His dad's voice was brusque. The voice of command.

"Hey, it's Ryder."

"Hello, son. Is everything all right?"

"Everything's good, Dad. I just thought I'd call and see how you're doing."

"I'm well. I was thinking of calling you tomorrow, in fact. I'm moving to a new posting and wanted to give you my new address and contact information."

Ryder relaxed. "Where are you headed?"

"D.C. It's a very coveted posting and I was lucky enough to snag it."

"Congratulations."

"You'll have to come see me once I'm settled. It's a great town—lots to see and do."

"Maybe I'll do that, though I doubt I'll be able to break away from this project for a while."

"Where are you again? Texas, I know, but where?"

"Cedar Grove. It's a small town outside of Dallas."

"Your mother is in Dallas now."

"I know. I drove over to see her a couple of times, and she's coming here this weekend. She's looking well."

"Your mother has always been an attractive woman."

"Yes, she is. She seems happy."

"And I'm happy about that. I know she blames me for what happened, but when we married she knew the kind of life I had to lead. She went into it with her eyes wide open. She couldn't expect me to give up a career I'd put years of my life into, simply because she changed her mind."

"Dad, you don't have to justify yourself to me." The last thing Ryder wanted was to be caught between his parents.

"I know, son. You were always the easiest of the kids. The girls would carry on and cry crocodile tears every time I announced a new posting, but you always took it in stride. Too bad you didn't opt for a military career. You'd have been good at it."

He'd been a "good little soldier." Ryder remembered how proud he'd been when his father used those words to describe him. But a military career wasn't for him. He didn't want a life that was so regimented, where other people made most of his decisions for him. "This is a better fit for me," he said. "You should come down and see me sometime, Dad. The country's wide open, with lots of ranches, and good people."

"Maybe I'll do that. I need to get settled into the new posting first. Tell your mother I said hello when you see her."

"I can give you her number, if you want to call her."

"No, that's okay. I'm sure I'm the last person she wants to talk to. Take my advice, son. Stay single as long as you can. There was a time when a woman married a man and took it for granted she'd follow him wherever he led. But those days are long gone. Women are more independent. I'm not saying it's wrong, but it makes it harder on a marriage—at least if a man's career requires him to move around."

"Did you ever think of doing something different—leaving the military and staying in one place?"

"What would I have done? I'm trained as a fighter—a military strategist. Even if I could translate that to the corporate world, I'm not cut out for the daily grind of staying in one place for years. I'd suffocate. You're the same way—you and I are just alike."

Ryder couldn't tell if his dad meant this as praise or not. He'd always admired and looked up to his father, but he didn't want to end up like him, alone and lonely in his fifties. "I hope you can come see me, Dad," he said. "I'd like us to spend some time together."

"I'd like that too, son. I'll say good night now. Have to get up early in the morning."

"Me, too. Good night, Dad."

He laid his phone on the coffee table; his gaze transfixed on the pattern of scars and cup rings. Was he really so much like his father? While he had always looked forward to going to new places and seeing new people, none of the places he'd lived had ever felt suffocating. His moves hadn't been driven by restlessness or boredom, but by the need to prove himself. He was moving up in his career. If anything, all that moving had been done to try to establish his place in the world.

He wouldn't be like his dad, always on the move. One day he'd find a location to settle. He'd have a home and family, and a position that would allow him to live where he wanted. It might be a big city, like Dallas, or even a small town, like Cedar Grove. He could see himself settling here, but not yet. He had other things he needed to do first.

CHAPTER FOUR

CHRISTA DIDN'T HAVE a chance to speak with her dad the next morning. Her parents left before dawn to drive to Dallas on some mysterious errand they refused to divulge. "We just have some things we need to take care of," Mom said as she finished her coffee.

"I could go with you," Christa said. "We could do some shopping after you finish with whatever you need to do, or have lunch—"

"We won't have time for that." Mom avoided meeting Christa's gaze.

"Besides, I need you to stay here and take delivery of a load of hay." Her father finished his own coffee and stood. "Rodrigo will help you. Adi, we'd better go."

They left before Christa could ask any more questions. She stood at the front window and watched until her dad's truck disappeared down the drive, feeling the same way she had when she was a kid and her parents went on a rare date, leaving her behind.

Ridiculous, she told herself. She wasn't a kid anymore, and her parents didn't have to take her everywhere. But it was her parents' secretiveness that hurt more than their going off without her. She'd expected to come home and easily slip into her old lifestyle, where she and Mom and Dad shared meals and laughter and confidences. But they didn't seem to want that.

Maybe this was a not-so-subtle way of telling her to grow up and move on. But she couldn't imagine ever being so mature she wouldn't want to be close to her family.

She pondered the problem as she changed into jeans, boots and a long-sleeved shirt and tied her hair back in a ponytail. Unloading hay was hot, itchy work, but it would be a better workout than any she'd achieve at the gym. When the tarp-covered eighteen wheeler turned into the drive, she was ready. When her parents returned, they'd see she hadn't forgotten her cowgirl upbringing.

Rodrigo, a forty-something cowboy, all sinew and muscle, who had worked for her family for as long as Christa could remember, helped unload the big square bales into the hay shed, while the terrier, Jet, sniffed for mice among the stacked bales. They slipped into an easy rhythm, dragging the hay from the truck and across the shed, muscles straining, nose itching. But the hard work felt good, and after an hour or so, the sweet-smelling hay filled the shed in neat rows, like bricks in a wall. Christa signed the manifest and the driver climbed into the truck and rumbled back down the drive.

Christa joined Rodrigo in the shade of the stacked bales. "Why isn't Duncan helping, too?" she asked. Duncan Walters had also worked for her family for many years.

"Old Dunc decided to retire back in March." Rodrigo swept off his hat, wiped the sweat from his brow, before replacing the battered Stetson. "Your dad figured we could get by with just him and me."

The Rocking M had always employed at least two hands—sometimes more. Was Dad cutting back because he really didn't need the help, or because he couldn't afford it? She checked the shipping manifest in her hand against the tower of hay stacked in the shed. "I'm surprised he's buying hay this time of year," she said. "He used to grow all his own."

"Hard to grow enough with the drought," Rodrigo said. "He sold off a lot of the stock last year because they were too expensive to feed. Might have to sell more this year. Prices are still pretty good."

"I didn't realize things were that bad." Her parents hadn't confided in her. She thought of all the money they had spent on her education. They could have used it here on the ranch. Maybe her being here now, another mouth to feed, was straining their budget, too.

"You don't have to worry about your dad," Rodrigo said. "He's one of the savviest ranchers I know. He plays it safe and always knows what he's about. When the rains come and the economy picks up again, he'll be ready."

"I'm sure you're right." She leaned back against the hay, the sweet, summery smell filling her head, reminding her of the days she'd spent helping in the hay fields. The hot, sweaty work was made bearable by the promise of swimming in the stock tank when they were done, and Popsicles on the back porch after that. So many memories.

"I guess there'll be a lot of changes

around here, with the new highway coming through." Rodrigo interrupted her thoughts.

The highway! She couldn't even get away from it here. "I guess so." She straightened. "What do you think of it all?"

He snorted. "I think people are in too much of a hurry to get to places. It's not like I left anything in Dallas that I need."

She hid a smile. Rodrigo wasn't alone in his disdain for the city. Once upon a time people in Cedar Grove had found everything they needed in the small town, and had no need to leave. Now they had to travel for everything from groceries to medical care. She hated that it had to be that way.

"What time are you expecting your folks back?" Rodrigo asked.

"I don't know. They didn't say."

"Looks like we've got company." Rodrigo nodded toward the dust cloud that announced the approach of a vehicle on the long drive leading to the barns and hay sheds. A late-model white pickup with some kind of seal on the driver's door crept toward them. Jet hurried to stand in front of Christa, barking, his tail wagging furiously.

The truck stopped and Ryder, dressed in his usual crisp khakis and white shirt, stepped out. Today he wore a tan Stetson, similar to the ones Rodrigo and her dad always sported, though much newer.

Christa scooped up the dog and shushed him as Ryder touched his hand to the brim of the Stetson in a salute. "Hello, Christa. Rodrigo. Is Bud around?"

"He's not here," Christa said.

"Is he up at the house?" Ryder glanced in the direction of the ranch house.

Clearly, he knew his way around the place. "He and Mom are in Dallas," she said. "Why did you want to see him?"

"Nothing important. How are you doing?"

Jet had quieted and was wriggling in her arms, so she set him down and resisted the urge to smooth her hair, which she knew was a mess, along with the rest of her. She wore no makeup and was dusty and sweaty, with hay sticking to her clothing, her hair a tangle. "We've been unloading hay," she said, by way of explanation.

"I've got some other work to do, so I'll get on with it," Rodrigo said. He nodded to Ryder, and sauntered away. Christa resisted the urge to call him back on some pretense. Last night she'd been easy with Ryder, in the café full of people, but now she couldn't seem to relax. Without the buffer of other people around them, would he sense her attraction to him and get the wrong idea? Even Jet deserted her, distracted by some scent he'd uncovered on the other side of the shed.

"So you grew up here."

He was still looking toward the house, which sat in the grove of oaks her grandfather had planted when he built the house. "I was born in a hospital in Dallas," she said. "But I came home to here and didn't leave until I went to Austin for college."

"What was that like—being a little girl here?"

"I don't think I could have asked for a better childhood. I mean, people pay big money to vacation in the kind of environment I lived in every day. I rode horses, swam, went to movies with my friends or hung out at the soda fountain. I knew almost everyone and could safely go almost anywhere in town." She'd been hoping to recapture a little of those stress-free, uncomplicated times when she'd moved back here. She'd lost more than her job in the city—she'd lost her place in life, her identity. She needed to return to the one place she was always sure of herself in order to figure out where she belonged and what she was supposed to be doing.

"You didn't long for malls and drive-throughs?" His dimples showed when he smiled and her heart did its trapped butterfly imitation again.

"Maybe sometimes I did," she said. "I mean, I was a teenage girl. When I left for college in Austin, I was excited about living in the city, being closer to shopping and restaurants and all the things we didn't have here. But after a while, I missed all of this." She gestured around her, at the wide-open prairie, the ranch buildings and the little house. "There's just something about home."

"I never felt that kind of tie to a place. I'm a little envious."

He was standing close enough she could smell the faint pine scent of the soap he used, or maybe it was aftershave. The sleeves of his shirt were rolled up to just below the elbows, revealing muscular forearms dusted with dark hair. She'd worked around men all the time growing up, riding horses, bucking hay and mending fences alongside Rodrigo and Duncan and the other cowboys, but none of them had seemed as masculine and desirable as Ryder did right now.

As if sensing her uneasiness, he stepped back, putting more distance between them. "Would you show me around?"

The request surprised her. "I thought you'd been here before."

"I have, but that was to talk to your dad. I'd like to see the place through your eyes."

She brushed hay from her jeans. "I'm a mess."

"You look fine to me."

She didn't dare look up, but she felt his gaze on her, like a caress. Quickly, she whistled for the dog. As she started walking. Ryder fell into step beside her. "These two hay sheds were built in 1979," she said. "My grandfather was ranching the place then. My dad was a teenager. He went to college at Texas A&M and got a degree in Agriculture Science, then married my mom and they lived in what everybody called the old home place, over near Jade Creek."

"Does anyone live there now?" Ryder took a long, deep breath and released it.

"Not for a long time. It's mostly used for storage," she said. "By the time I was born we'd moved to the main house. Grandpa had died and my grandmother lived with us." She smiled at the memory. "She was my favorite person in the whole world. She was half-Vietnamese, a tiny woman who still spoke with a lovely accent."

"How did she end up on a ranch in North Texas?"

Christa smiled. She loved this story. "She and my grandfather met when he was stationed in Vietnam. She was only fifteen, but he thought she was older. She worked doing laundry for the soldiers and he would give her food and treats like chocolate and peanut butter. When it came time for him to ship back to the United States, they were in love. He swore he wouldn't leave her behind."

"The war must have still been going on. How did he ever get her into the United States?"

"That's the wonderful thing about this story. It was almost impossible for adult Vietnamese to immigrate at that time, but some groups were able to bring in children—orphans. Somehow my grandfather convinced a group into taking her in and sponsoring her. By that time he knew how old she really was, but I think he lied and told them she was even younger. He broke all kinds of rules, spent all his savings and risked his career, his reputation, everything—all because he loved her so much." She had never tired of her grandmother telling this tale—how her grandfather had worked so tirelessly so the two of them could be together. "His parents objected to the marriage, and it wasn't as if anyone else was accepting. It was the height of the war and my grandmother was afraid to go out alone. People would say horrible things to her. But my grandfather didn't care about any of that. He loved her so much."

"That's an incredible story," he said.

"It's the most romantic thing I've ever heard." She sighed. "He wanted to start over in a new place, so they came here right after they married. He bought this land from another rancher and lived in the old house that was already here until he could build a new house—the one my parents live in now."

"Were the people in Cedar Grove more accepting of your grandmother?"

"By the time I was old enough to notice, people had accepted her," Christa said. "Though she still wasn't overly social. She preferred to spend most of her time on the ranch. She helped my mother with cooking and cleaning and gardening, and she looked after me. I never tired of hearing her talk, especially about the past."

"How long has she been gone?" he asked, his voice gentle.

"She died when I was a freshman in high school. I'd never lost anyone I loved before. I was devastated. I still miss her." She shook her head. "You asked for a tour of the ranch, not a family history. Sorry."

"No. I enjoy listening to you."

He was a good listener, and easy to talk to. "I told you about the hay sheds and the original house and the current house. To see anything else we'd have to take a drive, or saddle some horses."

"Maybe some other time." He rested one arm on the wooden fence that bordered the drive and studied her. He had a way of looking at her, as if he was seeing below the surface, to secrets she kept inside.

She tucked her hair behind one ear. "What are you looking at?" she asked.

"You seem so at home here. I'm wondering what you were like in the city. What did you do for this marketing firm?"

"A lot of different things. I worked with companies to design ad campaigns—everything from tech companies to nonprofits. I was part of a team. We did everything from idea generation to actually buying the ad space."

"What did you like best about the work?"

"I liked learning new things. The companies we worked with did so many things, and I had to learn about their products and services in order to design marketing campaigns for them. Every day was interesting and different. And I liked the people I worked with, too. Because the company was privately owned and still fairly small, we were like a family almost. I'm going to miss that."

"I'm sorry you were laid off. It sounds like you really enjoyed the work."

"I did. I not only liked the work, I had good co-workers I looked forward to seeing every day. I even liked our office. It was a light, airy space near my apartment. I was planning to buy a town home in a new development in the neighborhood next year. I thought I had it made, and that I'd stay there for years."

"It's even harder to leave a situation when you're so attached to it," he said.

She nodded. "It's scary, when things

change that we thought we could count on to remain stable."

"That's when you learn to count on yourself—and the people around you."

"I guess so."

Now it was her turn to take a step back, to move away from the connection she was starting to feel for him. "I have a bunch of things I need to do at the house before my parents get home," she said. "I'll tell Dad you stopped by. Do you want him to call you?"

"No rush. I'll stop by some other time." He straightened. "Maybe I'll see you again."

She took another step back. "Ryder— don't get any ideas, okay? I mean, I'm here for just a little while, to get my bearings and look for another job. You're here to oversee this highway project."

"And I'm part of all the changes you hate." He nodded. "I know you don't like what I do, but we can still be friends. That's all. You can't have too many friends, can you?"

What did he expect her to say to that? "No. I guess not. And I think—I think you're an okay guy, even if we don't agree on this highway issue."

"I'm still hoping to win you over to my

side." He nodded politely and then headed across the yard, back toward his truck.

She hugged her arms across her chest and watched him climb into the truck and drive away. She'd told him she liked it here on the ranch because life was simple. But lately, things had gotten very, very complex. Ryder was one more complication she wasn't sure she knew how to handle.

RYDER DROVE BACK into town, intending to return to his apartment and follow up on some paperwork he needed in anticipation of next week's ground breaking for the highway. He didn't want any last-minute glitches to delay the project. The townspeople, as well as his bosses with the state, would scrutinize every aspect of his work, so he wanted it to be perfect.

But instead of turning toward his apartment, he headed down Main Street and parked in front of the hardware store. Inside, he wandered the aisles, looking at displays of paint and supplies, then stopped in the aisle devoted to housewares. He fingered the edge of a red-and-blue braided rug.

"Thinking of doing a little redecorating?"

He turned and recognized Christa's

friend, Kelly. The petite brunette walked toward him. "I hope you don't mind my saying this, but you look a little lost, Ryder."

"My mother's coming to visit, and I thought I ought to try to fix my place up a little."

"Good idea." She glanced at the display of rugs. "You don't really seem like the braided rug type, though."

"Honestly, all I know about rugs is that you walk on them. And I don't care to learn more, except I'm trying to avoid giving my mom an excuse to lecture me about growing up and settling down. I figured having an apartment that looked like I actually lived there would help."

"You're in Vicki Harrison's garage apartment, right?"

"Yep. I take it one of her sons lived there for a while, so it still looks like a cross between a frat house and Grandmother's attic."

Kelly's laughter emerged as a snort. "Not a good look. So, what are you hoping for instead?"

"I just want it to look like someplace an adult man would live. One who's sort of… settled."

She quirked an eyebrow in a quizzical

manner. "Does this mean you're thinking about staying in Cedar Grove long term?"

"I'm only here for the duration of the road project."

She clucked her tongue. "And here I thought I had some juicy gossip." She studied the shelves, and then confidently pulled down a couple of navy blue rugs. "Start with these. I suggest you put them over any stains in the carpet."

"Okay." He took the rugs. "What else?"

"Are you seriously telling me you've never furnished an apartment before?"

"I never needed to."

She shook her head and added a stack of bath towels. "Hang these where your mom will see them if she uses your bathroom. That will keep her from focusing on the ratty ones you probably use every day."

"You're starting to scare me. Have you been peeking in my bathroom?"

"I don't have to. Most people—especially single men—use ratty bath towels for everyday, and save the good ones for company. Put these in the kitchen." She added dish towels and a matching pot holder. "Oh, and these will help dress up the sofa." She piled on four throw pillows in shades of gold, brown and blue.

Ryder peered over the top of the growing stack. "Anything else?"

"You need pictures. Art." She looked around. "I don't see anything here, but if you stop by Wildwood Flowers, she has a good selection. Buy a couple of plants, too. Ask her for anything that thrives on neglect. It would help if you framed a few photographs, too."

"Photographs of what?"

"You—with friends. Hanging out. Doing stuff. You know, to personalize the place. Let your mom see that you have a life."

He tried to remember if he had any photos of himself with other people besides his family. Maybe he'd been captured in some shots other people took, at work or casual gatherings with acquaintances. But he had no albums or computer files with candid shots of himself at parties or barbecues or dinners. Those were things people accumulated when they lived somewhere for a while—at least long enough to establish a history.

"Thanks," he told Kelly as they headed toward the checkout. "I'm sure this stuff will help warm the place up a little."

"Maybe you should ask Christa to help you," she said, her tone was casual, but the inference was not.

He smiled. "I thought she was in marketing, not decorating."

"She's a smart woman, so I'm sure she'd have good ideas for you. And it would give you an excuse to see her again."

Ah. More matchmaking. "I didn't know I needed an excuse to see her."

She set her purse on the counter and faced him. "Etta Mae said you two looked pretty cozy at the Blue Bell last night."

"We enjoyed talking."

"You could continue the conversation at your apartment."

If he was worried about his mom seeing where he lived, he definitely didn't want Christa to know what a failure he was at putting his own stamp on the place. "I think I'll leave Christa out of the decorating, thanks."

"Maybe that's a good idea. Get the place fixed up first, then invite her over."

"Christa and I are just friends."

"That's a good place to start. And I'm really happy for you. I think the two of you are a good match."

"We're not dating. She made it very clear she doesn't want to date me."

"And half the women in town would tell her she needs her head examined, but that's just Christa—it takes her a long time to warm up to anything new. She just moved back to town, so she has to adjust to that before she can move on to dating. But she'll come around. Trust me, I've known her all her life."

"So she's always been slow to accept change?"

"Are you kidding me? She carried the same backpack all the way through high school, even though it was falling apart, because she couldn't stand to get a new one. In ninth grade, she ate a cheese sandwich every single day for lunch. When the Dairy Queen closed down, she practically went into mourning. It's not that she doesn't like new things—she just wants all the old, familiar things to stay the same."

"Yet she moved to the city after she graduated."

"Yeah, that was a big step, but it was what her parents and everyone else expected her to do, so that made it kind of routine. Plus, she loved her job and established herself there pretty quickly. I think that's why this layoff has thrown her for such a loop. She thought she was settled for life."

"She seems pretty young to be so set in her ways."

"It's not set in her ways so much as anchored. She's very loyal to the people and places that are meaningful to her. And she's willing to change, if she has a strong enough reason to. There's something to be said for being steady and reliable and not flighty."

"I guess there is." He piled his purchases on the checkout counter. "Thanks again for your help, Kelly. Maybe all this…" He indicated the rugs, pillows and towels. "Will make me seem less, um, flighty to my mom."

A pink blush stained her cheeks. "I wasn't talking about you!"

"It's okay. I know Christa and I are pretty much opposites in our approaches to life."

"You know what they say—opposites attract."

"Why are you so set on setting me up with Christa?"

She made a face. "Well, you obviously

aren't interested in me, and if I can't have the most eligible guy to hit town in a while, why not root for my best friend? Also, if the two of you got together, she might decide to stick around, instead of running off to Houston again. I'd like that."

"Better not pin your hopes on me," he said. "I really think Christa isn't interested."

"But you didn't say you weren't interested in her."

"I don't see any long-term relationship in my immediate future." The words hurt to say, the tight pain in his chest a reminder that what he wanted and what he knew would happen didn't always mesh perfectly. "The timing just isn't right."

"Oh please! As if love answers to a time-table. There's such a thing as being too practical, you know."

He shrugged. "What can I say? I'm a practical guy—cold and logical."

Kelly wrinkled her nose. "You weren't supposed to hear that. And she didn't mean it, anyway."

"But I am practical. And I am leaving town in a year or two, so I'm not the right guy for someone who wants a life built around routine and constants."

"You say it, but I don't believe it. Anyway, good luck with your apartment and your mom. You never know—if you make the place comfortable enough, you might decide to stick around longer." She slid the strap of her purse onto her shoulder. "I have to run now. I just stopped to see if they'd gotten in the shelf brackets Mom ordered, but they aren't here yet. See you around."

"See you."

He paid for his purchases, and carried them to his truck. He had his doubts that a few towels and pillows would make much of an impression on his mom, but it was worth a try. And if he ever did bring Christa to his place, maybe she wouldn't think he was quite so cold.

CHAPTER FIVE

AFTER RYDER LEFT, Christa returned to the house and showered. She told herself she should pull out her laptop and start working on her résumé, but the thought of putting a positive spin on the fact that she'd lost her job made her want to crawl back into bed and stay there. She'd start the job hunt in earnest soon, but she needed more time to process what had happened. The job counselors had even said that getting laid off was like any other loss—she needed time to grieve.

Instead, she decided to make a special dinner for her parents. She couldn't compete with her mother's pot roast and peach pie, but she could grill steak and make baked potatoes and a salad. Mom and Dad would appreciate the meal after their long day in the city.

Jet alerted her to her folks' return, barking excitedly and standing at the front window, tail wagging. Christa stayed in the kitchen, slicing tomatoes, ears straining for the sound of the door opening. "I'm in the kitchen," she called.

No one answered. She moved to the door in time to see her mother hurry down the hallway. Her father removed his hat and turned toward her.

He had aged ten years in the few hours they'd been gone. Deep lines etched his face and his eyes were bloodshot, as if he'd been crying. But her father didn't cry—at least she'd never seen him do so, not even at his parents' funerals.

"Dad, what's wrong?"

"We'll talk about it later, pumpkin."

His use of his pet name for her only made her hurt more. "Dad, you look terrible. Something must have happened in Dallas. Are you hurt? Is Mom hurt?"

"Your mother is going to be fine." He spoke the words, not as reassurance, but as declaration, his voice almost angry.

"Do you need help unloading the truck?" she asked.

"There's nothing to unload."

So they hadn't gone shopping. "I made dinner, when you're ready."

"I don't think either one of us could eat. Thank you anyway. I'm just going to see to your mom."

He moved down the hall toward their bedroom, shoulders slumped, shuffling like an old man.

While her parents stayed behind the closed bedroom door, Christa sat in the kitchen with the untouched food. She'd never seen her father look so devastated. He must have gotten terrible news in Dallas. Had they gone to see their banker? Had the ranch been foreclosed on?

She'd been so focused on her own problems that she hadn't paid enough attention to all the signs that were right in front of her nose: he hadn't hired anyone to replace Duncan. He had sold off a lot of the stock. Even the orange survey flags she'd seen on her drive into the ranch were a clue. Maybe Dad planned to sell off part of the land. The last thing he needed was another mouth to feed. She couldn't have come home at a worse time.

She'd have to move back to Houston right away. She'd take any job she could find, whether it was in her field or not. And she'd get a roommate. She wouldn't burden her parents with her problems when they were dealing with so many of their own.

Well after dark, Mom and Dad emerged from their room. They came into the kitchen holding hands. Her mother had obviously been crying, and she looked shrunken, folded in on herself. Dad held out a chair and she sank into it. "Christa, we need to talk to you about something," she said.

Christa's chest hurt. "What is it?" she asked, in a voice that didn't sound like her own.

"I saw a doctor today in Dallas." Mom's voice sounded strange too—thin and whispery. "An oncologist."

Christa stopped breathing at the word. "A cancer specialist?"

"I have breast cancer." Mom drew in a shaky breath. "I'm going to have a mastectomy."

"When?" But the real question she wanted to ask was *How?* How could her strong, vibrant, *healthy* mother have cancer?

"Soon. Friday, if the surgeon can arrange it. We're waiting for a call."

"It's going to be fine." Dad rested his hand on Mom's shoulder.

"How long have you known?" Christa asked.

"We got the confirmation from the biopsy today, but the doctors have suspected something since I had my mammogram a couple of weeks ago."

"No wonder you seemed so distracted."

"The day you came home I had just had the biopsy. I was still a little out of it from the surgery."

"But why didn't you tell me? I could have come home sooner. Or I would have stayed in Houston, if that would be better." She would do anything for her Mom and Dad, if only they would let her.

"We didn't want to worry you," Mom said.

"I was already worried that you were acting so differently toward me—as if you didn't want me here."

"Oh, honey, that wasn't it at all. Of course I want you here."

"You'll be a big help in your mom's recovery," Dad said.

"Of course. I'll do whatever you need. All those times you nursed me when I was a kid, I can at least pay some of that back now."

Mom sat up straighter. "I don't need a

nurse. And I don't want anyone hovering over me. The doctor said I can be back on my feet a few days after surgery, and they have all kinds of new medicines to help cope with the treatments afterward."

Treatments. She must mean chemo and radiation—her mother couldn't even say the words. "What do the doctors say? I mean, how bad is it?" Christa tried to brace herself for whatever would come next.

"Stage two," her father said. "They caught it early."

"They won't know for sure until after the surgery," Mom said. "But they're cautiously optimistic."

"She'll be fine." She noticed her dad's fingers tighten on her mom's shoulders.

Christa's eyes stung, but she refused to let tears fall. Her parents were being brave about this; so would she. One thing was for certain, though. She wouldn't be going back to Houston any time soon.

"Two Barn Burner specials, coming up." Paul Raybourn dropped a white paper sack that smelled of beef and onions in front of Ryder and took a seat across from him at the picnic table. He opened a similar sack and pulled out a thick hamburger. "This is probably guaranteed to clog our arteries, but at least we'll die happy men."

"I plan on sticking around at least a little while longer." Ryder unwrapped his own burger. The two friends had run into each other outside the bank and decided to have lunch together. The Burger Barn, a local favorite, was a small stand near the school whose dining area consisted of three large picnic tables in the shade of ancient live oaks. The tables were splintered and uneven. Ryder thought of Christa's suggestion of a rest area along the new highway. Too bad that wasn't already a lunch option for them.

"You seem to be settling in here in Cedar Grove," Paul said. "That was quite a performance you gave at the public forum the other night. You won the men's respect and had the women all swooning."

"Swooning?" He choked back a laugh. "I don't think so."

"Don't play dumb. Most of the single women in town, and some of the married ones, are making eyes at you."

"New guys in small towns always attract attention." When he was first traveling on his own, Ryder had been flattered, until he'd figured out the women who went after him were more interested in the novelty of someone new than in getting to know him.

"Maybe so," Paul said. "Handsome guys with good jobs attract more. Or so my wife tells me. If I wasn't happily married, I'd probably hate you."

"How is Didi?" Ryder asked. "And the baby?"

"They're fine." Paul pointed a French fry at him. "Don't change the subject. Is it true you and Christa Montgomery are dating?"

"No!" He froze, burger halfway to his lips. "What gave you that idea?"

"Traci Schaeffer, who works at the bank, saw you two getting cozy over coffee in the Blue Bell after the forum, and Al Nelson, the mail carrier, noticed your truck out at the Rocking M yesterday afternoon."

Ryder's shock must have shown on his face. Paul laughed. "You can't keep secrets in a town this small."

"I don't have any secrets to keep. Christa and I are not dating. She barely tolerates me." For a while at the ranch yesterday, when she'd been telling him about her home, he thought they'd made a real connection.

Then she'd made a point of warning him off. Message received and understood.

"That must mean she really likes you," Paul said.

"You're crazy."

"What does she have against you?" Paul asked. "Is it because of the highway?"

"She doesn't like change. She thinks the new highway will kill the town."

"It's going to change the town. The main business area will probably shift. The bank is talking about moving out closer to the highway. And the town council is looking into annexing the land where the new shopping center will be, but it's going to require jumping through a lot of hoops. Christa will come around. Most people will."

"The town isn't the biggest problem," he said.

"Oh? Does she have a boyfriend back in Houston?"

Ryder's burger felt like a lump of lead in his stomach. He hadn't even thought of the boyfriend angle. But Christa had lived in Houston for years—maybe she'd left someone behind there. Maybe one of those co-workers she thought of as family. Still, wouldn't she have said so?

Then again, there were a lot of things between them that hadn't been said. "I don't
know if there's a boyfriend or not. I don't
think so. But when she finds out the deal
I've made with her father she's going to hate
me. And there's nothing I can do to stop
that."

"You haven't told her?"

"There's nothing for me to tell. The decision is up to Bud. I told her she needs to talk
to him about it, but apparently that hasn't
happened yet."

"I don't pity you when she finds out."

"I went out there yesterday to talk to Bud,
to tell him to discuss this with Christa. The
ranch is her home, so she deserves to know.
But he wasn't there. Christa said she's hardly
seen him since she got home."

"Maybe he's avoiding her. He doesn't
want to talk."

"Maybe you're right, but until she knows
what he's going to do about the ranch, there's
no sense in my trying to get too close to
her."

"So, what is he going to do with the
ranch?"

Ryder shook his head. "He hasn't said.
And I'm not going to push him. My plan is

to stay out of this as much as I can. And that means keeping my distance from Christa." Not that she'd given any indication that she wanted him closer—the opposite, really.

"Good luck with that." Paul picked up his burger again. "In my experience, women are more unpredictable than the weather."

Right. His best hope was that, when Christa did speak to her dad, Ryder managed to avoid the storm that was sure to follow.

BY THE TIME Friday arrived, Christa was a nervous wreck, though her parents had regained their equilibrium. They were a solid unit, supporting each other. That was the way a loving married couple should act, Christa told herself. Maybe one day she'd be lucky enough to experience that kind of support from her husband. In the meantime, she couldn't help feeling excluded from their intimate circle, struggling to deal with her worry and fears for her mother on her own.

On the long drive to Dallas for her mother's surgery, her thoughts drifted to Ryder. He probably would have pointed out how much shorter and more convenient the new route would make the trip. Shorter would be better today—though that didn't mean she agreed that the new highway was the best thing for the town.

The hospital was a modern, gleaming high-rise, as different from the little county hospital where Christa had had her tonsils out when she was six as a grand tabernacle was from a country chapel. After a flurry of paperwork and preparations, a nurse in pink scrubs whisked her mother off to surgery. Christa and her dad sat side-by-side in uncomfortable orange chairs in a waiting room, the sudden silence and stillness between them like the starkness after a tornado or other disaster. The world couldn't possibly be normal after this, yet it was.

A cooking show played on the television, the cheery hostess enthusing about the marvels of baked tomatoes or something like that. Christa had brought a book, but she was too keyed up to focus on it. Dad sat bolt upright in his chair, hands gripping his knees. He looked as if he might shatter if she touched him.

He must have felt her eyes on him. Suddenly, he turned and said. "What have you done about finding a new job?"

She'd been waiting all week for Dad to

ask about her job. When she'd first delivered the news about her reasons for moving home, she'd expected him to question her like a prosecuting attorney, wanting every detail of the layoff—the reasons given for letting her go, who else was laid off with her, what positions her co-workers had held, what kind of severance she'd been offered. Avoiding the grilling had been a relief at first, but had also made her feel that maybe he didn't care.

She appreciated his interest, but a hospital waiting room was the last place she'd expected to have this conversation. "Well, I attended the seminar my employer—ex-employer—offered to all the laid off workers," she said. "And I filed for unemployment, of course."

"Have you talked to anyone, put in any applications, let people know you're available?"

"No." She forced herself not to squirm in her chair like a little girl caught stealing cookies from the pantry. "I thought I should wait until I was settled here. And I need to update my résumé."

"You can't waste time. The longer you wait the worse it looks."

Said the man who had never worked for anyone but himself. "Dad, I—"

"I know you think I don't know anything about these things, but I read the paper. I've seen all the stories about the high unemployment rate. The people who land new positions are the ones who work all the angles. You did a good job for your old firm, didn't you?"

"Of course. The layoff was based purely on seniority, not performance."

"You'd be a real asset to someone else— just remember that." That was easy for her father to say—he'd have loved her if she'd been completely incompetent.

"Unfortunately, there are a lot of other capable people out there looking for jobs." Many of them her former co-workers, with more experience than she had.

"But they aren't you. Self-confidence. That's what these companies want to see."

Dad certainly sounded confident that he was right. But he had always been a man who could solve any problem, for himself, but also for his wife and daughter. Looking back, she could see how much she'd depended on him to do just that. But he couldn't solve her job dilemma for her, no matter how much he might want to. "I'm not feeling very self-confident right now," she confessed. "I mean, I loved my old job. I was good at it. I never saw the lay-off coming. I'm still trying to deal with that."

"You know the saying about if a horse bucks you off you have to get right back on, don't you?"

"I do, Dad." She refrained from rolling her eyes like an exasperated teenager.

"I know you think it's a cliché, but there's a lot of truth there. Do you remember when you were little and you got your first real horse—not the pony you rode at first, but a full-grown gelding?"

"Paco." She smiled, remembering the brown-and-white paint that had been her companion and friend well into high school, when he was finally retired from the saddle string and put out to pasture.

"Do you remember what happened the first time you tried to make him gallop?"

She winced. She remembered, all right. "He bucked me off and I broke my arm."

"And I made you get back on the horse the very next day, didn't I?"

"You did." Even though she'd been wearing a pink plaster cast. Even Mom had been concerned about Dad's plan, and Christa had shed more than a few tears, but her dad would have none of it, and in the end, he'd lifted her onto the back of the horse.

"I made you ride him again because if I hadn't you would have been scared of him—and he'd have gotten the idea that he got the better of you."

"No employer got the better of me, Dad. These things just happen."

"You need to remember that. Instead of moping at home, you need to get out there and apply for a job."

"I will." As soon as she figured out what she wanted to do. Houston was a big city, and there were probably plenty of marketing firms there, but her conversation with Ryder the other evening had her thinking more about the goals she'd started out with—she wanted to help people, and the work she'd done with non-profits had been the most satisfying in her old job. That kind of work wasn't the norm at most big marketing companies. What kind of work could she do that would combine her marketing skills and her desire to help others?

Her dad went back to staring into space and Christa pulled out her book and tried to read. She forced herself not to look at the time on her phone, so she didn't know how much time had passed when the doctor—a silver-haired man in blue scrubs—emerged from the double doors at the end of the hall. "Adele is doing great," he said.

Christa didn't pay attention to anything else he said. She was too full of relief that Mom had survived this first big hurdle. Dad listened and nodded and asked questions, until he, too, seemed satisfied with the news. "When can we see her?" he asked.

"She's in recovery now, but we've assigned her a room. You can go on up and wait for her there. But you have time to get some lunch first."

Christa's stomach growled. "Come on, Dad, let's find the cafeteria," she said.

"I don't want Adi arriving to an empty room," he said.

"I imagine they'll keep her in recovery a little while longer. She has to come out of the anesthesia." She took his arm. "We won't take long. You need to eat."

He let her lead him to the elevator, but when they stepped off on the ground floor he shook her off and led the way to the hospital cafeteria, which looked more like an upscale restaurant. They chose sandwiches and iced tea and ate in silence. Dad wolfed his food, then shifted in his chair and jingled his change, waiting for Christa to finish. She finally gave up. "I'm done. Let's go see Mom."

"All the rooms in this hospital are private," Dad said as they boarded the elevator again. "Your mom liked that."

Christa had trouble keeping up with her father's long strides as he hurried toward the cubicle assigned to Mom. The sag of his shoulders told her the room was still empty. He sat on the end of a narrow vinyl sofa against the wall while she took the only chair. "I'm sure she'll be here soon," she said.

Squeaky wheels, then a knock on the door. Dad and Christa both stood. "Come in," he called, though the door was already opening to admit an aide with a wheeled cart, on which sat a large vase of colorful flowers. "I have a delivery for Mrs. Montgomery," the aide said.

"Who sent those?" Dad asked.

"There's a card attached." The aide moved the flowers to a table at the end of the bed and left.

"What a gorgeous arrangement," Christa said. The orange birds of paradise, pink dahlias and purple lilies glowed against the dull sage walls of the room, like something out of a Van Gogh painting. She found the card among the lacy foliage and opened it. She blinked, unsure of the name on the card. It didn't belong here, in this room so far from Cedar Grove. "They're from Ryder."

"Now he didn't have to do that." Dad joined her beside the flowers. "Adi will like them, though. That was really thoughtful of him."

"Why is Ryder sending Mom flowers?" Christa asked.

"I saw him in town yesterday afternoon and told him Adi was having surgery." He returned to the sofa.

Christa tried to push down the hurt. Her parents hadn't even told *her* about her mom's diagnosis until Wednesday, yet her father had apparently volunteered the information to a man he scarcely knew. A man who wasn't part of their family or even a close friend.

She returned to her chair. "How did you and Ryder get to be such good buddies?" she asked, trying to keep her tone casual. As if she didn't care about the answer.

"We've spent a lot of time talking."

"About what?" What could her rancher father have in common with an itinerant engineer?

"The road project, for one thing."

"Do you agree with him that the road project is worth the risk to the town?"

"I think we can't predict the future. Things have already changed so much, what's a little more?" He shrugged.

"I know everyone says change is inevitable, but aren't some things worth holding on to and keeping the same?" Didn't people need those touchstones the way the ranch was her touchstone?

"Ryder's got a good head on his shoulders," Dad said. "He's traveled, seen a lot of the world. Maybe you should ask him for advice about your job search. He might know some people who could help you."

Christa thought they'd been talking about the highway, not about Ryder Oakes. The man had no business intruding on her family's problems this way. She was about to tell her father so when the door opened again and two aides wheeled in her mother.

Dad greeted Mom first, and kissed her cheek. She smiled weakly at Christa and squeezed her hand. "How do you feel, Mom?" Christa asked.

"I'm still pretty out of it." Her gaze shifted to the flowers. "Oh, how pretty!"

"Ryder Oakes sent those," Dad said. "The card says he hopes you're back home soon."

"How thoughtful of him." Mom turned her attention to Christa. "Have you met him? Such a handsome man."

"I was telling Christa she ought to talk to Ryder about her job search," Dad said. "He might have some contacts."

"Good idea," Mom said. Her eyes drifted shut, so she didn't see Christa's frown. The last person she wanted to ask for advice was Ryder Oakes.

CHAPTER SIX

SATURDAY MORNING, RYDER was up early. He'd spent the previous evening cleaning his apartment, and had stocked the refrigerator with bottled water and the diet soda his mother liked to drink. He'd arranged the rugs, pillows and towels, along with two potted plants the florist had assured him would thrive with very little care. But short of painting and buying new furniture, he could do little else to improve the rooms.

Promptly at eleven-thirty, his mother's car pulled into the driveway and parked beside his truck. He met her at the top of the stairs. "Come on in, Mom. Did you have any trouble finding the address?"

"Not at all. The town looks charming. Though I can't say the same about this place." She wrinkled her nose at the orange and brown plaid sofa set that filled the living room.

"It's not fancy, but it's clean and comfortable and that's all I need." He led her to a chair upholstered in brown-and-white stripes. "Why don't you sit here? Can I get you anything?"

"Not right now." She sat, ankles gracefully crossed, and looked up at him. At fifty, she appeared ten years younger, her hair colored a soft brown and styled in a shoulder-length bob. Her nails were neatly manicured, her jeans and jacket the latest fashion. She scarcely resembled the housewife who had cleaned his room and made peanut butter sandwiches and meatloaf for him all those years. "Sit down and tell me about the town," she said. "Do you like it here? Have you made friends?"

She'd asked the same questions dozens of times when he was growing up, after school during chats over glasses of milk and store-bought cookies—she'd never been a baker. He gave the same answer now that he'd given then: "It's a nice town. I get along fine."

But this time, the answer didn't smooth the lines on his mother's forehead. "Getting along with people isn't the same as having real friends," she said. "People you can count on in a crisis. It's only since I've moved to Dallas that I've made real friends like that."

He seized on this opportunity to shift the focus of the conversation off of himself. "I'm glad to hear it, Mom. I'm glad to know you really like it there."

"I love it. I have a job I enjoy. I've joined a book club and I take yoga classes—all the things I was never able to do before, moving around so much with your father."

"But you got to see the world." He had vivid memories of her in Japan, touring ornate temples and marveling at the landscaped gardens. Or in Germany, dancing at a local festival. She'd always seemed to be enjoying herself.

"That was exciting at first, but by the fifth time I had to pack everything we owned and start over a thousand miles or more away, the novelty was gone. About the time I felt I really knew a place and was beginning to settle in, we had to leave. But I was supposed to be a good army wife and not complain—your father never understood my feelings, anyway."

Ryder fought the urge to defend his father. "I always liked seeing new places and new people," he said.

Her expression softened, her lips curving in a fond smile. "You were the most adaptable of my children. You inherited your father's wanderlust, and his easy charm," she said. "Your sisters are more like me. They wanted marriage and children right away, and they were lucky enough to find men who know how to stay put. Sherry tells me Dale's about to be promoted to vice president of his company in St. Louis, and Megan and Todd are planning to buy a bigger house, closer to his job in Chicago."

"I'm glad you're happy, Mom." What else could he say? Though she didn't look particularly happy at the moment. Her gaze bore into him, as if she were examining a potential purchase for flaws. He fought the urge to squirm and returned the look, gazing into eyes the same shade of blue as his own. "What is it, Mom?"

"I know the divorce upset you," she said. "I've been doing some reading, about how divorce impacts even grown children. I'm sorry about that, but it couldn't be helped."

"You don't owe me an explanation." He stood. "I'm going to have some iced tea. Would you like some? Or a soda?"

"Sit back down. I know I don't need to

justify my actions to you, but I came here prepared to say some things, so hear me out."

He sat and forced himself to lean back against the sofa cushions, wanting to appear calm and relaxed, though he was anything but.

"I know your father blames me for ending our marriage," she said. "And I was the one who filed for divorce—that's true. But I also know I did the best I could for as long as I could. For a long time, I tried to be something I wasn't, because I loved him, and because I love all of you. But in the end, that wasn't enough. I couldn't live that nomadic, unstable life anymore."

"I had no idea."

"I tried not to make everyone around me miserable, too." She leaned over and put a hand on his knee. "I'm telling you this because I want you to think about the kind of life *you* want to live, while you're still young and can more easily change things. All this traveling may seem exciting when you're young and single, but who knows what may be in store for you in the future, what the picture might look like even a year or two from now?"

She sat back, hands folded in her lap once more. "You might get lucky and find a woman who shares your itchy feet. Or you could decide to settle down. After all, half your genes are mine."

"I don't think it's right to have a long-term relationship as long as I'm moving around. Maybe later, when I've established myself in my career." He had plenty of time.

"You certainly seem to be doing well here in Cedar Grove," she said. "Overseeing a big project like this new highway."

"I'm the youngest supervising engineer in the state." He wasn't one for bragging, but he couldn't keep the pride from his voice.

"How much more established in your career do you have to be, then?"

"If I do a good job on this, I could move up to overseeing multiple projects." Eventually, he might even head up the department.

"There's always something more to aspire to." She sighed. "For your father, it was always a higher rank or a better posting. He's still doing that."

"I talked to him the other night. He's being transferred to Washington D.C."

"He'll like that—at the center of the action."

"He seemed excited about it."

"Not that he was ever one to show much emotion." She shrugged. "It's none of my business now. But do me a favor and don't look to your father as the only example of how a man should live his life. There are more important things than titles and jobs."

"I know that, Mom."

"You do?" She leaned forward again. "Then what's more important to you? What one thing do you spend more time on and think about more than work?"

All the answers he knew were supposed to be right died on his lips—family, friends, hobbies—none of those received the devotion he gave to his work. "I guess I'll have to think about those things more," he said.

"You do that, darling." Her smile bloomed again, making her look younger, and more beautiful. "You really are so much like your father when we met. So handsome. Women swarmed around him like bees to honey. I felt so privileged to be singled out."

"He probably felt the same way about you."

She laughed at that. "Maybe so. But what about you? I know what you said about long-term, but still, do you have anyone special in your life?"

An image of Christa, leaning on the fence rail at the Rocking M, wind blowing back her hair, popped into his mind. But how special could she be when they'd only shared pie and coffee and a few conversations? He wasn't even sure she really liked him. "No one special," he said.

"I can't believe you have trouble meeting women," she said. "So it must be that you haven't taken the time to look for Ms. Right."

"*Ms. Right?* Mom, I'm happy with the way things are. I have plenty of time for that later."

"For years, I told myself I had time to do all the things I wanted to do, and then I woke up one day fifty years old and realized I had better get busy." She stood. "Why don't you take me to lunch and I'll see if I spot any likely candidates."

"I don't need you to manage my love life, Mom." He stood also, and took his keys from his pocket.

"It sounds to me like you don't have a love life." She patted his arm. "Besides, one of the advantages of living closer to you is that I can keep tabs on you. I might even be in a position to fix you up with some likely young women."

"Don't do it, Mom."

Her smile had turned sly. "Then you'd better find someone on your own, before I decide to take matters into my own hands."

THE COOL, AMMONIA-AND-PERFUME-scented air of the Cedar Grove Salon washed over Christa as she stepped out of the bright heat of Saturday afternoon. Kelly and her mom were both cutting hair at their stations, and two other women waited under the dryers. At the sound of the door bells, Kelly turned to greet the newcomer. "Christa!" She set aside her scissors and picked up a comb. "Mrs. Lytle, you know Christa Montgomery, don't you? Her folks own the Rocking M."

Mary Jane Lytle, one of the owners of the Seed and Feed, peered over her glasses at Christa. "Last time I saw you, you were just a skinny little thing riding in the rodeo parade," she said. "What have you been doing with yourself?"

"I lived in Houston a few years." Christa walked over to stand beside the salon chair. "I'm home for a little while."

"How is your mom?" Kelly deftly combed through Mrs. Lytle's newly streaked locks. "Is she still in the hospital?"

"No, they sent her home today. I can't believe they let her out so quickly, but she and Dad were both going crazy in there, so I guess it's for the best."

"I saw Adele's name on the prayer list at church," Mrs. Lytle said. "You tell her we're thinking about her."

"I know she'll appreciate that," Christa said.

"Is she doing okay?" Kelly asked.

"She seems to be." She didn't want to elaborate, with so many ears listening to every word. Janet had even turned off the blow dryer she'd been wielding in order to hear. "I just popped in for a minute to say hello. I dropped Mom's prescription off at the pharmacy and I'm waiting for them to fill it."

"You let us know if you need anything," Janet said. "I can even come out to the house to do her hair if she likes."

Kelly picked up a curling iron and began wrapping Mrs. Lytle's hair around the barrel. "Do y'all need any food or anything out at the house?" she asked. "I could make some soup or a casserole."

"Oh no, I think I've got that covered." Christa hadn't done much cooking in years, but between her and her dad, she was sure they could take care of the meals. "Mom really doesn't want anyone fussing over her." Including Christa. As soon as her parents were in the house, Adele had sent her daughter out to fetch the prescription. Not, Christa suspected, because she needed the pain medication so badly, but because she didn't want her daughter to have any part of settling her into a sickbed.

"I think Etta Mae planned to send something out to your mom," Mrs. Lytle said. "You might want to stop by the Blue Bell and check. She usually organizes volunteers to take meals to anyone who's been under the weather."

"We definitely don't need that," Christa said. Mom would be mortified if a bunch of women from town took turns stopping by to check on her. "I'll certainly speak to her. Thanks."

She took in the busy salon. She'd been hoping for a moment alone with Kelly, to unburden herself about the stress of the surgery, her worries for her mother, even her confused feelings about Ryder. He'd been so kind to her mother, and he'd accepted her stipulation that they limit their relationship to mere friendship—so why did she feel so unsettled around him?

But clearly, Kelly was too busy to talk. "I'd better get back to the pharmacy," Christa said. "I just wanted to let you know Mom is home and doing well."

"Come here and give me a hug before you go." Kelly held out her arms and the two friends embraced. "Hang in there," Kelly whispered. "I'll call you later."

"Thanks." Christa hurried from the salon before she gave into the tears that threatened. On the sidewalk, she took a deep breath and pulled herself together, then walked back to the pharmacy.

"The doctors never give refills on these things," the pharmacist, Liz Proctor, said. "So if your mom runs low, she needs to call a couple days ahead to get a new script approved."

"It's all Dad and I can do to get her to take one of these," Christa said. "I doubt she'll need a refill."

"You want me to give her a call and talk to her? I might be able to set her mind at ease."

"Not right now, but I really do appreciate the offer."

Back in the car, she closed her eyes and rested her head against the back of the seat. She felt like a football player, running interference between her mom and the line of well-wishers who wanted to descend on her to help. Life would be easier for all of them if they were able to accept the offered help graciously, but Christa understood her mom's need to keep life as normal and drama free as possible. She needed to pretend that nothing had changed; she was still the strong, healthy person she'd always been, a woman who didn't need anything from anyone.

She opened her eyes and started the car. She was almost out of town before she remembered Etta Mae's plans to organize volunteers to bring meals. She turned the car around and went directly to the Blue Bell.

Inside the café, she scanned the dining room for Etta Mae. The little woman was nowhere to be found, but Ryder greeted her from a table by the window. "Christa, how is your mother?"

Given the choice of shouting at him across the room or walking to his table, she chose the latter. He sat with an attractive older woman who shared his blue eyes and dimples. "Hello," the woman said. "I'm Ryder's mother, Peggy Oakes."

"Mom, this is Christa Montgomery. Her parents own a ranch near town, the Rocking M."

"It's good to meet you, Mrs. Oakes," Christa said.

"How is your mom doing?" Ryder asked again.

"Pretty good. The surgery went well and the hospital sent her home this morning. I just came into town to do a few things for her."

He smiled and indicated she should join them.

"No, I'm fine where I am. But thank you for the flowers you sent. They were gorgeous. And completely unexpected."

"I wanted to do something. I really like your mom and dad."

"And they like you."

"Why do you sound puzzled by that? I'm a likeable guy."

"I didn't say you weren't. I'm just surprised that you hit it off with them so quickly."

"Their high opinion of me means a lot."

Christa had no comeback. *Where was Etta Mae?* She turned instead to Ryder's mom. "Is this your first visit to Cedar Grove?"

"It is. Ryder's been showing me around town," Peggy said. "It's a lovely community. Everyone is so friendly."

"The pace is a little slower here than in the city," Christa said. "But we like it."

"Have you lived here long?" Peggy asked.

"Most of my life."

"And your parents are ranchers? For a while, when Ryder was a boy, he wanted to be a cowboy."

"Mom—every six-year-old wants to be a cowboy." He grimaced. "I also wanted to be a fireman and a race car driver."

"You must allow a mother to indulge her memories." She gave him a fond look. "How do you two know each other?"

"In a town this size, it's hard not to know almost everyone," Ryder said.

"Yes, but a casual acquaintance doesn't send flowers to a mother in the hospital, I don't think."

"Actually, Ryder knows my parents better than he knows me," Christa said. "I only just moved back to town a little over a week ago."

"Then maybe the two of you will get to know each other better."

Out of the corner of her eye, Christa spotted Etta Mae emerging from the kitchen. "I have to go," she said. "It was nice talking with you."

"It's always nice to meet Ryder's friends," she said. "I hope I'll see you again soon." But she looked at Ryder as she spoke, as if waiting for him to confirm that she would, indeed, be seeing more of Christa.

"Maybe so." She nodded to Ryder, and hurried away. She wasn't sure what to make of Ryder's mom. Ryder hadn't seemed all that comfortable with the conversation. He hadn't acted as if he was ashamed of Christa or anything that obvious, but he clearly hadn't wanted his mother to read too much into their relationship.

She glanced over her shoulder and saw mother and son, heads together, deep in conversation. She sympathized with Ryder's reluctance. Parents of single grown children had a tendency to want to pair them off. A lot of them tried to be subtle, but she'd seen the same light in her own and Kelly's mother's eyes that had shown in Peggy Oakes's eyes just now—a hopeful look that maybe this was the match they'd been hoping for for their child. Someone to partner them and care for them, and to provide the other half of the genes for future grandchildren.

"Just the girl I wanted to see." Etta Mae charged over and grabbed hold of Christa's hand. "How is your mother doing?"

"She's doing good. She's home from the hospital and determined to be up and about her normal routine."

"You tell her not to overdo it. And don't worry about meals. I've got that covered. Someone will be bringing by dinner every night this week."

"Oh, Etta Mae, that's so thoughtful." Christa gently withdrew her hand from the other woman's grip. "But it really isn't necessary."

"We're glad to do it, hon. Now, is there anything you all can't eat? Are you gluten free or dairy free or allergic to peanuts or anything like that?"

"Nothing like that, but really, I think Mom would prefer that people didn't fuss. You know how independent she is. She'd be mortified if anyone thought she was an invalid."

"My goodness, the woman just had major surgery. She deserves a break from the kitchen for a few days."

"My dad and I can handle the cooking. I'm really grateful, but the best thing you can do for Mom is not make any kind of fuss at all."

Etta Mae frowned. "Adele is a stubborn one. I remember when she had foot surgery several years back and was in a cast for two months. She wouldn't let anyone lift a finger to help."

"Then you understand. Maybe you could just send her a card to let her know you're thinking about her. She'd like that."

"All right. But I can't let you go without sending her something. You wait right here."

Christa waited behind a partition that separated the cash register area from the dining room. From here she had a view of Ryder and his mother, but they couldn't see her.

Without her there, he looked more comfortable. His mother said something and he laughed, his dimples and the lines at the corners of his eyes deepening. He took her hand in his, and she reached up to touch his cheek, with a look that reminded Christa so much of her own mother and grandmother that her eyes stung.

"There's a half a buttermilk pie in here." Etta Mae pressed a Styrofoam take-out container into Christa's hands. "I know it's Adele's favorite. You tell her if she needs anything at all, to give me a call."

"I will. And thank you."

Etta Mae pressed her lips together. "You tell her I had the same surgery almost twenty years ago. I imagine they've perfected their technique since then, but I made it through okay, and she will, too."

"I'll tell her." Christa hid her surprise by pulling the older woman to her in a hug.

"It's good to be independent and look after yourself," Etta Mae said. "But it's good to let other people help you, too. You don't have to tell her that, but let her know that we're here."

"I think she already knows it." Even if Mom never accepted the casseroles and counseling that others offered, just knowing they were available probably was a weight off her mind. Maybe it was easier to get through a crisis when you knew you had a whole town on your side.

CHAPTER SEVEN

CHRISTA HAD ALWAYS admired her mother's strength and independence. Adele Montgomery was a tough Texas cowgirl, able to hold her own in any situation. But those same qualities made her a terrible patient. She resisted being waited on, didn't want to stay in bed "like an invalid" and kept trying to do too much. Attempting to wash dishes her second day home from the hospital, she dropped a plate, which shattered at her feet. She burst into tears.

"Now, Adi, it's all right," Dad said, though he looked as if he wanted to cry, too.

"I'll get this, Mom." Christa grabbed a broom to sweep up the broken china. "I'm here to help, so you might as well let me."

"I never thought I'd see the day where I'd be useless in my own kitchen."

"Now, Adi, you are not useless." They both retreated to the bedroom, Mom weeping, Dad cajoling.

Christa swept up the broken plate, finished the dishes, and then turned her attention to supper. She'd agreed to take over the cooking for the time being. If only she was better at the job. Her father, accustomed to eating his wife's excellent meals three times a day, didn't hold back with his criticism.

That evening, while Mom slept, Dad stuck his fork in the mound of mashed potatoes on his plate and frowned. "You should ask your mother how she makes her potatoes," he said. "Hers are never lumpy like this." He took a bite and the frown grew more severe. "This gravy is scorched." He set down his fork in disgust. "Your mother taught you better than this, I know."

"She did, but I'm out of practice. There's no point in cooking a big meal when it's just me." Most nights she settled for frozen dinners, or take-out.

"You don't have a boyfriend to cook for?"

"If I had a boyfriend, don't you think I would have told you?"

"I don't know. I guess that depends on how serious things were." He scraped gravy off the potatoes and took another bite. But his eyes remained fixed on her. "You do date, don't you?"

"Yes, I date. But there's no one serious." She knew guys who were friends, and guys she went out with, but no exclusive relationships. Not because she didn't want to fall in love with someone, she just hadn't been lucky that way.

"Those men in Houston must be blind."

She held back laughter. "It's okay, Dad. I'm willing to wait for the right guy to come along."

He reached across the table and patted her hand. "You do that. I knew the moment I met your mother that she was the one for me."

Christa settled her chin in her hand to listen. She'd heard this story so many times over the years, but it never got old. Dad continued, "She was sitting in the Blue Bell with her friend from college, Raye Ann Taylor. She'd come from her home in Longview to spend a couple of weeks on the Taylor ranch. She laughed at something Raye Ann said and I froze from across the room. I thought she was the prettiest thing I ever saw."

Christa had seen pictures; her mother had been beautiful, with strawberry blonde hair and blue eyes. "I walked right over and introduced myself and asked her to the Kiwanis club dance that Friday night. She said yes. I borrowed the ranch truck and was so distracted by her I ran it into a ditch on the way home. We had to walk two miles up the road to a telephone, but we held hands and talked the whole time. Three weeks later, I asked her to marry me and she said yes."

And they'd been madly in love ever since. Anyone could see that. The depth of their love, and its longevity, amazed Christa. And maybe, in a way, the story of her parents' grand passion, along with her grandparents' fairy-tale romance, had spoiled her. Maybe, subconsciously, she'd been waiting for a man she could love at first sight—however uncommon or unrealistic such ideas might be.

"You should have wakened me for supper." Mom stood in the doorway, dressed in knit pants and a loose top, pale but steady on her feet. She moved to the table and sat while Christa rushed to add a place setting for her. "I can see we're going to have to work on your cooking," Mom said as she surveyed the lumpy potatoes, scorched gravy and dry pork chops.

"I'm out of practice," Christa repeated. She pushed aside her own plate. "Maybe we should have taken Etta Mae's offer to bring food. I'm sure it would have been better than this."

"I don't want half the women in town traipsing out here like mourners at a funeral, then going back to town to tell everyone how terrible I look."

"Mom, you make them sound awful, and they really just want to help. Most of them have known you for years."

"All right, maybe that wasn't very charitable. But I don't need their help. Besides, you clearly need the practice in the kitchen." She sipped her iced tea. "Besides working on your cooking, what do you have planned for this week?"

"I hadn't made any plans." Christa spread her napkin in her lap. "I thought I'd do whatever you need me to do."

"I won't have you moping around the house," Mom said. "Your father fussing over me is enough." She patted his hand to take the sting out of her words. "I got a call from Rhonda Benson this afternoon. She tells me the Chamber of Commerce is hosting a breakfast and a meeting tomorrow morning. They're looking for volunteers."

"Volunteers for what?" Christa asked.

"I'm not sure. You know Rhonda. She's

always involved in some project or another. I told her you'd be glad to give a hand."

"Mom! I really wish you hadn't done that."

Adele spooned peas onto her plate. "They could use your skills, I'm sure. And you'll meet a lot of nice people."

"Your mother's right," Dad said. "You should go."

"Fine. I'll go." But Christa couldn't help feeling this was just a way for her mother to get rid of her. The job she loved didn't want her and her parents only saw her as being underfoot. So much for thinking she'd fit right in here at home. Even Ryder, who was brand new to Cedar Grove, found a better welcome than she did.

"I DON'T KNOW what to tell you, Greg." Ryder clutched the phone tightly to his ear, trying to block out the sound of a backhoe scraping against rock. "I'm positive I'm going to have all the rights-of-way by the end of the summer, but I can't rush these people. Some of these ranches have been on their families' land for generations, and they don't want to give up even part of it too easily."

Greg Draycut, his boss, said something

about timelines and cost overruns, and all the things he and Ryder had been over half a dozen times already. From his office near the capital in Austin, Greg didn't always have a realistic view of what it took to persuade people to sell right-of-way for a highway they hadn't initially believed they even needed. Ryder had done a good job of winning over most of them to his point of view, but such persuasion took time. He wanted people to sell willingly, and not feel they were coerced. "Everything will be all right, Greg," Ryder said. "Don't worry."

But, of course, Greg's job was to worry. Ryder would leave that to him and get on with his task at hand, which was to shepherd this project through to completion. He pocketed the phone and rejoined the group of men and one woman who stood near a barrier of red ribbon stretched between two trees. The woman—the president of the Cedar Grove Chamber of Commerce—handed Ryder an oversized pair of scissors made of cardboard. "We'll do the real ribbon-cutting with real scissors," she said. "These are for the photo for the paper."

She positioned Ryder in front of the ribbon, with her next to him, Paul on his other side, and other prominent Chamber members gathered around. The reporter from the local paper shouted "Cheese!" and the camera flashed.

Still blinking from the blinding flash, Ryder handed over the cardboard scissors and thanked the woman. She snipped the red ribbon with real shears and everyone applauded. Paul clapped Ryder on the shoulder. "Let's go get some lunch."

"It's too early for lunch. It's barely after ten."

"Coffee, then."

"Don't you have work to do?"

Paul grinned. "Schmoozing the customers is part of my job."

"It's part of my job, too, but this morning I have other things to do."

"You're making me look bad, working so hard."

Ryder chuckled. "I could probably meet you later. I'll give you a call."

"Sure thing."

Ryder said his goodbyes and headed for his truck. He drove out of town, to a ranch that bordered the Montgomery property. The rancher, Melvin Nimichek, met him on the front steps of the ranch house. "Right on time." The stocky older man, dressed in a green-and-white striped snap button shirt, starched jeans and gray eel-skin boots, checked a heavy gold pocket watch. He then tucked it away in his jeans and offered a leathery hand. "Bud Montgomery told me I should talk to you again. You made a good impression on him."

"Thank you for seeing me. Mr. Montgomery's assistance had meant a lot to me." He couldn't say why he and Bud had hit it off so well. In many ways, the rancher reminded Ryder of his dad, with the same direct manner and rock-solid code of ethics. But Bud was quieter than Martin Oakes. Whereas Ryder's father was quick to tell Ryder what he should and shouldn't do, Bud listened to what Ryder had to say, and didn't try to push his own agenda. Maybe, since Ryder wasn't his son, Bud didn't feel the need to solve every problem or share every opinion.

"Let's walk up the drive and you can show me exactly how much of my property you intend to take."

"The state will pay the full market value for the land," Ryder said. "And we'll build fencing and even plant trees, grass and wild-flowers. You'll maintain your privacy and have great access to the highway. The value of your remaining property will likely increase."

"Don't know how I'll get used to hearing those big trucks zip up and down the highway all day and night." Melvin matched Ryder's stride. He was impressed the older man could keep up. "That's a big chunk of my land you want—a third of my acreage. Prime pasture."

After years of drought the pasture was reduced to dirt and stubby grass, but Ryder figured the older man didn't see it that way. He remembered when his cattle had grazed on lush grass. Maybe he even remembered when the only road into town had been a narrow dirt track. "We need enough land for the highway itself as well as utility right-of-ways and a buffer zone to protect the property owners on either side."

He stopped near the pink-flagged survey stakes the state had erected months earlier to mark the new route. "You see how there's a gentle curve up through here. We'll build up the roadway so water will drain off, with gravel catchments on either side to filter the runoff and keep oil, gas and other chemicals from washing into the groundwater."

"So I don't have to worry about all that stuff washing into my well," Melvin said.

"No, sir. The state is committed to protecting the water. We all know how precious that resource is."

Melvin grunted and both men stared across the pasture. Ryder pictured the highway to come, a sweeping curve of pavement built to the most up-to-date, exacting standards. He wondered if the rancher saw the same thing.

"My son doesn't want me to sell," Melvin said. "He thinks I should hire a lawyer and ask a judge for an injunction."

"You could do that," Ryder said. "But it could cost you a lot of money to fight this, and I don't think your chances of winning are very good. The state is really behind this project, and most of your neighbors have already agreed to sell the right of way we need."

"My son tells me if I sue, I could get my neighbors to go in with me."

"Is your son upset because he expects to inherit the ranch?"

"Oh, he'll inherit it, but he won't ever ranch." Melvin shoved both hands in the pockets of his jeans and rocked back on the heels of his boots. "He runs some tech company in Dallas, designing computer games. But you know how kids are—they want to know the old home place is still there, even if they don't have much practical use for it."

"How old is your son?"

"He's going on forty, but he's still a kid to me." The rancher looked Ryder in the eye. "You've been here long enough to see ranching isn't what it used to be. The old-timers say it was this bad in the dust bowl days, and we came back, but I'm not going to live long enough to see that, I don't think."

"I think we still need ranchers and farmers, but things have changed," Ryder said.

"I appreciate that you haven't pressured me like some slick salesman."

"I'm an engineer, not a salesman. I have a job to do, but I can appreciate that this kind of decision isn't easy." Ryder had never felt the close ties to a place the way these people, who had lived and worked here for generations, did. But he knew what it was to love his family, and he imagined love of a home could be like that.

"I told my son this was my decision to make, that I was looking out for my future as much as his. And I talked to my wife about it. We figure if we sell the land and take the money the state is offering, we'll be more secure in our old age. We won't have to depend on our son to pay the bills, and we can stay in our house. That's worth something in itself."

Ryder waited. He'd learned the value of silence when dealing with people. They needed room to weigh their thoughts and draw their own conclusions. "Do you have the paperwork with you?" Melvin asked.

"I have an agreement to sell. The state will draw up the closing papers and set a time for you to sign them and receive your check."

"Then let's get it and get this thing done."

They returned to the truck and Ryder retrieved the contract to sell the land to the state. Melvin signed it and let out a sigh. "My great-grandfather settled here in 1882," he said. "He took a section of land and his brother took a section. His brother sold out after only two years—that's the land the Montgomerys have now. Over the years different people sold off little chunks, so I suppose I'm no different. You should have seen it in the good years, though. Back in the seventies when we had rain and the grass grew knee-high, cattle really was king and we thought the boom would go on and on."

Now that the deal was done, it was as if the older man needed to review the history of the place, to justify his decision all over again. Ryder had had the same experience with others. He accepted their stories as he had accepted their signatures, as part of the process of passing along a legacy. "I appreciate the contribution you're making to this project," he said. "I'll stay in touch to let you know when to expect construction crews. We'll try to disrupt your life as little as possible."

"I guess I'll have a prime view of the roadwork," he said. "I worked a highway crew one summer, a long time ago. It'll be interesting to see how the methods have changed since then."

"Look me up anytime, and I'll give you a tour, answer any questions you might have." The men shook hands and Ryder climbed back into his truck. As he waited at the highway for a truck to pass, he thought of turning left, and stopping by the Rocking M. Maybe Christa would be there. But she'd be busy with her mother. The family didn't need him disturbing them.

Christa might not welcome his presence, anyway. She'd made it clear she didn't think of him romantically, and though he would have welcomed her friendship, he wasn't optimistic about that, either. She saw him only in the context of the highway project. To top it off, when they'd met in the Blue Bell last Saturday, he'd been so concerned with blocking any attempts his mother had at matchmaking, that Christa might have taken his protestations the wrong way.

He flipped his blinker for a right turn and eased onto the road. When you only lived in a place for a short time, staying only because your job took you there, people never really got to know you. And he never really got to know them. Keeping his distance had been a survival skill he'd learned at a young age; don't get attached and it won't hurt so much to leave. But the people in Cedar Grove—Bud, Paul, and even Melvin and yes, Christa—made him wish for roots that ran deeper.

THE CHAMBER OF Commerce met for breakfast at the Blue Bell on Friday mornings. Etta Mae directed Christa to a large table at the back of the room. "Christa! There's a seat over here by me." Kelly waved from midway down the table. Already feeling better about her decision to attend the meeting, Christa navigated a path through the chairs to join her friend. "You remember Didi Moffat, right?" Kelly indicated the dark-haired woman on her other side.

"It's Didi Raybourn now." Didi offered her hand.

"I saw Paul the other day." Christa shook hands, getting comfortable in her chair. "He said y'all have a new baby."

"We do." Didi leaned back so that Christa could see the infant carrier in the chair beside her. "This is little Alex."

"He's adorable." Christa offered a finger and the infant grasped it, and offered a toothless smile. She felt a brief stab of longing. She and Didi were the same age, yet Christa seemed years away from ever having a baby of her own.

"What are you doing here?" Kelly asked. "Are you that bored at home?"

"My mom volunteered me." She chose a biscuit from the basket in front of her, and looked around for the butter. "But I thought it might be good to hear how the Chamber feels about the highway project."

"Some are for it, some are against it." Kelly handed Christa a bowl of butter pats. "Though I think now that the project is a done deal, the Chamber has decided to do what it can to make the highway a positive, not a negative."

Rhonda Benson, tall and broad-shouldered with a crown of short brown curls framing a round face, loomed over the other end of the table. She tapped a fork against her water glass. "I want to call this meeting of the Cedar Grove Chamber of Commerce to order."

While Christa ate biscuits and eggs and sipped coffee that was better than any produced in a chain coffee shop, Rhonda quickly dispensed with minutes from the last meeting and a string of announcements about businesses that had closed or those that planned to relocate along the new highway. No one commented on the announcements; apparently such news was routine these days and they'd all accepted the changes as inevitable. Christa wondered if she'd come home when the highway was first announced would she could have made any difference? Would people have listened if she'd asked them to protest?

"Now we come to new business," Rhonda announced. "The Annual Summer Festival."

"Should we even have a festival this year, with so many businesses in transition?" Christa couldn't see the woman who spoke, but several people around her nodded.

"Absolutely we're going to have a festival," Rhonda said. "The money all goes to good causes—the Animal Shelter, the Food Pantry, and the Strangers' Aid Society."

Christa leaned over to whisper to Kelly. "What's the Summer Festival?" she asked.

"Rhonda and some others came up with the idea a few years ago," Kelly said. "It's really fun. All the money goes to charity."

"With fewer businesses to participate, we're all going to have to do our best to come up with clever ideas for the booths," Rhonda said. "We want to give people a reason to visit, and we want to raise more money than ever for these worthy causes. Now, I want to hear your ideas."

"A dunking booth is always good," someone said. "Especially if we can get a local celebrity, like the mayor or the school principal."

"Ned Yates always handles the petting

zoo," a woman said. "The children love that."

"Those are all splendid suggestions, but I'm looking for something new and different," Rhonda said.

"We should have a theme for the festival," Christa said. "Something we can use in advertising the event, to promote interest."

Rhonda nodded. "What do you suggest?"

Familiar faces turned toward her—some she had known since before she took her first steps. They were all waiting to see what the hometown girl with the big-city experience had to say. Christa hoped she lived up to their expectations. "Why not focus on local heritage?" she said. "We could feature displays about the ranches in the area, and organize the booths along a heritage trail. Each stop would highlight some interesting aspect of local history."

"I could make my booth like a little schoolhouse, and have pictures of early schools, and maybe an old desk and blackboard," a woman said.

"The bake sale booth could feature old recipes—and sell the historical society cookbook they put together a couple of years ago," someone else said.

"That's a wonderful idea," Rhonda said. "Thank you, Christa."

Kelly put her hand up. "Yes, Kelly?" Rhonda said.

"I think we should have a kissing booth."

Laughter greeted this suggestion. Kelly's smile never faltered. "But instead of women selling kisses, let's turn it around and have men."

"I can guess one man we all hope will participate," Traci, the bank teller, said. "Do you think we can persuade Ryder Oakes to offer up his lips for a good cause?"

"I don't think we want to risk any kind of sexual harassment claim," Rhonda cautioned. "But I like that you're thinking of new ideas for the booths." She scanned the table. "Does anyone else have an idea?"

"Instead of a kissing booth, maybe we have one of those bachelor auctions," Didi said.

"This town doesn't have enough bachelors," Kelly said. Several other women murmured in agreement.

"Maybe not bachelors, then," Didi said. "Maybe we ask guys to offer up their services for chores around the house. There are plenty of single moms and widows and older people who would love to have someone to paint or mend screens or something for the day. I think we'd get a lot of interest."

"Not an auction, a raffle," Rhonda said. "That way no one's feelings get hurt if they draw a low bid. We could ask the participants—men and women—to offer up four hours of their time for chores around the house."

"It's not as much fun as a kissing booth," Kelly said. "But I think people would like it. We'd probably sell a lot of tickets."

"I'd buy one," a woman at the opposite end of the table said. "I've been after my husband to paint the back fence for two years now. It would be nice to get it finally done."

"If I win Ryder, can I use the four hours having dinner with him?" Traci asked.

Rhonda brought her gavel down on the table, making the silverware jump. "Order."

Conversation died and everyone turned their attention to the chairwoman. "I think the handyman raffle is a great idea," Rhonda said. "Kelly, you and Christa take the lead on that. Find us some willing participants and we'll all help sell the tickets."

Christa opened her mouth to object to

being volunteered for this assignment, but Kelly kicked her under the table. "Come on. It will be fun," she said.

"All right." After all, she'd agreed to volunteer, and she'd rather work with Kelly than anyone else.

"We'll start with Ryder," Kelly said. "I can't wait to see his face when we tell him we want to raffle him off."

CHAPTER EIGHT

THE DIRT ROADS around Cedar Grove took their toll on Ryder's white truck, so most Saturday mornings he devoted to washing the truck, parked beneath a large live oak in front of his apartment. Barefoot, wearing old jeans and stripped to the waist, he enjoyed the fresh air and exercise and the end result of a clean truck.

When the blue sedan pulled to the curb midway through his Saturday morning ritual, he thought at first the driver was coming to visit one of his neighbors. But when Christa Montgomery, dressed in pink shorts and a pink plaid sleeveless blouse, slid out of the driver's seat, Ryder couldn't help hoping she'd stopped to see him. He dropped the sponge back into the bucket of soapy water and waved.

Christa returned the greeting and started toward him. Dark sunglasses hid her eyes, so he couldn't read her expression. She wasn't smiling, but she didn't seem angry, either.

He walked out to meet her. After the coolness in the shade, the sun felt hot on his bare shoulders. "Hello, Christa."

"Hello, Ryder." She stopped in front of him, but avoided his gaze.

"Are you looking for me, or is this just a pleasant coincidence?" he asked.

"I came to ask a favor."

"Anything for you." He wasn't normally a flirt, but she brought out that side of him. Standing here in the late summer sun, he was too aware of her long, bare legs and pink-clad curves. The light glinted off her hair and her cheeks flushed pink. From the sun, or from something else? Maybe he unsettled her; he liked the idea that he could do that.

She crossed her arms over her chest. Yes, she was definitely uncomfortable. "The Chamber of Commerce sponsors a festival every summer, in the town park. All the proceeds go to local charities."

So it wasn't a personal favor; he told himself he shouldn't be disappointed. "How can I help?"

"One of the committee members—not

me—thought we could raise a lot of money if we held a raffle."

"I think raffles are a pretty time-honored way of raising money. What are you raffling?" And where did he come into this? Did she want him to buy tickets? Surely that wouldn't make her so uncomfortable.

"We're asking men and women to offer their services doing things around the house—repairs and painting and house-cleaning, things like that. People can buy raffle tickets for a chance to win four hours of chores from a particular person."

"And you want me to be one of those persons?"

"You don't have to do it if you don't want to. After all, you don't even live here."

"I'm living here for the time being—probably for the next couple of years. I don't mind helping out. And I'm a pretty handy guy."

"All you have to do is show up at our booth on the day of the festival," she said. "You can work out the details with whoever wins you. I mean, whoever wins your services. Your *time*." Her cheeks blushed pink.

He searched for a way to put her at ease.

"How did you end up with the job of asking me to do this, if it wasn't your idea?"

"We drew straws. I got the short one."

"Ah." That explained a lot. "Well, I'd be happy to help."

"Thanks. It's the second Saturday of July—I think I forgot to tell you that. Does that still work for you?"

"I plan on being here, so, yes, that will be fine."

"Great. Someone from the committee will be in touch." She turned back toward her car.

"How's your mom?" he asked.

"Oh." She turned to face him once more. "She's about as well as can be expected. She won't rest as much as Dad and I think she should and she tries to do a lot and wears herself out. She's stubborn."

"That could work in her favor as she goes through treatment."

"I guess so. She's determined to beat this. And they caught it early. I'm sure she'll be fine."

"That doesn't make it any easier to get through it, does it?" Gone was the flirting tone; he wanted her to know he truly did care.

"It was fun meeting your mom the other day," she said. "She seemed nice."

"She is. And she likes having me close. That's a luxury we haven't had since I left for college, really."

"I had a hard enough time being in Houston, and that was only a few hours away from here. I can't imagine being separated from my family by whole states or even continents."

"You'd adjust. It seemed normal to me, but I'll admit, it's nice to see her more often. It's good to know she's happy in her new life."

"Was it hard for you, when they divorced?"

The real concern in her voice touched him. "It felt…unnerving," he said. "As if the world tilted a little, in a way it isn't supposed to. Your parents are always supposed to stay together. It made me wonder if everything I thought about my life, or at least about my childhood, was based on false assumptions."

"Now that you've had time to get used to the idea, do you still think that?"

"Sometimes. But I've never been one to dwell on the past." Growing up, his father had always advised looking forward. Actions could affect the future, but they could never change the past. And if you didn't think about all the things you left behind, it hurt less.

"How is it we always end up having these kind of conversations?" she asked.

"I don't know." He certainly didn't go around baring his soul to everyone. "Maybe it's because you're such a patient listener." Or maybe it was because he felt something for her that he'd never known with anyone else.

"Well, uh, I guess I'd better go, and let you get back to washing your truck."

He hated to see her leave. They'd started out awkwardly, and now that they were past that, he didn't want this visit to end. He glanced at the soap drying on his truck. "Are you in a hurry?" he asked.

She hesitated; he could almost see her debating whether or not to make up an excuse not to linger. Truth—or maybe curiosity—won out. "Not particularly."

"If you can wait just a little while I finish up my truck, I'd like to show you something."

"What do you want to show me?"

"Just something interesting. Wait for me, just for a minute?"

"All right."

He returned to the truck and rinsed the last of the soap, then gave it a quick dry with some old towels. He retrieved his shirt and shoes from the apartment and motioned her over. "Let's go for a ride," he said, and held the passenger door open for her.

She climbed into the truck, giving him an up-close view of those lovely legs. Smiling, he walked around to the driver's side. "Where are we going?" she asked.

"Just a place I found that I enjoy."

She remained quiet on the short drive across town, but he didn't find the silence uncomfortable. Christa was easy to be with. He didn't feel the need to prove himself to her or impress her.

He exited the road just outside of town and turned onto a dirt track that led up a small rise. At the top, he parked in the shade of a trio of oaks. Just below, a slash of raw earth marked the beginning of the new highway, and beyond that rolling hills and pastureland. "It seems like I can almost see all the way to Dallas from here," he said.

"Pretty view," she said. "In the spring there are probably lots of wildflowers."

"There will be more when we're done," he told her. "Part of the project calls for seeding wildflowers on both sides of the road. Drivers will want to make the trip just for the scenery."

"I never thought about highways being beautiful," she said. "I just thought of them as necessary and, utilitarian, I guess."

"They are that, but they don't have to be ugly, necessarily."

"I didn't realize you'd already started construction."

"We just broke ground this week. We have a long way to go."

"Are you trying to point out how foolish I am to be against the project?"

"No." He took her hand. "I just wanted you to see that maybe it won't be as bad as you fear."

She slipped from his grasp, almost reluctantly, he thought.

"Maybe it won't be as bad as I fear," she said. "And maybe you've already figured out—I don't deal that well with change. I need time to adjust."

"Feel free to come check the progress

anytime. I'll give you a tour—answer questions."

"Thanks." She stared out at the rolling landscape once more. "Did you always know you wanted to build roads?" she asked. "I mean, when you were a little boy, did you drive trucks through the sandbox and imagine yourself doing this one day?"

"If you'll recall, my mom says I wanted to be a cowboy."

She smiled. "And a fireman and a race car driver. All right, if not when you were little, what about when you were old enough to seriously begin thinking about a career. Did you try out different things before choosing engineering?"

"Not really. I think I was in high school when I decided I wanted to do this for a living." He nodded toward the road stretching before them.

"What is it about roads, do you think, that attracts you?"

"Roads take you places. They connect you with people. They lead to new experiences and help you revisit old ones."

"Maybe that's why I don't like them as much. I like to stay put, and I like things to stay the same."

"Then roads bring the people and things you love to you."

She laughed. "Do you always see the positive side of everything?"

"It's better than focusing on the negative."

"I wish I shared your optimism."

He took her hand again, and this time she didn't pull away. "What's wrong?" he asked. "I think more than just the highway project has you down. Is it your mom? Are you worried about her?"

"I am worried, but I believe she'll be all right."

"Then what is it?"

Again the laugh, self-deprecating and trying to make light of the sadness beneath the mask. "I guess I'm trying to figure out what I want to be when I grow up. My dad's been after me to get serious about my job search. Every day I tell myself I'm going to update my résumé and make some calls, but I end up frozen, doing nothing."

"Getting laid off had to hurt. Maybe it undermined your confidence a little."

"Oh, it definitely did that. My dad gave me this talk about how I needed to get right back on the horse that threw me—not let a tiny setback stop me. But that's not what's stopping me now. It's that I'm not sure I want to do the same kind of work I did before. At least, not for a big firm in the city. I'd prefer to find something where I was helping people more, not just selling them products."

"Have you thought any more about starting your own business?"

"Yes, but doing what?"

"I don't know. But whatever it is, I think you'd be good at it."

"How do you know?" She looked skeptical.

"I'm not just flattering you. Moving around so much all my life, I learned to size up people quickly."

"I can't imagine a life like that—never staying in one place very long."

"And I can't imagine a life tied to one place all the time."

"Don't you ever want to just...stop?"

"Maybe." Though he'd survived his own childhood all right, he wasn't sure he wanted to raise his children the same way. "When I find the right place I might stay put," he said. "Or the right person to settle with."

"Having another person to consider changes everything," she said. "That's why

I need to figure out my job situation. Then I can worry about the relationship stuff."

"You're not into multitasking?"

"You know what I mean—if one area of your life is unsettled, how can you focus on anything else?"

"Maybe that's why I'm still single. My life has always been unsettled."

"Maybe you'll do such a good job with this highway, you'll impress your bosses enough that they'll let you pick and choose your jobs. You can work in one area of the state and find a home base where you want to remain."

"I hadn't thought about it exactly like that, but I do think this job will be a good career move for me."

"Then that's one area of your life where you're definitely more settled than I am."

"You'll come up with something."

"Thanks for the vote of confidence. And thanks for bringing me here this afternoon. Talking this out—with someone besides my dad—helped."

"I'm always available if you need to talk more. You don't even have to buy a raffle ticket."

She laughed. The sound made him feel lighter inside—off-balance in a not-bad way.

"Let me take you to dinner or to a movie," he said. "We could have a lot of fun."

The request stole her breath. "I…I told you I wasn't interested in a relationship right now."

"I'm not asking you to marry me. I thought we'd just go out, take your mind—well, mine too—off of things. Nothing too serious."

She hesitated, and he thought for a moment she would relent. "No," she said.

"Why not? We get along well. We enjoy each other's company."

"I don't think we'd suit. We're too different."

"We never have trouble finding things to talk about. Aren't you tired of staying home all the time? I know I am."

"There are plenty of women in town who would go out with you if you asked."

"And every one of them would expect a long-term relationship. Since you and I both have no plans to stay in Cedar Grove—and you've made it clear you don't want anything beyond friendship—I'll be able to relax with you."

She shook her head. "I'm sorry. I...I can't."

He turned away and put the truck in gear. "I'm keeping the offer open if you decide to change your mind."

"I'm sorry, Ryder. I don't mean to hurt you."

"I'm not hurt. I just don't understand why you're being so stubborn." To hurt, you had to let yourself really care for someone. He hadn't gone that far with Christa. Not yet.

"HOW ARE YOU feeling today, Mom?" Christa knew her mom hated the question, but she couldn't stop herself from asking. A week had passed since her visit with Ryder and Adele had started chemo. Christa sensed her mom wasn't having an easy time of it, but she refused to admit it.

"I'm fine," Mom said. "How are you feeling? Are you sleeping all right?"

No, she was not sleeping well, but she refused to give Mom anything more to worry about. "I'm fine. Do we still have those old albums, with all the black-and-white photos of the ranch?"

"I think they're probably up in the attic. Why?"

"The Summer Festival this year has a theme of our ranching heritage. I thought it would be cool to enlarge some of those photos and use them to decorate some of the booths."

"I'm glad you're helping with the festival. I know they can really use your talents."

"I am having a good time." She liked working on a project that would directly benefit the town and the people she loved. "Thanks for pushing me to do it."

"That's how it always was when you were a little girl." Her mom smiled at the memory. "Swimming lessons, 4-H, even the beauty pageants—you never wanted to try anything new, then once you were involved, you loved it."

"I guess I'm still trying to learn to expand my comfort zone." She'd been doing well in Houston, but apparently the layoff, and her mom's cancer, had pushed her back into the comfort of the familiar. "Anyway, do you think we have some pictures I could use?"

"You're welcome to look up in the attic, though it's awfully warm up there this time of year. Don't let yourself get too hot."

"I won't, I promise."

She pulled down the stairs and climbed

into the windowless attic. Mom was right—
it was an oven up here. Well, she didn't intend to stay long. She yanked the chain to
turn on the single light bulb suspended from
the rafters and surveyed the stacks of boxes,
old lamps and unused furniture.

She spotted two trunks pushed against the
far wall and crawled to them. The lid of the
first lifted easily and the aroma of honey-
suckle surrounded her, instantly transport-
ing her to her girlhood, and long summer
afternoons shelling beans or shucking corn
on the back porch in the company of her
grandmother.

Grandmother Swan always wore honey-
suckle perfume, the scent infused into her
clothing, as much a part of her as her black
hair and eyes and her accented English.
Though she had come to Texas from Vietnam as a girl of only sixteen, she had never
mastered the language of her new country.
To Christa, her grandmother was the most
exotic and interesting person she had ever
known.

She lifted an apron from the trunk, an
old-fashioned kind with a bib front and deep
pockets. Grandmother had worn this apron,
or one like it, every day as she worked in

the kitchen and garden. The pockets held tissues and wrapped pieces of candied ginger, which she shared with her only granddaughter.

The next item she pulled from the trunk was her grandfather's Army uniform. William Montgomery had died before Christa was born, but he was as real to her as any living person, thanks to Grandmother's stories. He had been a soldier in the Vietnam War when he and Swan met, and, according to Swan, he was the most handsome, smartest and bravest man who ever lived.

Next came the sky blue *áo dài* in which Thiên Nga had married her GI. No one ever called her by her Vietnamese name after that, using instead the English translation—Swan. Embroidered images of cranes and lotus flowers in silk and gold threads covered the tunic and trousers—symbols of good fortune and happiness for the newlyweds.

"First time I see my Billy, I was washing shirts in wooden tub out behind the barracks. I look a mess, but he doesn't care. He try to talk to me in English and Vietnamese. I thought he was handsome and funny and *old*." Grandmother wrinkled her nose to show her disdain for Corporal William Montgomery who had been only eight years older than she was, but her diminutive size and delicate features made her appear younger

"He comes back the next day and brings great present—American chocolate. I tell him I want to learn English and he promises to teach me. He come every day after that and we fall in love."

A tender look came over Grandmother's face at this point in her story, and Christa knew she was lost in memories of her soldier boy. After a bit, Grandmother returned from her memories to continue the story.

"Billy say he want to marry me. I say yes, but when he ask for permission to marry me, his commanding officer say no.

"Then Billy get word he being sent home. No time to marry, make me dependent. I cry and cry, thinking I will never see Billy again."

Even though Christa knew what happened next, her heart always beat a little faster at this point in the story.

"Then he comes to me very early one morning," Grandmother continued. "He say I must pretend I am fourteen and an orphan.

I say okay, and he take me to a school—a place where many orphans live. A church in America has raised money to have these orphans taken there. I will go with them and wait for Billy. He will come and marry me."

The memory still made Christa sigh. Faced with the prospect of losing the woman he loved, her grandfather had gone to extraordinary lengths to rescue her. The story was incredibly romantic, but also a little daunting. She wanted that kind of deep, lifelong love, but she didn't know if she would be willing to risk so much for someone else.

A drop of moisture landed on the *áo dài* in her lap—not tears, but sweat. Christa realized she'd probably been up in the stifling attic too long. Reluctantly, she put the clothing away and opened the second trunk, where she found the photo album.

Her mother, who had been lying on the sofa with Jet at her feet, struggled to sit up when Christa walked into the living room with the pictures. "You don't have to get up," Christa said. "Lie down and rest."

"No, I'm fine." Mom sat up, her expression drawn but determined. Jet moved up beside her, the little dog's eyes full of concern.

"Mom, it's okay to admit you're human. You're not super woman."

"I won't let this cancer get the better of me."

"And it won't. But that doesn't mean you can't rest when you're tired, or admit when you feel sick. We won't think any less of you."

"I've spent a lot of years being tough. You can't expect me to change now." She frowned at her daughter. "You're all flushed. You stayed up in that heat too long."

"I lost track of the time. I found a trunk full of Grandmother and Grandfather's things—his Army uniform and the *áo dài* she wore at their wedding."

"Definitely not a conventional wedding outfit. I can only imagine what people had to say about it."

"But they loved each other so much they didn't care what other people thought." Christa settled into an armchair. "I think that's beautiful."

"As many years as she lived with us, I never felt I knew her well."

"It must have been hard for her; she couldn't have had much in common with other ranchers' wives."

Mom stroked Jet's back over and over. "Some of them were not nice to her, especially when she first came here from Vietnam. But she seemed happy to devote herself to her home and family. She adored your grandfather, and she spoiled Bud shamelessly."

"Grandfather saved her. He was her hero. And he must have loved her very much, to risk so much for her."

"They did love each other very much. But being rescued never sounded that romantic to me."

"No?"

"No. I like to think I could always save myself. There's something to be said for a love that survives between two people who are on even footing."

Her mother made love sound so practical. "I still think Swan and William are the most romantic couple I know. I'd like to think a man would go to such great lengths for me one day."

"Maybe he will. Or even if he doesn't have to, you'll believe he would. And he should believe you would do the same for him."

Her parents' marriage was like that, an

even match between two people equally de-voted to one another. A steady, sure love didn't sound as exciting as an all-consuming passion—but maybe that fantasy only lived in movies and books, not real life. Christa only knew about her grandparents' marriage from her grandmother's stories. Still, she couldn't help believing that when love found her, it ought to feel big and special, even if in the end it was a quieter, deeper devotion.

CHAPTER NINE

CEDAR GROVE DIDN'T look quite so sleepy the Thursday afternoon before the Summer Festival. As Ryder made his way across the town park, the echo of hammers on wood, the whine of circular saws and the shouts and laughter of volunteers filled the air. Paul Raybourn waved to him from a spot near the bandstand. "Glad you could make it." Paul clapped him on the back in greeting when Ryder reached the group gathered around stacks of lumber and a pile of hand tools. "We need all the help we can get."

Ryder nodded hello to Paul's wife, Didi, and Christa's friend, Kelly. "I heard you needed volunteers, so here I am."

"That's really sweet of you," Kelly said. "We have to get all these booths built and in place so the different clubs and other groups can decorate them for the fair on Saturday."

"Usually, we just use those pop-up canopies," Paul said. "But Christa thought we should have wooden structures, to make it look like an Old West town." He nudged a stack of lumber with his foot. "It's more work and expense, but Christa swears it will help set the festival apart, and she got businesses to donate most of the materials."

"I think it's a great idea," Kelly said. "We're lucky to have someone with Christa's marketing background to help us."

"I don't see her here with a hammer," Paul grumbled.

"I'm sure she'll be here any minute." Didi nudged him. "Besides, you're the one who said you could handle the construction details."

"That's before I saw what a big job we had ahead of us," Paul said.

Ryder picked up a hammer and studied the piles of precut lumber and premade corner brackets. "I think if we frame up the walls lying flat on the ground, then we can lift them into place and brace them at the corners with metal brackets. That will make them relatively easy to disassemble. Stack the pieces flat for storage, then put them together again next time you need them. You could even put several smaller structures together in a different configuration or to make a bigger booth."

"That's it. I'm resigning as the volunteer in charge of construction and handing my golden hammer over to you." Paul bowed low, to the laughter of those around him.

"You're going to need that hammer to help me with this. Come on." Ryder hefted up the first corner post. "We'll form teams—you and Didi against me and Kelly. Let's see who's fastest."

They were well on their way to having the first two booths assembled when Christa joined them. "Sorry, I'm late. The print shop took longer than I'd anticipated."

"You're just in time." Paul finished pounding in a nail. "Ryder's come up with a great idea for these booths." He repeated Ryder's suggestion that they assemble the booths in sections they could brace together. "It's going to make things so much easier."

"Whatever you think, Paul," she said. "You're in charge of construction."

"I've handed that job over to Ryder. Clearly, he's the expert."

Ryder shifted the hammer from one hand to the other, aware of Christa's intense gaze fixed on him. "It just seems like the most practical approach," he said.

"Well, thanks for helping out."

"Did you get the photographs you needed?" Kelly laid aside her tools and approached Christa.

"I did. I'm going to distribute them among the different booths. Some other people are bringing additional pictures, as well as things like chaps and saddles. The Seed and Feed is lending us some hay bales and we've got some old milk cans and buckets to put sunflowers in. The different groups will come in Friday to put the finishing touches on their booths and we'll be all set for Saturday."

"What's the weather forecast?" Ryder asked.

She frowned at him, as if he'd somehow jinxed her project by mentioning bad weather, but before she could say anything, Kelly flashed Ryder a warm smile. "I'm sure Christa ordered sunshine for this weekend," she said. "And a little rain won't stop folks. They'd probably welcome it."

"No kidding." Paul mopped the sweat from his brow with a bandana. "And rain would cool things off."

"The park has lots of shade, and we'll have plenty of cold drinks for everyone," Kelly said. "I know a lot of people who are especially going to turn out for the handyman raffle. I'm sure you're both going to draw a lot of bids."

"Y'all did set some limits on what kinds of jobs the volunteers will do, right?" Paul asked.

"We figured we'd leave that up to the individuals," Kelly said. "They know where their talents lie."

"Just don't ask me to balance anybody's checkbook," Paul said. "People come into the bank all the time wanting help with that, and I have to send them to a teller. They can't imagine a banker who's not good with math. But my specialty is really my people skills."

"I'm thinking about bidding on you and forcing you to paint the den," Didi said.

"Maybe you can win Ryder for that one," Paul said. "He's probably good with a paintbrush."

"Paintbrush, hammer or scrub brush, I'm your man," Ryder said.

"This raffle is going to be the best fundraiser the fair has had in years," Kelly said.

She nudged Christa. "We'll have to make it an annual tradition."

"Let's make sure we get through the first year before we make any plans." She snagged a tape measure from the jumble of tools on the picnic table. "I'm going to work on putting these pictures into the frames I bought. I'll check with y'all later."

For the rest of the afternoon, Ryder and Paul and other volunteers worked on knocking together the wooden booths. The structures were crude, but Paul assured Ryder they were going for the rustic look—all part of Christa's master plan for the event.

"Christa definitely has a talent for organizing," Ryder said as he watched her direct the garden volunteers in arranging planters filled with flowers and small shrubs around the completed booths.

"You should have seen her in high school. I always wanted to be on her team for group projects. She's smart and creative and scary organized." Paul shook his head. "That marketing firm she worked for made a mistake when they let her go."

Just then, Christa turned and met Ryder's gaze. She smiled and started toward him, and his heart sped up. "You look like you're all finished here," she said. She'd tucked her hair under a ball cap that advertised horse feed and her denim shirt was smeared with black poster paint. A pink petunia blossom peeked jauntily from behind one ear. She looked young and fresh and so adorable Ryder had to look away, afraid his eyes might betray too much.

"Thanks for your help, Ryder," she said.

"You're welcome." Silence stretched between them. He felt hot, almost feverish. Maybe he was coming down with something. Usually, he didn't have any trouble finding things to say to people, but this afternoon, with Christa, he was suddenly tongue tied.

"Where are these photographs you were talking about earlier?" he asked.

"Come see." She started toward the other end of the row of completed booths and he followed. "I tried to match them up to the theme of the booth," she said. "So the bake sale booth has a photo of ranch women in the kitchen." She pointed to a framed poster-sized image of a trio of women in flour sack aprons who were rolling out pie crust and peeling potatoes.

"This booth will feature local crafts,"

she said. The picture here was of a group of cowboys around a campfire. One man whittled while another played a harmonica. These weren't movie-star cowboys, but rough, somewhat homely men in worn shirts and patched jeans, horses picketed behind them.

"Are these all pictures from your family's ranch?" he asked.

"Yes." She led him to the next booth and pointed to a photograph of a young couple posed in front of a low wooden house. "That's my grandmother and grandfather, in front of the original ranch house."

Ryder leaned forward to examine the photograph more closely. The man resembled Bud Montgomery, with the same square chin and unruly cow's lick of hair dipping down over one eye. The woman, however, was nothing like he would have expected. She stared at the camera with small, knowing eyes and delicate Asian features. She was tiny, reaching only to her husband's shoulder, and she didn't look comfortable with the attention of the camera.

"Are your grandparents still living?" he asked.

"No, they both died relatively young.

Grandfather died of cancer before I was born. Grandmother passed away the year I graduated college. I really miss her. I grew up hearing her stories and I loved them all."

"I've heard of war brides from World War II, but not any from the Vietnam War."

"I guess it was pretty unusual. Maybe the equivalent would be an American World War II soldier marrying a German girl—even though the South Vietnamese were our allies in the war, most people around here didn't make a distinction."

"How did she and your grandfather manage?"

"It wasn't easy."

"That must have been a bit of culture shock for her."

"It was, but she was very focused on family. I think she would have been happy anywhere, as long as she was with him. She came here because it was my grandfather's home, but she did it knowing the heroic effort he made to be with her—that he was willing to risk everything—his money, his reputation, the good opinion of his family—in order to be with her. It's just so romantic."

Some people probably called her grandfather's actions foolish. But in the end they had worked out.

"Would you take those kinds of risks for someone you loved?" she asked.

"I don't know. I've never been in a situation where I had to make that kind of choice. I can't imagine that I ever would be."

"But what would you have done, if you had been in my grandfather's place?"

"I tend to make safe choices." Her expression clearly showed this wasn't the answer she wanted to hear. "That's my personality," he said. "I don't act on impulse. Knowing the difficulty of a romance between an American GI and a Vietnamese girl, I probably never would have approached her."

"Not even if you were attracted to her?"

"I'm attracted to a lot of people. But I don't start things I can't finish, whether it's jobs or relationships."

"I think love is worth any kind of risk," she said. "It's more important to follow our hearts than to always listen to our heads."

"I think it's smarter to let our heads rule our hearts. Maybe there would be fewer divorces if people thought more before they married, instead of relying on raw emotion."

"No wonder you aren't married. No woman is practical enough for you."

"You're still single, too."

"I'm holding out for a man who will take my breath away."

And that man clearly wasn't him. If he'd really meant what he said, about not getting involved in a relationship that he knew from the start would cause problems, then how did he explain his continued attraction to Christa, and the pain that her rejection caused him, though he'd never in a million years admit as such to her?

Maybe his heart wasn't as good at paying attention to his head as he liked to pretend. In any case, with at least two more years in Cedar Grove, he'd have plenty of opportunities to spar with Christa, and maybe make her see him and his practicality in a better light.

DESPITE RYDER'S QUESTIONS about the weather, the day of the Summer Festival turned out perfect—sunny and not too hot, with enough of a breeze to fill the air with the scent of all the flowers the Garden Club had distributed in planters around the park. Christa closed her eyes and inhaled deeply, the aroma of roses and petunias competing with the mouthwatering scents of barbecue, kettle corn and baked goods from the food booths. She opened her eyes again as a trio of children raced past, laughing. All around her, people filled the picnic tables to enjoy everything from the Elks Club's secret recipe barbecue ribs to the Methodist women's brownies and red velvet cupcakes.

Right now, the biggest crowd surrounded the community garden's booth, where high school principal Ray Gardiner was taking his turn in the dunking booth, much to the delight of his students, who eagerly lined up to buy tickets for a chance to dunk their principal.

As Christa stopped to watch, a tall boy wound up and let the ball fly. It hit the bull's-eye with a satisfying thwack and Ray plunged into the water, to the cheers and giggling of the crowd. Christa applauded and moved on, past the metal water trough the Boy and Girl Scouts had set up as a fish pond, where kids could cast their line and try to catch prizes, to the Garden Club's display of herb plants for sale. "At this rate, we'll be all sold out in another hour or so," announced Didi, when Christa asked how things were going.

"Christa, there you are!" Christa turned at the sound of the familiar voice and hurried to where her mom waved from one of the tables. Adele Montgomery wore a pale straw cowboy hat with a teal band over her increasingly thinning hair. Just that morning she'd announced that she was going wig shopping after her chemo appointment next week. Though new medications were helping her deal better with the nausea the treatments induced, doctors could do nothing to prevent her from losing her hair. Though she may have shed tears in private over this loss, in front of her husband and daughter she maintained a reserved calm, which they felt compelled to emulate.

But right now none of them needed to fake happiness. Mom looked well, and her smile was genuine. Judging by the ribs and potato salad on the paper plate in front of her, she even had a good appetite. "I think this is the best festival yet," Mom said.

"Roberta tells us you had a lot to do with it," Dad said. "She said you had a lot of great ideas."

"Many people volunteered to help,"

Christa said. "I only made a few suggestions I thought would work."

"You don't have to be so modest around us," Mom said. "Here, eat some of these ribs for me. I can't possibly finish them all."

"You eat them, Mom."

"I've already had two. I'll bet you've been too busy to even stop for lunch."

True. "Well, they do look wonderful..."

When Christa had finished her ribs and half the potato salad, Mom stood. "Come walk with us. I want to see the rest of the booths."

"The crowd seems bigger this year," Dad said, as they made their way past a row of games operated by the Kiwanis Club—ring toss, target shooting with pellet guns, and skee ball.

"I persuaded the committee to put an ad in the Dallas paper, and on a couple of Dallas radio stations." Christa savored a heady feeling of pride as she counted six people waiting in line at one booth, and eight at another. She'd designed the print ads herself, putting a modern family into an old black-and-white photo of cowboys playing an impromptu baseball game on the ranch.

"Guess you haven't lost your touch," Dad said.

"I guess I miss work more than I thought—or, at least, I miss creating something and then seeing how it helps people."

Her dad nodded. "You're too good to waste your time hanging around on the ranch."

She didn't consider time spent helping her parents a waste, but Dad was right—she needed to get serious about her job hunt soon, while she still had recent, fresh material to show a prospective employer. If only she was more certain about the direction she wanted to take in her career. Making a mistake and ending up at a job she hated would be worse than getting laid off. At least the layoff wasn't her fault. If she chose the wrong job this time, she'd have no one to blame but herself.

"Is this the famous Handyman Raffle everyone's talking about?" her dad asked as they neared one of the largest booths at the fair. Kelly and Christa and some others had decorated the structure to look like an old blacksmith shop, with large posters of cowboys branding cattle on either side of the entrance, and old branding irons hanging from the beams inside.

"We have some women offering their services, too," Christa said. A large whiteboard in front of the booth displayed the names of the people who had agreed to offer an afternoon of their services for the raffle. A line of clay flowerpots filled a long bench inside the booth, each pot labeled with the name of one of the volunteers. Anyone could purchase a raffle ticket for one dollar and put the ticket in the pot corresponding with the person whose services he or she wanted to win. The winners could avail themselves of the volunteers' talents at painting, auto repair, carpentry or other household skills.

"This must be the most popular booth at the fair." Mom nodded to the row of flowerpots. "They're all getting full. A couple of them are almost overflowing."

"I'll admit I was skeptical about the idea at first," Christa said. "But it looks like we're going to raise a lot of money for charity."

"And a lot of people will be getting those odd jobs they've been putting off completed before winter," Dad said.

"I see Ryder is drawing a lot of interest." Mom pointed to the pot labeled with the engineer's name. Tickets spilled out of it onto the table.

"He has a knack for drawing people to him," Dad said. "You can't help but like him."

Christa followed her father's gaze to a picnic table nearby, where Ryder stood, surrounded by a crowd. Most of the single women in town had ended up there, she noted, an uncomfortable tightness in her chest. Ryder laughed at something someone said, his blue eyes crinkling at the corners, mouth open to show straight, white teeth. He wore his Stetson pushed back slightly on his head, and his customary white Western-cut shirt with the sleeves rolled up to reveal tanned forearms. Pressed jeans and boots made him look as if he'd lived here all his life, working a ranch and joining endless debates about the weather and politics.

Did he blend in this seamlessly everywhere he went? The idea unsettled her. Was his friendliness just a costume he put on to fit in, with no real feeling to back it up? After all, how much could you really care about other people when you knew you wouldn't be around them very long? Maybe Ryder got along with everyone so well because he never truly let himself get involved. That would be the practical approach, wouldn't it? The kind of thing a man who valued thinking over feeling might do.

The crowd shifted to reveal Peggy Oakes standing beside her son. She wore a stylish shift and designer sunglasses, her hair pinned in a neat chignon. "Who is that with Ryder?" Mom asked.

"That's his mother. She lives in Dallas."

"I'd love to meet her." Mom, with Dad in tow, started toward the crowd around Ryder. Christa hurried after them.

As they drew closer, she couldn't help overhearing the conversation taking place. "What are your particular skills?" asked a petite redhead Christa didn't recognize.

"Oh, I'm good with my hands," he said, to much laughter.

He was clearly in his element.

He looked up at their approach. "Hello, Bud, Adele, Christa." He put his arm around his mother. "This is my mom, Peggy. She drove over from Dallas for the festival."

"Mrs. Oakes, these are my parents, Bud and Adele Montgomery," Christa said.

"You must call me Peggy." She clasped

their hands, her smile a copy of her son's. "I'm so happy to meet you."

"I didn't know Ryder had family so close," Mom said. "How nice to meet you."

"Christa, Ryder tells me this raffle was your idea," Peggy said, her enthusiasm could be heard in her tone.

"Oh no. I did help pull it together. The credit should go to Didi Raybourn. She was the one who made the suggestion."

"Well, whoever came up with it, I think it's brilliant." Peggy looked around her at the crowded park. "Of course, I just got here. I'm anxious to see more of the fair."

"I'll show you around, Mom," Ryder said.

"Will you come with us, Christa?" Peggy turned to Bud and Adele. "Do you mind if I borrow your daughter for a while?"

"Not at all," Bud said. "Adi and I plan to go visit the stage and listen to the music for a while." He nodded toward the stage set beneath a trio of spreading live oaks, where a local bluegrass band was setting up.

Christa would have rather gone with her parents, but she couldn't think of a gracious way to refuse Peggy's invitation. "We'll see you later, when it's time for the raffle," Mom said, giving her hand a reassuring squeeze.

Christa fell into step on one side of Ryder, his mom on the other. Though he didn't touch her, she felt touched by him, aware of him next to her, his broad-shouldered, definitely masculine shadow merging with her smaller form in the bright sunlight. She forced her attention away from the man who unsettled her so, to their surroundings. This was the first chance she'd had to tour the various booths on display, and she had to admit, the Festival was turning into a big success. Every booth was busy, people smiling and chatting and having a good time. She and Ryder and Peggy bought snow-cones from the School Booster's booth, and laughed at the antics of a group of rowdy boys as they pounded each other with pillows at a games booth.

"I love all these black-and-white photos at the booths," Peggy said, stopping to admire a poster of a trio of girls on horseback in front of a ranch gate.

"Most of them are of Christa's family's ranch," Ryder said. He looked to Christa for confirmation. "Isn't that right?"

"Yes. We have albums full of pictures in the attic at home. I had some of them made into posters to illustrate the area's ranching heritage."

They moved to the next booth, and Peggy paused again, this time in front of the photo of Christa's grandparents. "Who are these people?" she asked.

"That's my grandmother and grandfather."

Peggy studied Christa. "Your grandmother was Asian?"

"Vietnamese. They met and married during the war."

"Fascinating." She turned to Ryder. "Your father had a friend who married a Vietnamese woman during the war. The top brass really frowned on such relationships, so it meant the end of his military career. I think he went back to school and became a pharmacist or something."

"He must have loved her very much," Christa said.

"Making sacrifices in the name of love always sounds so romantic," she said. "I'm not sure the reality is so sweet and easy. Then again, love can make people do some crazy things."

"Do you think your marrying dad was a crazy thing?" Ryder asked. He wore a

pinched, cautious expression, as if he wasn't
certain he wanted to hear her answer.

"No, we weren't crazy. We had some wonderful years together, and I'm very proud of
my children." She patted his arm. "In the
end, it didn't work out, but I don't believe
in wasting time with regrets."

So Ryder's practical side didn't only come
from his military father. Christa checked
the time on her phone and was surprised to
see that more than an hour had passed since
she'd joined Peggy and Ryder on their tour
of the festival. "I have a few things I need
to check on," she said.

"We'll see you at the raffle," Peggy said.
"Did you buy any tickets?"

The question caught her off guard. "Oh
no. I mean, what would I need a handyman
for?"

Peggy looked amused. "Why, indeed?"

"I'd better go. See you later." She turned
and started across the park, toward the stage,
where she hoped to find her parents.

"Christa!" Kelly waylaid Christa before
she'd gone more than a few yards. She hurried up to her friend, a little breathless. "Isn't
it great?"

"The festival?" Christa said. "Yes, it's going even better than I'd hoped."

"Oh, that, too. But I was talking about the raffle. We're raising all kinds of money. All the volunteers are getting lots of bids."

"So maybe this is even better than a kissing booth," Christa teased.

"Oh, I don't know about that, but it did turn out to be a good idea." She leaned closer, her tone confiding. "I hope you don't mind, but we bought a couple of tickets in your name."

Christa narrowed her eyes. Kelly's cheeks were flushed, the picture of guilt. "And just whom am I bidding on?"

"We wanted to get the bidding going for Ryder, so we didn't figure you'd mind."

She did mind, but Kelly obviously meant well. A couple of raffle tickets wouldn't hurt. "Let's just hope I don't win," she said.

"Oh, don't tell me you couldn't find something to do with Ryder for four hours," Kelly said. "It's not like he's hard to be around."

"Right." Except that Christa did find it difficult to be around Ryder sometimes. On one hand, he was a good listener and a thoughtful conversationalist. On the other hand, his outlook on life was so different

from her own. The things she valued—
home, family and stability—didn't seem
to mean as much to him. Her attraction to
him confused her. After a year filled with so
many changes, she wanted a man she could
depend on to always be there for her. Ryder
wasn't going to ever stay in one place too
long, so he clearly wasn't a man she could
count on.

"I gotta go," Kelly said. "I promised
Mama I'd help with the Ladies Auxiliary
booth. They're selling popcorn and lemon-
ade."

"I'll stop by in a bit and say 'Hi'," Christa
said. "I'm going to find Mom and Dad."

She spotted them in the crowd around
the stage, standing together arm in arm,
her mother's head on her father's shoulder. The knowledge that they were still so
much in love after almost thirty years together brought a lump to Christa's throat.
That was the kind of love she wanted, with
a man who would move mountains to be
with her.

She shifted her gaze to the rest of the
crowd, made up of both familiar faces and
strangers. The shady oaks offered respite
from the heat of the day, and the band's

music was lively; people nodded and tapped toes in time with the music. Dads held little children up so they could see better, and a few couples on the edges were dancing.

This was the way she remembered things from her childhood—Saturday fairs in the town park, where she ate too much cotton candy while her mother sold cookies at the church booth and her father played dominoes with his rancher friends.

Everything about those days had been idyllic—and maybe a little too perfect. Her father often accused her of having a very selective memory about her childhood. Truthfully, Cedar Grove had already passed its prime by the time she was old enough to remember much. Even as a small child, she recalled boarded up buildings on Main Street and having to drive fifty miles to a department store to buy good shoes for church.

Still, today was how it should be, and it had all been inspired by her memories of her childhood. Though her father and Ryder had accused her of looking at the world through rose-colored glasses, sometimes those glasses could provide a better vision of what the future ought to look like. She liked to aim for that vision, even if the results were less than perfect. That was much better than never bothering to try at all.

CHAPTER TEN

RYDER HAD ATTENDED his share of small town festivals over the years, but he had to admit Cedar Grove's Summer Festival was better than most. The setting—in the green park in the shade of oaks and elms—was particularly inviting. And everyone he met seemed to go out of their way to welcome him. The food from the various booths was delicious, and he'd had fun trying his hand at tossing bottle caps into cups and trying to hit a target with bean bags, all in the name of contributing to local charities.

Having his mom there made the day special, too. He'd forgotten how much fun she could be. Today brought back memories of attending village Fetes in England and touring Saturday markets in France. Though his father had often been away on tours of duty, his mother had tried to entertain her three children and teach them about the areas where they'd lived.

"That was very thoughtful of you to volunteer for the raffle," his mom said as they browsed a booth full of hand-dyed scarves and T-shirts.

"I was flattered to be asked," he said. "I can certainly spare an afternoon to re-hang a crooked door or paint a fence or install a ceiling fan."

"My guess is that a good number of the tickets in that overflowing flowerpot are from local single women." She held up a scarf dyed in shades of teal and pink. "A man like you, good-looking and employed, is considered quite the catch, I think."

"Mom, please." He looked around, hoping no one was listening. "It's a handyman raffle, not a bachelor auction."

"Still, I've seen how the women around here look at you. You could have your pick if you were interested."

"There's no sense getting involved with someone when I'm only going to be here a little while."

"Hmmm." She folded the scarf over her arm. "I think I'll get a couple of these for your sisters for Christmas. Do you want to buy one for Christa?"

Did she purposely pretend not to hear

what he'd said? "I don't need to buy a scarf for Christa."

"You could call it a thank-you gift, for getting you involved in the auction."

"She wouldn't see it that way." He pictured her throwing the gift back in his face, or at least accusing him of going too far.

"You two seem to be good friends," his mother said.

"Not good enough for me to buy her presents." A gift would definitely send the wrong message.

Despite the closeness he felt to her sometimes, she acted as if she didn't trust him. Her reaction when he'd asked her out had wounded his pride a little, he could admit. If he was going to date while he was in Cedar Grove—and that was a big if—he'd be better off finding someone whose opinion didn't matter to him quite so much.

"Attention, everyone!" came the announcement over a loudspeaker. "You'll want to start making your way to the Handyman Raffle booth. In a few minutes, we're going to begin drawing names for the raffle winners. And we need all our volunteers at the booth right away."

"I guess that means me," Ryder said.

His mother set aside the scarves and hooked her arm through his. "I'll come back for the scarves later. I don't want to miss a minute of this."

As they neared the booth, Paul Raybourn caught up to them. "Are you ready?" he asked.

"I guess so." Ryder could admit to a few butterflies. After all, he wanted to make a good showing in front of his new friends.

"I can't believe some poor winner gets me to do their chores," Paul said. "I hope they don't expect a professional job."

"Maybe your wife will win," Peggy said.

"That would be worst of all. At home, I can put off jobs, saying I'm too busy. But if she paid cash for my services, I don't think I'll be able to get away with that excuse."

They joined the crowd around the raffle booth. Someone had brought the Public Address system to the booth, so that everyone in the park could hear the announcement of the winners. Ryder spotted Christa standing with her mother and father near the front of the crowd. "The woman who's going to draw the names is Janet Jepson, Kelly's mother," Paul informed them.

The trim, white-haired woman took up

a position behind the table lined with the names of the people who had volunteered their time. "Let's begin!" she announced, and plunged her hand into the first flowerpot.

"The handyman in question is Paul Raybourn," Janet told the crowd. "And the winner for Paul is…Monica Makepeace."

Paul let out a muffled groan, but strode forward to claim the ticket. A woman with long, flowing hair, even longer skirts and a vibe that was somewhere between Flower Child and Earth Mother, threw her arms around him in a hug. "We've got a new solar system at our yurt and I know you're just the man to help us set it up," she said.

"Sounds like fun," Ryder whispered when Paul returned to his side.

"Monica's all right," Paul said. "Just a little…unique."

Janet chose a series of names in quick succession and men and women of all ages were paired with couples, older men, younger women and grandmotherly types. The biggest laugh of the day was drawn by a girl, all of six or seven years old, who won the services of a burly ranch hand. "I want you to build me a playhouse," she declared, and the man solemnly promised that he would do exactly that.

Finally, only one flowerpot remained on the table, belonging to the last name on the list—Ryder. His mother nudged him. "They're saving the best for last," she said. Was it his imagination, or were tensions running especially high as Janet stirred the raffle tickets? "In case some of you don't know who Ryder Oakes is, he's in charge of the new highway construction project," Janet said as she stirred. "The girls running this raffle finagled him into participating and he was a good sport about it. Looks like he drew a lot of bidders, too." She closed her eyes and pulled a ticket from the pot. "And the lucky winner is…" Janet's smile widened. "Christa Montgomery."

All the breath left Ryder as he tried to process this information. Christa was the last person he'd have thought would bid on him. He searched the crowd for her, wondering what job she had planned for him.

A large man moved to one side and there she was, staring right at him. And she didn't look happy about winning. He moved toward her, wary. "Congratulations," he said. "I didn't know you cared."

"I had nothing to do with this," she said. "My friends bought the tickets for me." She glanced toward the end of the booth, where Kelly and Didi giggled together.

"Guess they think we deserve each other." Some of the tension left him. If Christa hadn't tried to win him, that gave him the upper hand. "What would you like to do with four hours of my time? I can wash your car. Or maybe take you on a picnic."

"My dad needs help re-stringing some fencing. You can do that."

"But you're the one who won my services, not Bud."

"I was going to help him. You can take my place." She turned away, but not before he read the emotion reflected in those brown eyes. Christa looked almost regretful, as if at least part of her wished she'd chosen the picnic, instead of pawning him off on her father.

"I'M GLAD YOU finally made an appointment. I've been dying to work on your hair." Kelly ran her fingers through Christa's long dark locks.

Christa had been so busy getting ready for the Summer Festival she hadn't had much time for primping. With the festival passed, she was overdue for a haircut. "A trim will be fine," she said. The excited gleam in Kelly's eyes made her nervous.

"Oh, come on. You've got to let me do more than that. After all, you want to look sharp for all those job interviews you're going to be getting soon."

"I guess you're right." Christa shifted in the salon chair. "I've got an interview in Dallas next week." The call had surprised her. She'd only sent out a few résumés, and she hadn't expected to hear back so quickly.

"You don't sound very excited."

"I am. But it's…it's with a really big marketing firm. They have some huge clients—oil companies and multinational corporations. A lot different from the boutique company I worked for in Houston."

"It's still marketing work." Kelly began combing out Christa's hair. "I bet they have great benefits. And think of the people you'll meet."

"I'm not sure big corporate work is what I want to do."

"Maybe you'll find out things at the interview that will help you decide."

"That's what I'm hoping."

"But first, I'm going to give you a terrific cut and some highlights—you're going to wow them. Not to mention a certain hunk whose services you won at the raffle."

Christa moaned. "I'm still not sure I've forgiven you and Didi for setting me up this way. How many tickets did you buy?"

The mirror reflected Kelly's smug grin. "I'll never tell. Besides, one day you'll thank me. You and Ryder make a great couple, even if you don't see it yet. What are you having him do with the four hours you won?"

"He's going to help my dad string fence. I might not even be there."

"Christa!" Kelly's tone was scolding. "You have to be there. Your dad didn't win the raffle—you did."

"That's what my dad said when I told him. I said I was having Ryder fill in for me, so I could have a day off, but he said I have to be there, too. I'm at least hoping I can slip away early."

"You might change your mind after you spend a little more time with Ryder." Kelly spun the chair around so that Christa faced away from the mirror. "He's a really nice guy."

"I don't have time for men right now," Christa said. "Nice or otherwise. I need to find a job and a place to live and all those things. What are you doing?" She tried to turn the chair back to the mirror, but Kelly had locked it.

"No peeking until I'm done." Kelly picked up her shears. "It would be great if you got a job in Dallas. I could see you all the time. With the new highway making the commute time shorter, you might even decide to live here."

"I really hate to admit there's anything good about that highway, but I guess you're right."

"Although, now that you've lived in the city, small town life might be too boring for you."

"It's not that. I just wish the town wasn't changing so much—it feels like everything is moving away from me when I've only come back. Even my parents."

"Your parents are moving?" Kelly stopped snipping and put a hand on Christa's shoulder.

"No! At least I don't think so. They've both been so distant I don't really know what's going on in their lives."

Kelly squeezed her shoulder. "Your mom is probably focused on getting well. And your dad is focused on your mom."

"Yes, that's true. And I'd really like to help them, but they won't let me. Mom only wants Dad to take her to her chemo and doctor's appointments. And something's going on with the ranch, but every time I try to ask about it, Dad brushes me off. He'll talk to me about my job, or something in the news, but not about how he's feeling, or what's really going on in his life."

Kelly returned her attention to Christa's hair. "He's a man. And a rancher at that. They don't call them the strong, silent type for nothing. You're used to those touchy-feely city guys."

Christa tried not to pay attention to how much hair was falling around her shoulders. "Trust me—I never met one of those in Houston. I think they're a myth."

"Maybe so. And speaking of guys I'd like to touch and feel, let's get back to Ryder. What's going on between you two, really?"

Christa resisted the urge to squirm under her friend's questions—questions she'd avoided asking herself. "Nothing is going on," she said. "He's a decent guy, but I'm not interested."

"You've been avoiding him."

"I'm not avoiding him." This wasn't one hundred percent true. Earlier in the week, when she'd seen Ryder's truck parked at the Blue Bell, she'd decided to eat lunch at the Burger Barn instead. "I just have no reason to talk to him."

"Yes, you do. You won him in the raffle."

"My father is making the arrangements for that." With luck, she'd have another job interview, and spend that day away from the ranch.

"You don't even appreciate the big favor we did for you," Kelly said. "Fixing you up with the best looking guy in town."

"I'm sorry you wasted your money buying all those raffle tickets, but I'm not interested in Ryder Oakes."

"Why not? He seems interested in you."

Her heart beat a little faster. "You're imagining things."

"I am not. I've seen how he looks at you. I figured out pretty quick that I didn't stand a chance with him."

"He doesn't look at me any special way." But she had a sudden image of Ryder's blue eyes studying her with an intensity that felt warm and intimate.

"Maybe I was wrong," Kelly said. "But I could have sworn he seemed interested in you. But I guess if he hasn't asked you out…"

"He did ask me out." Christa couldn't stop herself from telling this news; she never had been able to keep anything from her best friend.

Kelly gripped Christa's shoulder again. "Please tell me you said yes."

"I told him no. I'm not interested and I won't lead him on."

Kelly moved around in front of the chair and frowned at her friend. "Christa, what is wrong with you? He's good-looking, decent, intelligent, has a good job—what more do you want?"

"I want a man with whom I have something in common. Ryder and I are too different."

"Oh, please! You're both intelligent, good-looking and single. That's all it takes to build a good relationship."

"We're too different," Christa repeated. "I'm emotional. He's practical. Home is really important to me, and he's never really had a home."

"Haven't you heard that opposites attract?"

"Not in this case."

Kelly shoved her shoulder. "I think you're afraid."

"I am not!"

The hairdresser returned to her spot behind the chair, her scissors moving quickly. Christa prayed she'd have some hair left. "You're afraid. Come on—what's the worst that could happen if you went out with him?" Kelly asked.

Christa had lain awake more than one night thinking about this. "I'd fall for him and he'd leave me behind."

Kelly's frantic cutting slowed. "Then you admit you could fall for him."

"I didn't say it would happen. Only that it could. And I've had enough rejection for one year, thank you."

"A job is a far cry from a man. Getting laid off was not personal."

"It felt that way, whether it was or not." And her parents hadn't exactly rejected her, but they hadn't welcomed her with the open arms she'd expected. Was it so wrong of her to want to avoid any more hurt?

"But you're going to get a new job. Why not a new boyfriend while you're at it?"

"Maybe I only want to deal with one challenge at a time. Job first. Then figure out where I'm going to live. Then, maybe I'll be ready to get involved with someone—but not a man who doesn't believe in emotional attachments to people and places."

"I don't think Ryder is as cold as you make him out to be. Why not give him a chance? Dating him might even help you decide what you want to do about your job situation."

"I don't see how Ryder has any relation to my job. Besides, he'd probably be like every other man I know—including my father—and try to tell me what I should do. Men always think they have to fix things."

"Think of dating Ryder as practice at taking risks," Kelly said. "You risk going out with him and it isn't so bad. So that inspires you to take a career risk—applying to some place you really want to work that you thought was out of reach, or something equally frightening."

Kelly was right about one thing. Christa

didn't like risk. "I hate to say this, but you're almost making sense."

"Certainly, I am. I may not have a degree in psychology, but I've spent my life listening to women confess their deepest, darkest secrets within the sacred confines of a beauty shop. I know what makes people tick."

"So you think you know what makes me tick?"

"Of course. You need to take more chances in your life."

"I'm taking one big chance now, trusting you blindly with my hair."

"That's not a risk at all." She stepped back and studied her work. "So far, so good. Let me mix some color and get to work on your highlights. And you can tell me all about what you and Ryder are going to do on your date."

"I never said I was going to date him."

"But what I said about risk made sense. You need more risk in your life. Why not start with Ryder?"

Why not, indeed? "Maybe I'll give him a call," she said. Saying the words out loud made her feel slightly light-headed. "But only to get you off my back."

"Perfect. Now lean this way a little and let me work my magic."

She needed some magic in her life. She didn't think Ryder was going to pull any rabbits out of a hat, or make the kind of change in her life Kelly said she needed.

But she'd never know if she didn't try. She'd go out with him and prove to herself that they were wrong for each other. Then she'd be able to see her next move more clearly.

RYDER DIDN'T EXACTLY look forward to spending a hot, bright Saturday fence building, but he'd made a bargain and keeping it was important. "I'm cashing in Christa's raffle winnings," Bud had explained when he'd telephoned. "Come out Saturday and I'll put you to work."

Ryder's hands tightened on the steering wheel as he drove toward the ranch just after breakfast. He'd have felt better about the work if Christa had been the one to call. Every time he felt the two of them were getting closer, she backed away. He'd never had a woman behave so skittish around him; she was a puzzle he needed to solve, if only so he'd know what not to do the next time he was attracted to a woman.

It didn't help that his mother had gotten involved. Every time they talked now, she asked about Christa. "The two of you seem to get along so well," she'd said the last time they'd talked. "She's interested in you, even if she's not ready to admit it."

"I asked her out once and she turned me down," he said. "I know how to take no for an answer."

"I don't think she meant it," Peggy said. "The raffle win gives you both a second chance."

His mom had sounded hopeful, but Ryder really couldn't see the point. Christa had pawned him off on her father; he didn't need any more proof that pursuing her would lead to a dead end.

He parked his truck in front of the ranch house; no sign of Christa's car. Adele answered his knock at the door. She didn't look much different to him than she ever had, which in itself was a relief. "Bud said to meet him out at the north pasture," she said. "Just follow the dirt road up past the windmill and the stock tank. You'll see Bud's truck parked up there."

"Thanks."

"When you're done, come on up to the house for lunch," she said.

He began to relax as he guided the truck slowly down the dirt track that cut through the ranch. So what if he wouldn't see Christa today? The day was clear and hot, the dry fields and rolling hills bathed in a golden summer glow. He drove past a small herd of glossy black Angus cows, yellow tags clipped to their ears like modish fashion accessories. He passed the stock tank and the windmill, the blades turning lazily.

He understood Christa's reluctance to let all this go, even as he understood that things never stayed the same. Not the way people wanted them to. Change came whether you wanted it to or not; learning to adapt was a gift in itself, one he wanted to share with her.

He spotted Bud's black Chevy parked in the shade of a cluster of post oaks, and pulled in beside it. As he climbed out, someone called his name, and he turned to see the rancher striding toward him. Christa followed a few paces behind him, her expression unreadable in the shade of a pale straw Stetson.

He settled for trying to read her emotions in her walk. She copied her father's long stride, arms swinging at her side. Her straight-cut jeans showed off her figure. A sleeveless snap-button shirt in a pink-and-blue plaid was the latest in cowgirl chic; how like her to be fashionable even when doing chores.

Father and daughter were almost to him before he caught a glimpse of her face. The corners of her mouth turned down, almost in a pout. "Dad didn't tell me you were coming today," she said when she stopped in front of him.

"Must have slipped my mind." Bud shook Ryder's hand. "I figured this was as good a time as any to collect your raffle winnings."

"Have you ever strung fence before?" Christa asked.

"No. But I'm a fast learner."

"It doesn't take a degree from Harvard," Bud said. He handed Ryder a pair of fencing pliers. "The first step is taking down the old wire. You pull out the staples. Christa, you roll up the old wire as it comes loose."

"What are you going to do?" she asked.

"I'm going to lay out the new wire." He

nodded toward the rolls of new wire standing a few feet from the fence.

Ryder followed Christa to the first post. "I
like your new hairstyle," he said. She'd cut
several inches off her long hair, and added
lighter brown highlights.

She put one hand to the shorter hair.
"Thanks. Kelly surprised me with this. I
wasn't sure what to think."

"It's flattering. Very stylish."

"Thanks." She turned her attention to the
fence. "Be careful with the staples. They
tend to go flying."

The pliers made fast work of pulling out
the old staples, though a few were stubborn,
clinging to the hardened oak fence posts as
if they'd been welded in place. "How old is
this fence?" he asked.

"I think my dad said his father put it in
sometime in the seventies."

"He did a good job." He grunted as he applied pressure to a stubborn staple.

"He built things to last. My dad is the
same. They didn't want to have to come back
in ten years and do things all over again."

Was this another route to reminding him
that he couldn't understand that kind of per-
manence? "I always took pride in doing a

good job," he said. "Even if I wouldn't be around to enjoy the results." He straightened and moved on to the next post. She followed behind, rolling up the wire. "I saw your mom earlier," he said. "She looked good."

"She's having a good day. The new wig cheered her up a little."

"I wouldn't have known she was wearing a wig. What do the doctors say?"

"Not a lot. It's too early to tell, I guess."

She didn't elaborate, and they moved on to the next fence post. Though the silence wasn't uncomfortable, he wasn't going to let her cut him out. Not when the one thing they'd always been good at was talking to each other. "How's your job hunt going?" he asked.

"I have an interview on Friday in Dallas."

Not Houston. Did that mean she planned to stick around? "That's great. Congratulations."

"Don't congratulate me yet. I'm not even sure this is something I want."

"Oh?" He glanced at her. Beneath the shade of her hat, her eyes filled with worry.

"I've been thinking a lot about what you said, about finding what I really want to do."

"And what have you decided?"

"Nothing, yet. But I have some ideas. I may be able to make them work in a new job, or I may have to try something completely new for me. Right now, I'm open to all options."

"Sounds like a good plan." He yanked hard on another staple.

"I'm sorry I was so harsh with you the other day," she said. "When you took me out to look at the highway, I know you were only trying to help."

The words were as welcome as a chill breeze, but he tried to play it cool, not wanting to startle her. "I did want to help," he said. "But you didn't ask for my advice, so I shouldn't have offered it."

"Still, I overreacted. If the invitation to go out with you is still open, I'd like to take you up on it."

"Really?" He couldn't hold back a smile. So much for keeping cool. "You'll go out with me?"

"There's no reason we couldn't have dinner. Get to know each other better."

"That's terrific. How about next Saturday evening?" He didn't want to give her too much time to change her mind. "You can tell me how the interview goes."

"All right."

That settled, he felt no need to press her for more. They continued to work easily together, until all the old wire was off between the corner posts. Together, they rolled up the old wire and Ryder carried it over to Bud's truck, along with the bag full of old staples he'd collected. Bud had unrolled the new wire in front of the posts, ready to be stapled in place.

"The important thing is to stretch it tight between posts," Bud said, as he clamped a fence stretcher onto one section of wire. "Christa, you pound in the staples while Ryder stretches the wire."

"What are you going to do?" she asked.

"I promised your mother I'd take her shopping. She's feeling good today and didn't want to put it off."

Before she could protest, or Ryder could respond, Bud climbed into his truck, started the engine and drove away.

Ryder pushed his hat back on his head and watched the older man hightail it down the dirt track. "Do you think your father planned this—leaving us alone together?" he asked.

"Oh yeah." She removed her own hat and

smoothed back her bangs. "If Mom hadn't wanted to go shopping, he probably would have come up with some other reason to leave." She picked up a hammer and turned toward the fence. "Let's get back to work."

Muscles straining, he pulled on the fence stretcher while she pounded staples into the hard posts. "I wouldn't call this a romantic way to spend the morning," she said as they rested between posts. "It's really hard work."

"You're holding your own," he said.

She selected another staple from the bag. "I may have lived in the city for a few years, but I'm still a ranch girl. Dad expected me to work as hard as the hands."

"Maybe it would have been different if he'd had a son."

"I doubt it. Women on ranches work as hard as the men. They have to."

"I'm glad I'm not having to do this by myself," he said. "We make a good team."

"Well, at least you don't make fun of how I hold a hammer. Rodrigo, our old hand, always told me I used tools like a girl. He gave me a hard time about it."

"I'd much rather be working with you than some old cowboy. Hold the hammer any way you want."

She laughed, and pounded in the next staple.

By the time they reached the corner post, the sun was high overhead and they were both hot and sweating. Ryder looked at the remaining rolls of wire. "What now?" he asked.

"You've done your four hours and I've had enough. Dad and Rodrigo and I can do the rest later." She picked up the hammer and the rest of the fence staples. "We need to take the tools up to the barn. I can offer you a cold drink."

"That sounds good."

He moved aside a box of files, a camera, and a surveyor's transit so that she could ride in the passenger seat of his truck. "Welcome to my office," he said.

She slid onto the seat and fastened her seat belt. "This morning I had to wait for my dad to unload a snaffle bit, two quarts of oil, a drencher and his barn jacket. So I'm used to it."

The cows stood in a clump by the windmill now, and turned their heads to watch the truck as it passed. "Stop by the house first," Christa said. "I'll get us some iced tea. Then we can go to the barn."

CHAPTER ELEVEN

RYDER FOLLOWED CHRISTA through the back door into an old-fashioned kitchen with dark wood cabinets, speckled Formica counter-tops and a red linoleum floor. A feed store calendar hung on the wall by the back door, and a row of ceramic canisters shaped like ears of corn sat by the stove. Ryder had sat in similar kitchens all over the country, talking to ranchers and farmers and friends. Christa filled two glasses from old-fashioned ice trays, and then poured tea from a crockery pitcher. "Do you take sugar?" she asked.

"No. Plain is fine."

"There's sliced ham, if you want a sandwich."

"No thanks. Not just now." He didn't want her to make him a sandwich, or do anything other than stand here with him in this serene place, at ease, no longer running away.

Except that she wasn't really at ease, and

part of her still wanted to run. "We'd better get those tools out to the barn," she said, and moved past him, out the back door.

She started to climb into the truck, but he leaned over the tailgate and took out the hammer, pliers and fence stretcher. "I can carry these," he said. He tucked the hammer and pliers into the pockets of his jeans and hefted the stretcher in one hand. "Let's walk."

"All right." She fell into step beside him, matching her stride to his own. A breeze carried her scent to him: floral perfume, shampoo and the faint underpinning of clean sweat. Feminine and earthy. Provocative.

A horse greeted them as he pulled open the barn door. He left the tools on a work bench just inside the door, and moved to the stalls. A quartet of horses stood watching them with alert brown eyes, silky tails switching back and forth. Ryder smoothed the nose of the closest animal, a tall bay with a black mane and tail. "That's Peanut, my dad's favorite." Christa moved in beside him, almost close enough to touch.

She held out her hand and a second horse, a brown-and-white paint, stepped over. "This is Susie, my horse. The other two are

Cinnamon and Buster." She drained her tea glass and set it atop the fence post. "Do you ride?"

"I'm no expert, but I've ridden some."

"Want to try out Buster?"

"You mean it?"

"Sure. The horses need the exercise."

"Then let's go. You promised to show me the ranch once. I'd like to see it." Most of all, he'd like to see the land through her eyes, and try to understand what this place meant to her.

They saddled the horses and he swung up on the chestnut gelding named Buster. The horse danced sideways for a few seconds, then seemed to accept the stranger on his back and followed Christa and Susie out of the barn. "Where to?" Ryder asked.

"Want to see the original ranch house, where my grandparents lived when they first came here?"

"I'd like that."

She dug her heels into the horse's ribs and took off. Ryder followed, his eyes fixed on her erect figure in the saddle. Her dark hair gleamed beneath the brim of her hat and the faded jeans hugged her curves. He had a new appreciation for cowgirls.

He spotted the house long before they reached it. It was a low, rectangular structure huddled against a small rise. Christa reined her horse to a stop in front of it and swung down out of the saddle.

"Does anyone live here now?" Ryder asked when he joined her.

"Not now." She wrapped her horse's reins around a post beside a water trough. Ryder did the same for his mount. "We use it for storage," she said. "Dad replaced the roof a couple of years ago to keep it from falling in."

"So this is where your grandparents lived?" He remembered the couple from the picture—the weathered, bowlegged man and the tiny Asian woman.

"They lived here when they first married. But the house is a lot older than that. I think my grandmother told me it was built about 1920."

A faint dirt track ran in front of the house. A windmill turned lazily, pumping water into a rusting metal tank. The only sound was the snuffling of the horses as they drank. "It's pretty remote," Ryder said.

"It is. I like to visit sometimes to be alone and think." She walked over to some flowers that bloomed at the base of the metal tank. Roses, he thought. Pink, with small, open blooms. "My grandmother planted these. Even after they moved, she came out here to tend them. After she died, my dad punched a hole in the bottom of the tank so water would trickle out and keep them alive."

He tried to imagine the taciturn, practical rancher and his delicate, foreign born mother. No matter how many years she lived here, Christa's grandmother would have always stood out as different. "Do you think she missed Vietnam?" he asked.

"She never said. But then again, she lived here far longer than she lived there." Christa stopped and stared at the old house, the empty windows staring blindly back. "I think she thought of this as home." She glanced at Ryder. "Do you miss any of the places you've lived before?"

"When I was little, I was always homesick for the place we had just left. But after a while I stopped doing that."

"You learned not to get attached."

"I guess so."

"It doesn't sound like a good way to live. Always holding back."

He heard the disapproval in her voice,

judging him and finding him wanting. "I don't think of it that way," he said. "I think of it as living in the moment. Enjoying what I have right now. Appreciating who I'm with." He moved over beside her, almost but not quite touching, and looked down into her eyes. "I get the feeling you're the one who's holding back with me."

A small V formed between her brows. "Because I'm not throwing myself at you like half the women in town?"

"I like that about you."

The frown deepened. "I'm not playing hard to get."

"I know that. I also know that I'm really attracted to you." He touched her arm, a gentling gesture. "And I think you're attracted to me."

She stiffened, but she didn't move away. "I said I'd go out with you. Isn't that enough?"

"I guess I'm greedy. What if I said I wanted to kiss you?"

She wet her lips. The tip of her tongue slicked across her luscious mouth and got his blood pumping. "I'm not afraid of a kiss," she said.

He bent his head and covered her mouth with his own. Her lips were smooth and cool and tasted of cherries. Sweet and a little surprising. She rose up on her tiptoes, leaning in, and slid one hand up to steady herself against his chest. She kissed him back, as ardently as he kissed her. Another surprise.

Even after their lips parted, they stared into each other's eyes for several seconds. They were both breathing hard, as if they'd run a long way.

She turned away first. "I think we'd better go back to the house now," she said. She moved away; he didn't try to stop her. Maybe she was right. No telling what might happen if they kept on kissing like that.

She untethered her horse and swung into the saddle, then galloped away, as if pursued by bandits.

Ryder followed at a more leisurely pace, savoring the memory of that kiss, the feel of her in his arms. She'd been right when she'd guessed he'd learned at an early age not to attach himself to places. He found it hard to be close to most people, too. He was always friendly, but he kept an emotional distance. Good-byes were always easier when the people you were leaving didn't know the real you.

Christa was the exception. He wanted her

to see him as he really was. And he wanted her to like what she saw.

FRIDAY MORNING, CHRISTA drove to Dallas for her job interview. As the miles rolled by, she told herself she should be thinking about her résumé and the questions an interviewer might ask, but what filled her thoughts was Ryder. Ryder, muscles straining against his shirt as he stretched the fence wire. Ryder on Buster looking as at home in the saddle as any cowboy. Ryder looking into her eyes, stripping away all her attempts to hide from him. Ryder's lips on hers, kissing her until she was dizzy.

She was crazy to let him get that close. Crazier still to invite more closeness with their date tomorrow night. She needed home and stability and familiarity; he wanted none of those things. Even if he would commit to one person—commit to her—he'd expect her to follow him around the country like a nomad. The thought tied her stomach in knots.

Her grandmother had followed the man she loved halfway across the world, but she'd been younger, and willing to make changes. Christa was neither of those things, and she didn't want to get involved with a man who required such negotiations. Either she'd be unhappy moving to follow him, or he'd be restless, stuck in one place with her.

And she couldn't afford to think about any of this now. She had to focus on this job interview. Despite her natural inclination to resist change, she wanted to keep an open mind about this position. Maybe it was exactly what she needed to get her moving forward again.

She found the office she was looking for, a sleek glass-and-steel high rise jutting out of the flat prairie like a candle on a cake. She parked in the garage and took the elevator up to the thirty-fourth floor. Already the high heels she'd chosen were hurting her feet, after weeks in flat boots and sandals.

"Ms. Montgomery, so nice to meet you." The man who greeted her was only a few years older than her, with a dark goatee and sandy hair. "I'm Chad Bremer. And this is Joyce Palmyra and Randall Selvin." The other two, who stood slightly behind him, were older: Joyce a sleek blonde in her forties, Randall a distinguished, swarthy fifty-something.

"You have some very nice work in your

portfolio," Joyce said as they walked down a gleaming hallway between rows of cubicles. "Some very interesting small projects."

"We tend to work on a large scale here," Randall said before Christa could comment. "We're involved in national and regional campaigns for some of the top Fortune 500 companies."

"I'm especially interested in work for nonprofits." Christa regretted the words as soon as she'd said them. It was far too early in the interview process to mention anything like that. She didn't miss the frowns that passed between the two older members of the team.

"We've done some of that, too," Chad said. "We did a big campaign for a charity with a national profile last year."

Christa kept quiet this time. They passed more cubicles. She'd probably end up in one of them if she took this job. She thought wistfully of the open loft where her former company had been headquartered. She'd had a workspace with a view of a greenbelt, and had set up a bird feeder right outside her window.

"We employ a team approach, and if you were selected for this position, you'd work on as many as a dozen campaigns at once,"

Randall said. "Most people really enjoy the variety. For instance, right now we're working with a private contractor who specializes in building toll roads, a major oil company, a baby food manufacturer, and several political campaigns."

"It sounds very interesting," Christa said. Also stressful and a bit daunting. She had interviewed at a company like this while she was still in college. Back then, she'd been excited about the prospect of being part of a large group. She'd be able to learn so much, and eventually advance so far. She'd even been disappointed to land the job with a smaller concern instead.

She tried, but couldn't muster any of that original excitement. Had she changed so much in only a few years? "Let's step in here and get to know you better." Joyce led the way into a large conference room. Christa sat on one side of a long table, Chad next to her and Joyce and Randall across from her.

The usual battery of interview questions followed, examining her strengths and weaknesses. "What's your favorite part of marketing work?" Joyce asked.

"I enjoy working with clients to discover their core message and to find creative ways to communicate that message to others," Christa said. "For example, I once worked on a campaign designed to encourage more parents to vaccinate their kids. I designed advertisements that focused on parents' desire to protect their children even when they weren't around, so we showed kids wearing bicycle helmets and skateboard pads and other protective gear, and related vaccinations to the same kind of proactive decisions."

"What about commercial clients?" Randall asked. "What kind of experience do you have with things besides public service announcements?"

"Actually, I have quite a lot of experience in that area." She tried not to let his disdain for public service work rattle her. "I designed a social media campaign for an up-and-coming dress designer that doubled her business. And I was part of a team that launched a line of seasonal brews for one of the largest breweries in the state."

"What is your least favorite aspect of the job?" Chad asked.

Christa hated questions like this. You couldn't be honest and say you hated meetings or being micromanaged or any of the annoyances that came with every job. You had to find an answer that was more positive than negative, something like "I hate when I don't just wow the client with my brilliance."

She smiled weakly. "I hate when the results of a campaign aren't as good as expected. I want to do a great job every time."

This answer seemed to satisfy them. Joyce closed the file with Christa's résumé and other information. "Thank you for your time today, Ms. Montgomery. We'll be in touch if we decide to offer you the job."

"Thank you." They stood and shook hands.

Chad escorted Christa into the hall. "You did well," he said, his smile encouraging.

"Do you really think so?" She glanced over her shoulder at the now-closed conference room door. The briefness of the interview alone told her she hadn't impressed them.

"You did fine," he said. "You haven't worked with the kind of big clients we usually handle, but that could be in your favor— fresh blood and new ideas and all that."

"Thanks for the encouragement."

He checked his watch—a Rolex. "Would you like to have some lunch? My treat."

"Oh, I…is this part of the interview?"

He laughed. "No. I just like you and I'd like to get to know you better. This has nothing to do with the job."

So he was asking her on a date? She should probably be flattered. He was good-looking, nice and apparently well off. But really, all she wanted was to escape to her car and drive back to Cedar Grove. She wanted to change into jeans and boots and go riding. "Thanks," she said. "But I have another appointment. It was good to meet you."

"Could I call you some time?" he asked. "Maybe we could get together for drinks or a movie."

"Sure." She couldn't think of a way to tell him no without seeming rude. And he was a perfectly nice guy, even if he didn't set off any sparks. "Now, I'd better be going."

He walked her to the elevator. Only when she was safely in her car did she let herself sigh and relax. One thing she'd learned from this experience; she wasn't cut out to work for a big corporation. She needed to find a smaller, private firm, where she worked with nonprofits and small businesses.

On the way home, she kicked off her heels, turned up the radio and rolled down the window to let the wind blow through her hair. The farther she drove from the city, the more relaxed she began to feel. In Cedar Grove, she headed straight for the Burger Barn, starving for a cheeseburger and onion rings. She'd just collected her order from the window when Paul Raybourn waved to her from one of the picnic tables. "Hey, Christa!"

Ryder sat across from Paul. He moved over as she approached. "Have a seat," he said. "How did the job interview go?"

"An interview. That explains why you're so dressed up," Paul said. "Who'd you interview with?"

"A very big, very successful marketing company in Dallas." She slid onto the bench and arranged her lunch before her, very aware of the man beside her, the bench creaking as he shifted his weight.

"Sounds like a step up the career ladder," Paul said.

"It could be." She nibbled an onion ring. "But I don't think it's for me."

"Why not?" Paul asked.

"Would you leave Cedar Grove to work for a big bank in the city?"

"Duh! Yes."

"But you know all your customers here," she said. "You can make a difference in their lives, if you give them a loan or help them when they bounce a check."

"I'd learn to know my customers in the city. And sometimes it's easier if you aren't so personally involved in people's lives. Sometimes I have to turn down friends who want loans, or tell people they're overdrawn."

"Okay, I see that. And I don't have anything against the city. I'd just rather help small businesses and nonprofits than big corporations."

"Maybe it's time to hang out your own shingle," Paul said. "Small marketing 'R' us."

"That's not a bad idea," Ryder said, smiling. "Everyone's probably going after the big companies—you could build a niche market."

"I'll think about it." Though the prospect of starting her own business sounded daunting, like a big risk.

"Speaking of work, time for me to get back to mine." Ryder stood and gathered up the remains of his lunch. "See you tomorrow night." He nodded and left them.

Paul leaned across the table toward her. "What's happening tomorrow night?" he asked.

"None of your business." She took a bite of cheeseburger.

"You have a date, don't you? Are you and Ryder secretly seeing each other?"

She swallowed and sipped from her cup of iced tea. "There's nothing secret about it." Especially since Paul would go home and tell Didi, who would tell all her friends. Pretty soon the whole town would know that she'd agreed to go out with Ryder. "We're going on one date. As friends."

Paul grinned. "You may think that, but I don't think he does. Ryder has plenty of friends. What he doesn't have is a girl-friend."

He winked, then gathered his own trash and left. She ate the rest of her burger and onion rings, pondering this. Ryder had admitted he was attracted to her, and that kiss certainly hadn't been a platonic gesture. So all right, they had some chemistry. But not every experiment led to an explosion. Sometimes things fizzled out. The fizzling was what she was afraid of, but she'd vowed to take more risks with her life. Ryder was risk number one, but she wasn't about to throw caution to the wind when it came to the handsome engineer. If he wanted her trust, he'd have to earn it, just as her grandfather had earned Swan's love all those years ago.

CHAPTER TWELVE

RYDER ALMOST FELT as if he should be carrying a corsage in a plastic florist's box as he walked up to the Montgomery's front door Saturday evening. The last time he'd picked a date up at her parents' house must have been prom or some other high school dance. He had that same sense of nervous anticipation now, as if he wasn't quite sure what to do with himself. He wanted the evening with Christa to go well, more than he'd admit to himself even.

Bud answered his knock, the little dog, Jet, at his heels. The rancher looked tired, the lines around his eyes deeper, his shoulders more stooped. "Come on in, Ryder," he said, holding the door wide. "Christa's still getting ready."

Ryder followed Bud into the comfortable living room and sat on the sofa while the older man settled into a worn recliner. Jet curled onto the ottoman at Bud's feet and watched Ryder with a solemn expression. "How's the road project coming?" Bud asked.

"Great. The weather's been cooperating and we're making solid progress."

"These budget cuts going to affect you any?" Bud muted the sound on the television, which was tuned to the news.

The Texas legislature had made a pledge to slash state spending in the wake of some revenue shortfalls. Lots of people were worried, but so far no specific programs had been cut. "I don't think it's going to affect the Highway Department," Ryder said. "Especially not a project that's already started."

"That's good to know."

Bud fell silent, staring at the muted television. Ryder shifted on the sofa. "How's Adele?" he asked.

"She had a bad day today. She's resting now."

"I'm sorry to hear that."

"Christa wanted to stay home with her mom, but I told her not to be ridiculous. There's nothing she can do, and if she's here, Adele thinks she has to be strong—pretend everything's all right. She'll rest better if she knows Christa's out enjoying herself."

Not good. Christa had been reluctant to go out with him to begin with; now she had an even better reason to be distracted all evening.

"Hello, Ryder."

He stood as Christa came into the room. As always, she was dressed stylishly, in a short skirt and high heels. He forced his attention to the rest of her, which looked just as good in a silky blouse, her newly styled hair curling up at the top of her shoulders. "Hello, Christa," he said. "You look nice."

"Thanks." She turned to her father. "I checked on Mom. She's sleeping."

"That's fine," Bud said.

"There's some chili in the refrigerator you can have for supper," Christa reminded her dad. "And some fruit salad."

"I'll be fine. You two go on now."

She bit her lip, but said nothing more. Ryder followed her to the door and held it open for her. Outside, he put a hand on her elbow to steady her on the uneven ground. Unnecessary, probably, but he wanted to touch her, to offer some kind of silent comfort.

He opened the passenger door of his truck for her and waited until she was belted in before he walked around to the driver's side. "Where are we going?" she asked, as he started the truck.

"You know this area better than I do," he said. "I thought maybe you'd like to choose."

"What if I said I didn't know? Or I don't care?"

She wasn't hostile, exactly, but this wasn't the warm reception he'd hoped for. "I know you're preoccupied. Your dad said your mom had a bad day."

She pressed her lips tightly together and nodded. "The chemo is really affecting her now. She can't keep anything down."

She was fighting tears. Part of him wanted to hold her and let her cry, but he didn't think she'd take such a suggestion well. He settled for squeezing her arm gently. "Adele is a strong woman. She'll get through this."

"I wish she'd let me help her, instead of sending me away." Christa's voice rose, an anguished wail.

"Sometimes it's hard to show weakness to the people we love the most."

She sniffed and nodded. "Right. So I'm supposed to go out and have a good time, knowing she's lying at home, miserable."

"You're not going to make her any less

miserable if you stay home. Why not try to take your mind off your problems for a few hours? I'll do my best to distract you. It's the only way I know to help."

She nodded, and forced a smile. "Sounds okay. So what do you have in mind?"

"We could have dinner at the steakhouse, or at the Blue Bell."

"Not the Blue Bell. Everyone in town will see us. Next thing you know, the gossips will have us eloping."

He laughed. "I hope you're exaggerating."

"Maybe a little. But not much."

"Well then, the Blue Bell is out. Would you rather go to Dallas and take in a movie?"

"A movie's not a bad idea, but Dallas is so far to drive." She looked thoughtful. "I know where we should go."

He put the truck into gear. "Where to?"

"The drive-in, on the old Dallas Highway."

He vaguely recalled an oversized screen situated in a pasture. He'd passed it on his drives around the area and thought it was a relic from days past. "I didn't realize that place was still open."

"It is on weekends. Bill Omar runs it. His wife and daughter operate the concession

stand—they do really good barbecue sandwiches, and the best popcorn, with real butter."

"This is sounding better all the time.
What's showing?"

"Bill chooses the movies, and he tends
to favor Westerns, but as long as you're not
picky about the show, it's a lot of fun."

"I've never been to a drive-in movie,"
Ryder said. He'd been to theatres in France
and Japan and Germany, but never one in
an old cow pasture.

"Now you can check it off your bucket
list."

They arrived at the single-screen pseudo-
movie theater right at full dark, a sliver of
moon rising up behind the big screen which
was indeed set in the middle of a pasture.
Ryder paid the gum-chewing teenager at the
entrance, then dodged more than one cow
patty as he steered to a parking space next
to a speaker on a stand.

"Roll down the window partway and clip
the speaker on the glass," Christa told him.
She unbuckled her seat belt and stretched.
"Looks like it's going to be a beautiful
night."

"This place is pretty popular," Ryder

said. All around him, spaces were filling up with trucks and cars. Families, teenagers and older couples stood among the vehicles, chatting and eating. Some people brought picnic suppers, but most formed lines at the little trailer that served as a concession stand.

"Saturday nights in Cedar Grove, it's either this or the bowling alley, or maybe a high school dance."

"Want to grab dinner before the show starts?" he asked.

"Sure." Christa opened her door and slid out of the truck.

He met her at the front bumper. "Those heels probably aren't the right footwear for a cow pasture," he said.

"They aren't that high, and I'll be careful." She hooked her arm in his. "I can lean on you."

"Anytime." They started toward the concession stand, but had to stop three times to speak with people who greeted either Ryder or Christa, or both.

Melvin Nimechek was there, with his wife, Beryl. "Good show tonight," the old rancher said. "It's John Wayne."

"I'm sure we'll enjoy it," Christa said,

and leaned closer to Ryder. He put his arm around her and she didn't object. He was beginning to feel a lot better about tonight.

At the concession stand they waited in line for paper boats of barbecue sandwiches and coleslaw. The enticing aroma of spicy barbecue sauce and buttery popcorn filled the air. "Do you want popcorn now?" Ryder asked.

She shook her head. "Maybe at intermission."

"There's an intermission?"

"Bill has to change the film reels."

"So he hasn't gone digital."

"He probably won't. It's too expensive and this is merely a hobby. He likes movies and likes to share them with others. Whenever he can't get film to fit his old projector, he'll have to shut down."

Ryder looked around at the crowd of locals, everyone friendly and relaxed, visiting among the cars. Modern movie theaters weren't conducive to this kind of socializing among all ages, with everyone keeping to their seats in each little theatre. "I'm glad I got to see this spot before it's gone," he said.

"Me, too."

They gingerly made their way back to the

truck and spread their meal out on the console between them. Good thing he wasn't a teenager looking to score, Ryder thought as he fit his drink into the cup holder. The console was a solid barrier between him and his date, and the truck had no backseat. "Maybe drive-ins died out because cars changed," he said. "No more comfortable bench seats."

"When I was in high school, some of the boys would back their trucks into the slots and bring quilts to make a kind of bed in the back," Christa said. "They told Bill they wanted to be more comfortable, but, of course, they really just wanted to make out. He made a rule they couldn't do that anymore."

"Being teenagers, I'm sure they found other methods to sneak in some necking," he said.

"Do you speak from experience?" she teased.

"Oh, I'll never tell."

The speaker blared to life, startling him. Christa laughed again. Such a lovely sound; he was glad she was able to put her worries about her mother behind her for a while.

The evening began with a classic cartoon. "My sisters and I used to watch this," Ryder said. "Saturday mornings, when we were living on base in Texas."

"How old were you?" she asked.

"Eight or nine. Sherry and Megan were six and four. We spent all morning in our pajamas, watching cartoons and eating giant bowls of sugary cereals. During commercials, we'd stage battles with our Ninja Turtle figures."

She laughed more, covering her mouth with one hand and rocking back and forth. "I'm picturing it now—so cute."

"I had buck teeth and a cowlick that made my hair stick up in back."

"On an eight-year-old, that qualifies as cute."

"Good thing I had braces when I was older, and grew my hair out to hide the cowlick. What about you? Did you watch cartoons?"

She nodded. "With my grandmother."

"She liked cartoons?" He never remembered his parents as part of those Saturday mornings. They were still asleep, or otherwise occupied.

"She did. She told me when she first came to the United States, she improved her English by watching TV."

"What did she think of Westerns?" He nodded toward the screen as the intro for the main feature appeared. "Did she like John Wayne?"

"She did. She had a thing for cowboys. Maybe that's why she married one."

The feature began and they settled into an easy silence. Ryder had seen the movie before, years ago, but he found himself caught up in the story again. In the cars around them, people applauded at familiar lines, or even recited them along with the actors. Children raced between the cars, some folks sat on lawn chairs between the vehicles, while others shared popcorn and candy in the front seats of pick-up trucks and sedans. The atmosphere was as relaxed and comfortable as a living room.

At intermission, Christa sat up straight and stretched. "What do you think so far?" she asked.

"About the movie? It's better than I remembered."

"I meant about the Cedar Grove Drive In."

"I like it. I hope Bill can keep getting the movies he loves to show. Want to get some popcorn?"

"Not really," she said. "But I wouldn't mind a walk."

"Sounds good."

Once more, she let him take her arm. They picked a route across the pasture to more level ground near the concession stand and port-a-cans. "Tell me about Friday," he said. "Do you really think the job you interviewed for is a no?"

"The interview wasn't long enough. And my answers were too honest. I didn't tell them what they wanted to hear. I doubt they'll ask me back, but that's okay. I don't think it was a good fit for me."

He recalled her words at the Burger Barn. "The company's too big and impersonal?"

"Something like that. I think I was spoiled by my first job and now I don't want to settle for less. I know I can't have exactly what I had before, but I want something I can feel good about."

"Sometimes it's not the job itself, but the attitude you bring to it," he said. "For instance, I know you think what I do is harming the small town you love, but I see my job as helping people to communicate and connect and stay relevant."

She squeezed his arm. "As much as I hate

to admit it, I like that about you. I didn't believe it at first, but now I know you really do believe those things."

Her words made him feel about seven feet tall. "I'm glad I was able to convince you."

"That still doesn't mean I'm happy about the new highway, but I can sort of see your point," she said. "When I was driving to Dallas Friday morning, I couldn't help but think it would be nice if the commute was shorter."

"I won't say I told you so because I'm too much of a gentleman."

"Oh, of course you are. And I get your point about an attitude changing how we feel about things. But if I had to work on a marketing campaign for a politician I didn't like, I'd have a tough time."

"Whereas, I might try to see it as making a contribution to the overall political process."

"Oh please." She punched him playfully. "Are you always so positive?"

"Call it a survival mechanism. My life growing up was one of constant change. I had to choose to be either miserable or happy, so I chose happy. My father was the same, so I had a good example to follow."

"I think you have a special gift, and you don't even realize it."

"Some people have accused me of being shallow." The criticism stung, but he'd learned not to let it show. He braced himself for Christa's reaction.

She looked at him, her expression serious. "No, I don't think you're shallow."

"But you're still not sure about me."

"You give the impression that everything is easy for you. That you never have to push yourself or do anything that makes you uncomfortable."

Never let them see you sweat. That had been his dad's motto. "I'll admit, I don't put myself into situations where that's necessary."

"Exactly. But I think life is only that easy if you never let anything touch you." She released her hold on him and stopped. "You remain aloof. Uninvolved."

"Are you saying you don't think I would take a risk for anything? For anyone?"

She faced him. "I don't know. Would you?"

"I suppose that depends on what kind of risk."

It wasn't the answer she was looking for.

He knew it as soon as the words were out of his mouth. "I'm being honest with you," he said.

"I know you are." But the disappointment didn't leave her eyes. She patted his arm again. "Come on, let's go back to the truck and see how Wayne gets out of his predicament."

"That's right," he said. "In the movies, the heroes always know what to do." He couldn't be the kind of rash, reckless hero Christa seemed to want. He was a man who planned his next move carefully, and didn't take chances unless he was sure of the outcome. But people weren't always that predictable. He couldn't be sure about Christa, and that made him less sure of himself.

CHRISTA TRIED TO concentrate on the movie, but her thoughts kept drifting to her conversation with Ryder. More than anything, she'd wanted him to tell her he was willing to go out on a limb for the things that were important to him. She wanted to believe he was a man like her grandfather, who would risk everything for the woman he loved.

A romantic notion, maybe even outdated, but that was the kind of man she wanted in her life. Risk was so hard for her, she needed a man who could balance out her hesitancy with a more daring nature. This was one case where she'd hoped Ryder's opposite traits would complement and mesh with her own.

He slumped beside her, eyes focused on the movie screen, expression guarded. He could talk all he wanted about her resistance to change, but he was just as unwilling to do anything that would unsettle the uncomplicated, unconnected life he'd made for himself.

The screen went black, and then the words "Brief Intermission" appeared. "Must be time to change another reel," Christa said.

"I could go for some popcorn about now," Ryder said.

"That sounds good. If you don't mind, I'll stay in the truck." She glanced at her feet. "Walking in these heels is more challenging than I thought."

"I'll be right back."

She watched him walk away, moving effortlessly through the crowd, greeting people he met as if they were old friends. She would have thought a man who adapted so well to new situations would be someone who wasn't afraid of risk.

A tap on the side of the window interrupted her thoughts. She smiled as she recognized Janet Jepson. "Hey there. Is Kelly with you?" She looked over Janet's shoulder, expecting to see her friend.

"Actually, I'm on a date." Her cheeks pinked, making her look years younger.

Christa recovered her surprise. Janet had been a widow for four years now. It wasn't so odd that she'd want to date. "Anyone I know?" she asked.

"I don't think so. His name's Chuck Bailey. He's part of the crew working on the new highway."

So Kelly had been right when she'd predicted the highway project would bring eligible men to town. "Are you having a good time?"

Janet tucked a stray lock of her bleached blonde hair behind one ear. "He's nice. Though I'm not a big fan of Westerns."

"You should have told him that."

She made a face. "You young girls would do that, but I come from a generation where we were taught to let the man make all the decisions. It's the way it was when Steve and I were married and it still feels comfortable."

Christa remembered Steve Jepson as a portly, smiling man who had sold used cars from a small lot that had since been vacant for the past several years. He hadn't struck her as a particularly authoritative man but then, who knew what went on behind closed doors?

"Don't make that disapproving face at me," Janet said.

Christa hadn't realized she'd been making any kind of face. "I guess I'm surprised that you wouldn't want to admit you didn't like a movie a man had picked out."

"Tell me—who paid for your tickets tonight?" Janet asked.

Christa flushed. Ryder had opened his wallet and she hadn't objected.

"You don't have to be embarrassed," Janet said. "There's nothing wrong with a woman who likes a man to take the lead every now and then." She checked her watch. "I'd better go. I just saw you on the way back from the ladies' room and thought I'd say hello."

She left and the message on the screen flashed that intermission would be over in one minute. Christa scanned the crowd for

Ryder, confused by her interaction with her friend's mother. Sure, she wanted a masculine man, but that didn't mean he had to be her boss.

"Take this so I don't spill it." Ryder handed two bags of popcorn through the open window, then opened the driver's side door and climbed in.

"You should let me reimburse you for this," Christa said. "And for my ticket."

"When you land a new job, you can take me out." He juggled a handful of kernels into his mouth.

"So it wouldn't bother you if I paid for a date?"

"No. Should it? But I asked you out, so tonight is my treat." The screen darkened and music blared. Ryder settled into his seat. "Looks like I got back just in time."

Christa munched popcorn and watched the end of the movie, but the plot barely registered. No wonder her friends complained about how arduous dating had gotten. Instead of worrying about who should pay—or who should take more risks—maybe for now she'd focus on simply having a good time and stop analyzing Ryder for character flaws. Since she wasn't ready to make a commitment, dating a guy who'd spent a lifetime avoiding permanent relationships might be the best idea she'd had in a while.

CHAPTER THIRTEEN

"HOW WAS YOUR date with Christa last night?" Paul Raybourn handed Ryder a cup of coffee, then climbed into the passenger seat of Ryder's truck. The two friends were headed for a local fishing hole that Paul had promised would be teeming with fish. Though Ryder wondered if Paul hadn't scheduled the trip for this particular morning in order to get the scoop on Ryder's date.

"We had a good time. We went to the drive-in."

"The drive-in?" Paul laughed. "I haven't been there since high school. Is Mr. Omar still showing those old Westerns?"

"He is. Last night was John Wayne." He cautiously sipped the hot coffee. "I'd seen it before, though that was years ago."

"But you wouldn't have cared what was showing, as long as you got to spend the evening with Christa. So are things heating up between you two?"

Ryder nestled the coffee in the cup holder and gripped the steering wheel with both hands. Though he and Christa had parted pleasantly enough—she'd kissed his cheek and thanked him for a fun evening—he'd replayed her words over and over until he finally fell asleep early this morning. "She thinks I'm distant and uninvolved."

"She said that?"

"Not in so many words." Though he was sure that's what she'd meant. "And maybe she's right. I've spent my life never really a part of any place. Rootless."

"It's not like you're some old set-in-his-ways curmudgeon. You can change that."

"It's not only a matter of staying in one place."

"Are you worried you'll be bored? I'll admit, small towns aren't exciting. But you could just as easily settle in the city."

"That's not it exactly. I've spent so many years learning not to get attached to people and places, I don't know if I can unlearn that."

"You won't know unless you try."

"Maybe." Except if he tried and failed, he might not be the only one hurt by the experiment.

"What's the latest on the highway project?" Paul asked. "All this fuss in the legislature about the budget isn't going to affect you, is it?"

"I'll admit I haven't been paying too much attention. What exactly is happening in the legislature?"

"Someone miscalculated and they've got a six-billion-dollar shortfall they've got to recoup somehow. Apparently, no department or project is safe."

"We're already broken ground on the highway, negotiated deals. Stopping the project would cost more in the long run than it would save in the short term."

"Since when do politicians take the long view?" Paul said. "They're worried about making an impression on people now, before the next election."

"Still, I think we're safe."

"So, no stress."

Ryder shook his head. "That's not my style."

"Then I envy you." Paul finished his coffee and put the empty cup in the holder. "But hey, my plan is definitely not to stress about anything today. Wait until you see this place.

A beautiful gorgeous lake, shade trees and lots and lot of hungry fish."

"Sounds good to me."

"You can come to my house tonight for fish dinner. Though I warn you, Alex is cutting his first tooth and tends to be fussy."

"I don't mind." Though truthfully, he'd never spent much time around babies. "Are you sure Didi won't mind?"

"No. She's been after me to have you out for dinner. All women are convinced that as soon as single men see their married friends' blissful lives, they'll immediately want to settle down themselves."

"Maybe she's right." But Ryder thought it would take more than a home-cooked meal and the company of an infant to convince him he had what it took to change his life so completely. If settling down in one place sounded risky to him, then giving his heart to one woman was downright terrifying.

"How was your date with Ryder last night?" Mom shook out the bedsheet and passed one end to Christa, who stood on the other side of her parents' king size bed. Jet stood beside Mom, watching the proceedings intently.

"It was fine," Christa said. She buried her face in the sheet, savoring the aroma of sun-warmed linen. Though Mom had a clothes dryer, she insisted on hanging the linens on a line out back. No fabric softener or fancy linen spray could smell as sweet and fresh. "We went to the drive-in. He'd never been to one before."

"Your father and I used to go there when we were dating." Mom spread the sheet over the bed. Christa did the same with her side.

"Bill was probably showing the same films back then," Christa said. "Last night's was a John Wayne movie that was a lot older than I am."

"They're still good movies. Did you have a nice time?"

"I did. It's fun seeing everyone. I ran into Janet Jepson. She was on a date with one of the highway workers. She said the strangest thing, though."

"Oh? What was that?"

"She didn't like Westerns, but she said she believed in letting the man take the lead and make the decisions, so she hadn't told him. She said that was how women of her generation believed they should act."

"I'm the same generation as Janet and I

don't believe that. I don't think any relationship benefits from one partner always holding back and failing to be honest. Whether or not you like a movie may seem like a very little thing, but all those little things build up over time."

"I guess you're right. Everybody has so much advice on how to date, how to find the right person, how to have a good relationship—it's hard to know what's right."

"It's easier than you think," Mom said. "Follow your heart and listen to your head. You know better than anyone how you really feel about someone, and you're smart enough to figure out if this man is the one for you. Focus on what you know, not what you fear."

"Is that what you did with Dad?"

"I hope so. It was so long ago, I can't honestly remember." She smiled. "We fell in love so quickly. Once I moved to Cedar Grove, we spent every spare moment together."

Christa tucked the sheet in all along the edges of the mattress, meeting her mother at the foot of the bed. "What else did you and Dad do when you were dating?"

"Oh, the usual—dinner, or dancing. The

Kiwanis Club had a dance every Friday night and we tried to make them all. We went to the rodeo when it was in town, and once, he took me into Fort Worth for a fancy dinner. Sometimes we just went for a ride."

"And you were staying with a friend when you two met?" It had been a long time since Christa had heard the story from her mother. She wanted details she might have missed before.

"Yes, I'd come to spend a couple of weeks with Raye Ann Taylor and ended up staying the whole summer. I got a job at the county clerk's office to earn my keep. By the end of the summer I felt as if I knew everyone in town."

"You were used to a bigger place."

"Longview was bigger, but it still wasn't a city." She handed Christa the top sheet and they spread it over the bed. Jet wagged his tail. "Cedar Grove was a good fit for me. Or maybe I saw it so favorably because by that time I knew I was in love with your father."

"Do you think you'd have loved him as much if he'd lived in a big city, or an ugly town?"

"Probably." She finished tucking in her side of the sheet and straightened.

Christa shook out the blanket—a new blue one she didn't remember seeing before. "I think a lot about Grandmother," she said. "Coming all the way from Vietnam, on a promise from a soldier she didn't see again for weeks."

"She probably felt she had nothing to lose. Young people often feel that way."

Was Mom saying that, now that she was older, she realized she had a lot to lose? Christa looked up from smoothing the blanket. "How are you really doing?" she asked. "Are you worried? Scared?"

Mom picked up a pillow and fluffed it. "I thought we were talking about your grandmother."

"We were, but now I want to know about you. Not what you want me to hear, but the truth."

She arranged the pillow on the bed, taking her time placing it just so. "Of course I'm worried. Sometimes I'm scared. But mostly, I try not to think about what could happen. I'm going to get through this and be all right."

"Yes, I believe that, too." Christa took the pillowcase her mother handed her.

"Something like this changes you, though,"

Mom said. "I'm not only missing a breast, I'm missing some of the confidence I had before. That sense of invincibility."

Losing the job she'd loved felt that way to Christa—though she couldn't say that to her mother. Compared to cancer, getting laid off seemed like such an insignificant thing. She set the pillow in its place at the head of the bed.

"I'm going to get through this, Christa," Mom said. "I know it's hard on you and your dad, seeing me on the bad days, and I'd give anything to change that. But I'm going to get through it."

"I believe that, Mom. You're the strongest woman I know."

Mom laughed. "Maybe the most stubborn, as your father likes to point out." She turned to the dog. "All right, Jet, your turn."

Jet barked and leapt into the middle of the bed. He ran first to Christa, and then to Mom, who scratched his ears. "Now that the bed's made, how about a nap?" Christa asked.

Her mom's gaze stayed on Christa for a split second. "I think I will lie down for a while."

"Sleep as long as you like. I can get dinner."

"I heard about that last dinner of tuna casserole you cooked. Your father was not happy."

"How am I going to get better if I don't practice?"

"There's not much to practice tonight. I already put a lasagna in the refrigerator. All you have to do is put it in the oven at five."

"I'm sure I can handle that. And maybe I'll make a salad."

"Don't make a big one. You know your father isn't a fan of lettuce."

Christa started toward the door, but stopped. "When do you see the doctor again?" she asked.

"Next week." Mom made a shooing motion. "Now go. Jet and I want to sleep."

Restless, Christa left the house and walked to the barn, where she found her father. He stood in the middle of the tack room, studying a collection of saddles. Some of them were more than thirty years old, the leather burnished by decades of wear. Some bore the initials of long-ago riders, cowboys who had once worked for the ranch or relatives who had once lived here. One English-style riding saddle had sat in the corner for as long as Christa could remember, though no one ever used it. The others saw duty from time to time, when visitors wanted to ride, or when neighbors came to help during round-ups. "I was thinking I ought to sell some of these old things," Dad said.

"You don't think you'll need them?" She ran a hand over the worn pommel of one of the oldest saddles.

"Nah, they're just taking up space. Maybe I'll ask Nate at the feed store if he knows anybody who might want to buy them."

Christa's stomach knotted. "What's with all this downsizing, Dad? Selling off the cattle, not planting as much hay? Are you trying to cut expenses?"

He stiffened. "You don't need to worry about my finances. Your mom and I are fine. But I've been meaning to ask you if you need any money. It can't be easy for you, with no income coming in."

"I don't need any money." Once more, he'd conveniently deflected the conversation back to her. "I have savings." Those funds were getting low, but she wouldn't admit that to him.

"How's the job hunt going?" he asked.

"Have you heard back from that interview you went on?"

"I don't think I'd want that job, even if they offered it to me," she said.

"Why not?"

"I don't think we'd be a good fit."

Her dad snorted. "What do you care about 'fit'? A job is a job. You do your work and get paid."

She could have predicted her father would say this. To him, a job was a means to an end. The few times he'd taken outside work, he'd been focused on supporting the ranch. He never cared about making friends or having a career or advancing to a higher position.

"I've been thinking about maybe starting my own business," she said.

He frowned. "I'd say in this economy, that's pretty risky. And where are you going to get the money to get started?"

"I wouldn't need much. And I could get a loan…"

Already, he was shaking his head. Debt was another thing Dad was against, if it could be avoided. "If you go to work for a big company, you'd have a good salary, guaranteed," he said. "Health insurance, retirement. Those kind of things are worth a lot."

"I think I'd like being my own boss. Yes, I'd take all the risks, but I'd reap the rewards, too."

"You've only been out of school four years. Why would someone hire you when there are other people out there who have more experience?"

Why, indeed? "I think I could offer things big companies wouldn't. Personal service. New ideas."

"I'm not trying to be negative, honey. But you've got to consider this carefully. I'd hate to see you set yourself up for failure."

She was already broke, unemployed and living with her parents, so how much worse could it get? "I'll be okay, Dad."

"I'm sure you will, hon." He returned to contemplating the saddles.

Don't sell them, she wanted to say. *Don't change anything else about the ranch.* She'd had too much change lately.

Ryder would probably remind her that life was all about change. The problem with him was, he was so used to change, she didn't have faith that he'd ever settle. While all she wanted to do was find a place to grow some roots again—in a home and a job that she wouldn't have to leave. With people who wouldn't leave her.

"THEY'VE FAST-TRACKED this section of the new shopping center and, if the weather co-operates, they're hoping to have it open after the first of the year." Ryder spread a set of plans on the hood of his truck and pointed to a shaded area along one side of the page. "There's a natural drainage route through here. We're laying corrugated culvert, which should take care of diverting water from the roadway and the parking lot."

Ryder's boss, Greg Draycut, a tall, wiry man with close-cropped blond hair and thick, black-framed glasses, squinted out across the newly paved lot, toward the row of stores taking shape. "The businesses going in are good. They'll want to be sure and have access. Good. Good." He bobbed his head, and shifted his gaze to the graders and back-hoes at work on the future roadway. Greg had driven up from Austin this morning to meet with Ryder. "I thought it would be useful to see how things are going," he'd said on the phone, but now he seemed agitated. Distracted.

"Is something wrong?" Ryder asked.

"No, no. It looks fine. You're doing a great job." He nodded toward the center. "Do they know yet what's going to be in these buildings?"

The future shopping plaza was still only a latticework of steel beams and concrete. Hard-hatted construction workers carried plywood, sheetrock and power tools in and out of stores in various stages of construction. "I'm not sure," Ryder said. "The usual chain stores, I guess. And, I hear some businesses are moving out here from Cedar Grove. Near the highway, they're going to put in some restaurants."

"That's good. This should be a popular place." He shoved his hands in his pockets and rocked back on his heels. "Let's make this a priority. We want to complete this section as quickly as possible."

"Of course." Ryder began rolling up the blueprints.

"Maybe we should put on extra shifts," Greg said. "Bring in some floods and work nights."

That sort of addition would run the budget for the project into the red. "What's the rush?" Ryder asked. "We're already ahead of schedule."

Greg stared at the dirt between his feet. "The legislature is really focused on slashing the budget. They're cutting everywhere," he said. "That could mean some pretty drastic cuts across the board."

"They wouldn't cut funding for a project that's already this far along."

"Don't be so sure about that. There's a faction within the statehouse that thinks we ought to concentrate on maintaining and improving the roads we have, not building brand-new ones."

Was Greg exaggerating, or were things really that bad? "I've been so busy I haven't been paying much attention to politics," he said.

"I can't get away from it." He clapped Ryder on the shoulder. "Do what you can. So far, everything looks great."

"Can I take you to lunch?" Ryder asked. "Show you some more of the town?"

"I wish I could, but I have to get back for a meeting this afternoon." He pulled his keys from the pocket of his khakis. "I'll be in touch."

He walked to his truck, head down, shoul-

ders bent; he was the picture of a man bur-
dened by responsibility. Ryder directed his
attention to the crew positioning one of the
giant culverts that would handle the runoff
from even the most torrential rains. Surely
Greg was exaggerating the threat that any
of this would be stopped. They'd already
started pouring concrete. They still had
miles of roadway to go, but it didn't make
sense to abandon things once they'd begun.

"Hey, Ryder!"

He turned and saw Kelly and Christa
striding toward him across the new parking lot.

"What are you two doing out here?" he
asked, as they neared his truck.

"We came to take a look at the new location of the Cedar Grove Salon." Kelly was
smiling from one ear to the other. "Mom and
I signed the lease yesterday and I couldn't
wait to show Christa."

"Hello, Ryder." Christa looked genuinely
pleased to see him. He'd meant to call her
later in the week, to see how she was doing
and feel her out on the possibility of another
date. He'd fully expected to have to employ
all his charm to get past her reservations
about him, so he'd put off the call. But now,

she looked so welcoming, he wondered if he'd imagined her earlier resistance. When her eyes met his, all the tension that had been building over his meeting with Greg dissolved, and he couldn't stop himself from grinning.

"However, there's not much to see yet," Kelly continued. "But the builders have promised we'll be able to move in after the first of the year."

"It's a super location," Christa said. "Between a cosmetics boutique and a kids' clothing shop."

"And right across from the coffee shop," Kelly said. "Handy for when I need a caffeine fix."

"Congratulations," Ryder said, forcing his gaze away from Christa to her friend.

"Mom's scared to death about the move, and frankly, I'm kind of nervous myself, but this could be a great thing for us. I'm hoping we'll pull in lots of new customers, and that our established clients will be willing to make the drive out here, with so many other stores close by."

"I'm sure you'll do well," he said. "You did a sweet job on Christa's hair."

"Thanks." They both looked at Christa

again. "She was great to let me experiment with her," Kelly said. "but I think she's happy with how it turned out."

"I am." Christa ran her fingers through the shorter, streaked locks. "It's easier to manage than I thought it would be."

"Oh, and Christa's going to help me with my plans to expand my business." Kelly clutched her friend's arm. "Show him, Christa."

"Show me what?" Ryder asked, amused.

She opened her purse and took out a slim, gold card case. She extracted a business card from the case and handed it to him.

He studied the logo of two stylized M's superimposed on each other. "Montgomery Marketing," he read.

"That's Christa," Kelly said. "Isn't it exciting? She's going to open her own marketing company, and I'm her first client."

"My only client right now." Christa leaned in for the card.

Ryder held it out of reach. "Can I keep this?" he asked.

"Oh. Sure."

"She's helping me design a whole new logo and signs," Kelly continued. "And we're going to hand out coupons for the grand opening, and run some ads in the paper. It's going to be amazing."

"Congratulations to you, too," Ryder said. "I know it's a big step."

"Thanks. I figured I didn't have anything to lose, giving it a try. I'm going to talk to the leasing agent about getting a list of other stores and contacting them about hiring me, too," Christa said. "It's scary, but exciting at the same time. And I'm going to see what I can do to help the businesses that are staying downtown. I'm hoping we can encourage people to pull off the highway and take a detour into Cedar Grove proper."

"That's an excellent idea," he said.

"Thanks." Her smile dimmed a little. "My dad isn't so keen on this plan."

"Dads worry," he said.

"I know. I want him to see that I'm serious about this. And it's a way for me to stay in Cedar Grove, which should make him and Mom happy."

"You're happy here," he said. "That's what counts."

"It's home." She shrugged. "I went away for a while, but I'm ready to stay now."

"And you're going to be here for a while, too, aren't you Ryder?" Kelly asked.

"A couple of years at least." After that… well, he'd learned not to look too far ahead into the future.

"You never know," Kelly said. "You may come to like it so much you decide to make it your home."

Lively pop music blared from Christa's purse. She reached in and pulled out her phone. "It's my dad," she said.

"His ears must have been burning," Kelly joked.

"Hello, Dad? What's wrong? You sound upset."

Christa's face paled, and Ryder put out a hand to steady her. Her eyes met his, fear and confusion mixed. "Okay," she said. "I… I'll be there as soon as I can." She dropped the phone back in her purse. Ryder held on to her arm, afraid she might crumple.

"What is it?" Kelly asked. "What's wrong?"

"My mom…" She swallowed, and took a deep breath. "An ambulance is taking her to the hospital."

CHAPTER FOURTEEN

HER FATHER'S WORDS on the telephone echoed in Christa's head like a song that refused to leave. "Your mother collapsed and I called an ambulance. They're taking her to the hospital." *Collapsed...Hospital.* Only Ryder's steadying hand on her arm kept her upright. "I've got to go to her," she said, and fumbled in her purse for her keys. If only she could fly to her mother's side.

"I'll drive you." Ryder put his hand over hers. "Where's your car?"

"It's back at the beauty shop," Kelly said. She put her arm around her friend. "She'll be all right. Your mom is tough. She's a fighter."

Christa nodded, trying desperately to breathe normally. She couldn't panic. She wouldn't lose it. Not yet. "I'm sure this is merely a precaution. But Dad sounded so upset."

"Where is he now?" Ryder asked. "Do we need to go out to the ranch and get him?"

"He's following the ambulance." She turned to Kelly. "Take me back to my car."

"We'll go in my truck." Ryder took her hand.

"He's right, Christa," Kelly said. "You shouldn't try to drive yourself. What if you had an accident?"

She wanted to protest that she was fine; she could do this. But her hands shook and she had trouble focusing her vision. Obviously, she was in no condition to drive. She looked into Ryder's eyes, drawing on the strength she found there. "What about your job here?"

"I can leave, no problem." He put his arm around her. "I want to do this."

She leaned against him, resisting the urge to bury her head in his shoulder and weep. After so many weeks of worry, this was too much. But she had to stay strong, for her mom. "Thanks," she said. "But let's hurry."

He pulled out his keys. "We'll leave now. Do you know what hospital?"

"Park Haven. On the south side of the city."

He helped her into the truck and made

sure she was buckled in before he raced around to the driver's side. As they pulled away, Kelly waved, a worried look on her face.

Christa closed her eyes and sent up a silent prayer that her mother and her father would be okay. "Now I really wish the highway was complete, so we could get there faster," she said.

"By the time we get there, maybe she'll have seen the doctor and we'll know something more," he said.

"She was doing great over the weekend," Christa said. "My dad barbecued steaks Sunday afternoon and we were kidding her about how much she ate. Then she had her regular chemo appointment yesterday and that seemed to go okay."

"Maybe this was a reaction to one of the drugs they gave her. Something they can quickly correct."

His words filled her with hope. "Do you think it could be something like that? Something so simple?"

"I'm no doctor, but doesn't that kind of thing happen all the time?"

She collapsed back against the seat once more. "I hope that's all it is. I mean…I know she's really sick. She has cancer." Just saying the word was hard. "But I never let myself think about that. We say things like 'when your treatment is over' or 'when you're well again'. It's too frightening to think anything else."

"That's how you should think of it," he said. "Cancer doesn't mean she's going to die. A lot of treatments these days work."

But they all knew of people for whom treatment didn't work. She bit her lip and blinked against the stinging in her eyes.

"What does her doctor say?" Ryder asked.

"I don't *know* what her doctor says!" She took a deep breath, regaining control of her tattered emotions. "I'm sorry. I didn't mean to snap at you. I'm just frustrated my parents won't tell me anything. Or they only tell me things they want me to hear."

"They're trying to protect you."

"But I don't need them to protect me. I need them to be honest with me. I'm a grown woman. I won't crumble at bad news."

"It's hard when our parents can't see us as adults."

Something in his voice made her more alert. "Do your parents treat you like a child, still?"

"Sometimes." He smiled. "My mother always tells me I'm not eating right, and my dad wants to give me advice and money."

She laughed—a sound that was part relief, part sympathy. "My dad does the same thing. He's certain that because I'm unemployed, I must be nearly destitute. Although, I suppose living at home with them again doesn't do anything to make me seem less dependent. So I try not to argue with them."

"That's what I do—nod and thank them and then do pretty much what I want. I tell myself that one day I'll say the same things to my kids. It's how parenting goes."

She wondered what kind of dad Ryder would be. Calm, she thought. Protective, but considerate. The same way he was with her. Her heart gave a little flutter, like something lovely waking up.

"It won't be too long now," he said. They were on the highway leading into the city. She checked the speedometer; he was doing eighty miles an hour, but traffic was light and the speed didn't feel reckless.

"Are you sure it will be all right, your disappearing in the middle of a workday like this?" she asked.

"I'll call my assistant and my boss once we're at the hospital," he said.

"Thank you. I'm glad I don't have to do this by myself."

"I'm sure if I hadn't been there, Kelly would have gone with you."

"She would have. But I'm glad it's you with me now."

He reached over and squeezed her hand. "I'm glad I could be with you, too."

She held on to him, his grip so reassuring and firm.

"I think that's the hospital, up on the left." He put on his blinker to exit the highway. Christa released his hand and wrapped her arms around her shoulders. As soon as he stopped the truck, she wanted to leap out, run into the building and demand to know what they had done with her mother.

But she restrained herself and settled for walking briskly toward the entrance, Ryder close behind her.

This was a different hospital from the one where her mother had had her surgery, and was disorienting, with many corridors branching off from the main lobby. "This way." Ryder pointed toward a small information desk set in a back corner.

"I'm looking for Adele Montgomery," Christa said, as soon as they were in earshot of the woman behind the desk.

The woman's fingers clicked on the keyboard. She shook her head. "I'm sorry, I don't see a patient by that name."

"She was brought here by ambulance just a short while ago," Ryder said.

"Oh, then you'll want to go to the emergency department." The woman pointed. "Down that hall on your left, through the double doors, then onto the second set of doors. Ask at the triage desk there."

Their footsteps echoed on the tile floors as they hurried through the corridors. Everything smelled faintly of rubbing alcohol and floor polish—antiseptic and impersonal. At the emergency department, Christa waited impatiently for the woman behind the glass partition to look up. "May I help you?" the woman finally asked.

"My mother, Adele Montgomery, has been brought here by ambulance."

"Let me check." She consulted her computer and nodded. "Mrs. Montgomery was transferred to the MICU. Third floor."

Christa turned and raced out of the department, back toward the elevator. "We're certainly getting our exercise, running all over this place," she said, as she punched the up button. She glanced over her shoulder at Ryder. "Thanks again for staying with me. You don't have to if you need to get back to work. I can get a ride home with my dad."

"I'll stay until I make sure you're okay. And I want to find out how your mother is doing, too."

"Thanks."

He took her hand and squeezed it, and she fought the urge to lean into him. If she did so, it would be too easy to stay there, head on his shoulders, his arms around her. She wouldn't want to move for hours, and she didn't have the luxury of relaxing just now.

A sign on the third floor pointed the way to the Medical Intensive Care Unit. Yet another woman at a desk guarded the entrance. "My mother was just admitted here," Christa said. "Adele Montgomery."

"Yes. She's in room five."

"Thank you." Christa started toward the door.

"Wait a minute," the woman called. "Who is he?" She pointed to Ryder.

He opened his mouth to answer, but Christa spoke first. "He's my husband."

She grabbed Ryder's arm. "Come on, honey. Let's go see Mom."

Once they were through the double doors, she leaned close and whispered, "I hope you don't mind. They probably wouldn't have let you in if you told them you were a friend."

"I would have understood if I needed to wait outside."

"I'd rather have you in here with me."

He put his arm around her. "Then that's where I want to be."

She located room five halfway around the circle of rooms. Steeling herself for the worst, she knocked gently on the partially open door.

"Come in," her father said.

"Hello, Christa. And Ryder, how nice to see you." Mom greeted them as if she was welcoming guests in for a glass of iced tea. She sat up in bed, eating from a bowl of soup. Only the various tubes and monitors attached to her—and the blue hospital gown—gave a clue that anything was wrong.

"Mom! You look great," Christa said.

"I don't know about that." She smoothed the hospital gown. "This was all a lot of fuss over nothing."

"She needed a transfusion." Dad stood and shook hands with Ryder, then gave Christa a quick hug.

"The chemotherapy drugs are working a little too well," Mom said. "They killed off a few too many red blood cells along with the cancer."

"That doesn't sound good." Christa perched on the edge of a chair beside her mother's hospital bed.

"They can pump me full of new blood," Mom said. "The good news is they're killing the cancer."

"That's what they're supposed to do, right?" Christa said.

"The new blood tests show the cancer marker levels are dropping," Mom said. She sounded almost giddy.

"Mom, that's fantastic news." Christa jumped up and hugged her. The tears she'd been holding back all afternoon finally overflowed. "That's the best news I've heard in weeks."

"There's nothing to cry about." Mom patted her shoulder. "They're giving me some medicine to help with the anemia. I can probably go home tomorrow."

"That is good news," Ryder said.

"Thanks for taking off work to bring Christa here," Dad said.

"I hate that you went to so much trouble." Mom pushed the empty soup bowl aside and lay back against the pillows. "I'm going to be fine."

"Yes, you are." Dad moved to her side and took her hand. "I hope you never need to be in the hospital again, but if you do, it won't take over an hour to get you there."

"That's right," Christa said. "Once the new highway is in—"

"I'm not talking about the new highway," Dad said. "Your mother and I are going to be moving closer to the city."

Christa blinked, sure she hadn't heard him right. "But the ranch…"

"We're selling the ranch to the state for the new highway project. Ryder and I have talked about it for a while now, and your mother and I agree it's the right thing to do."

She stared at Ryder. "You never mentioned this."

He looked uncomfortable—like a guilty man caught in a lie. "I thought your parents should be the ones to tell you. And nothing was decided for sure." He sounded so calm, so untouched by the fact that she was devastated by this news.

"It's decided now," Dad said. "Ryder, you bring the paperwork by tomorrow and I'll sign it."

"Daddy, you should think about this more," Christa said. "The ranch has been in your family for years."

"I've had months to think about it and I know what I want to do." He clenched his jaw in a stubborn line.

"We were considering this even before I got sick," Mom said. "The money the state will pay will give us a secure retirement, and we'll have money and time to travel and do other things." She smiled. "We know you're not interested in raising cows and hay. And our neighbors and friends will get a lot more benefit from the new highway than from another piece of property sitting vacant."

Christa sat back in the chair, reeling. When she closed her eyes, she had a vision of a swath of concrete cutting through her childhood home. The fields where she'd ridden horses, her grandparents' house—all paved over.

She opened her eyes to find her parents

and Ryder staring at her. "I can't believe you'd do this," she said.

"That's one reason I didn't tell you before." Dad said. "I knew you'd be upset."

"We know you need a little time to get used to the idea." Her mom's voice was soft and low. "But it's for the best. Your father and I are happy about the decision, we hope you'll be happy for us."

"I'll never be happy about this." She stood and faced Ryder. "And I can't believe you would do this to me." Blinded by tears, she raced from the room and out of the MICU. Bad enough that she was losing her home—but the man who was taking it from her was the one man she'd come to believe she could trust.

CHRISTA RAN BLINDLY until she reached the parking lot, then common sense returned. She couldn't get back to Cedar Grove without a car. Why hadn't she come to the hospital alone instead of letting Ryder drive her?

She knew why—because he'd been there, the big, strong man, happy to take charge.

But taking charge apparently also meant that he decided what she did or didn't need to know. All those times they'd been together, on and off the ranch, and he'd never even mentioned the possibility that she might lose her home soon. Maybe places didn't mean much to a nomad like him, but he had to have known what her family's ranch meant to her.

She moved around the corner from the hospital's main entrance, into a shadowed alcove, and pulled out her phone. Scrolling through her contacts, she found the number she needed and punched it in. A few moments later, a familiar voice answered. "Hello, Kelly? This is Christa. I need a really big favor."

"Sure. How's your mom?"

"She's doing great. She needed a transfusion, but she should get to come home tomorrow. The good news is the chemo seems to be working. The numbers for the cancer markers in her blood are dropping."

"Oh, that's wonderful!"

"Yeah, it is." At least one positive thing had happened today. She needed to cling to that bit of good news in the midst of her loss. But why couldn't she have her mom well and her home intact? If Ryder hadn't come to town—if he hadn't visited her parents and charmed them into selling out—her home would be safe, and her parents would be happy there.

"What's the favor?" Kelly asked.

The double doors leading into the main lobby slid open and Ryder stepped out. His expression was grim as he scanned the parking lot. Christa shrank into the shadows and lowered her voice. "Can you come pick me up at the hospital in Dallas? I need a ride home."

"What about Ryder? Did he leave already?"

"I'm not speaking to Ryder." As she watched, the man in question turned and went back into the hospital.

"Christa! What happened?"

"I'll tell you when you get here. Can you come?"

"Sure. I was about to close up the shop early. Where exactly are you?"

Christa gave her directions to the hospital. "There's a coffee shop on the ground floor, near the main entrance. I'll wait there."

"I'll be there as soon as I can. And you have all the way home to tell me what's going on."

Christa returned the phone to her purse. No more sign of Ryder. She went back inside the building and headed for the coffee shop. He'd probably already checked there, so she should be safe enough.

She ordered a cup of tea and settled at a table in a quiet corner. She tried reading from a novel she'd downloaded to her phone, but thinking about anything but how her whole life had been turned upside down—again—was almost impossible. Still, brooding wouldn't do any good, and if she thought about things too much she might break down and cry—something she didn't want to do in public. So she forced her attention to the book.

She was reading a page for the third time when the chair across from her scraped back. "How do you intend to get home if you don't let me take you?" Ryder asked.

She glared up at him. Did he have to look so imposing, looming over her table like that? Well, he wasn't going to intimidate her. "Kelly is coming to get me."

"She didn't have to drive out here. I would have taken you."

"I don't want to see you. And I definitely don't want to talk to you."

She shoved back her chair and started to stand, but he motioned for her to sit again.

"You can't keep running away," he said. "I'll just come after you again. I can be very determined when I have to."

"So can I." But she sat. After all, her only alternative was to wait in the parking lot, and he'd probably follow her there, too.

He lowered himself into the chair across from her and rested his forearms on the table. "I understand you're upset with me," he said. "But I promised your father I wouldn't say anything to anyone until he made his decision."

"I'm not *anyone*."

"I didn't like keeping this from you, but after you came home, Bud expressly asked me not to say anything to you. I tried to convince him to talk to you himself, but he said he wasn't ready. He didn't want to upset you when he hadn't made up his mind yet."

That explained why her father seemed to know Ryder so well; they'd obviously spent a lot of time talking. "You should have warned me somehow," she said. "You know how much the ranch means to me."

"Your memories won't go away just because the ranch isn't there for you to come back to," he said.

"Oh, that is such an infuriating, insensitive thing to say." As if some trite platitude could switch off her feelings. "Just because you've never had a real home that meant something to you doesn't mean that my feelings aren't real and deep and important."

He drew back, his eyes reflecting what might have been real hurt. "I never said that."

"You didn't have to. It's all there in your attitude. You never let yourself get attached to anything—or anyone. So you think if everyone else was like you, life would be so much easier. Well, it might be easier, but it wouldn't be the kind of life I'd want to live."

She jumped up and shoved past him, brushing against his shoulder as she did so. It was like brushing past a brick wall. An apt comparison, since he was just as cold and unfeeling as a wall. So what if he'd promised her father not to tell her about his plans for the ranch? His feelings for her should have outweighed his loyalty to her father.

That was her biggest mistake, of course— thinking he had feelings for her.

Thankfully, Ryder didn't follow her outside. She was waiting on a bench in front of the hospital, shaded from the hot afternoon sun, when Kelly pulled up a half hour later.

"I thought you were going to be in the coffee shop," Kelly said.

"I changed my mind." She climbed into the passenger seat. "Thanks for coming to get me. You're a true friend."

"I'm a true friend who wants the scoop on what's going on with you and Ryder. A few hours ago, you two were getting along great."

Christa fastened her seat belt. "I found out he's been deceiving me. He pretended to care about me, but his actions prove he didn't care at all."

"Ouch! That's harsh." Kelly exited the hospital parking lot and headed toward the freeway. "What did he do?"

"He knew my dad was considering selling the Rocking M for the highway project and he never told me."

"Wait—your dad is selling the ranch?"

"Yes. He announced it this afternoon, right after we got to the hospital. Ryder had known all along, and he never said a word to me."

"That's bad," Kelly agreed. "But your dad never even hinted to you before today?"

"No. And every time I tried to ask him about anything going on at the ranch, he changed the subject." Her voice cracked and she blinked, her vision blurry from the tears she couldn't hold back any longer.

"There are tissues in the center console."

Christa found one and wiped her eyes and blew her nose. "Dad's not at the top of my list of favorite people right now, either," she said.

"That was a pretty big bombshell to drop." Kelly signaled and slid the car into the left lane. "What did he say, exactly?"

"That he was selling the ranch to the state and he and Mom are going to move closer to the city."

"Did he say why he decided to sell?"

"They want to be closer to the city for Mom's treatments, and they want the money from the sale for their retirement and to travel. Honestly, I've never heard either of them mention those things before. I thought they'd be happy staying on the ranch forever." Sure, maybe they'd take a vacation every now and then, but couldn't they do that and keep the ranch?

"Wow," Kelly said.

"Wow is right. I'd barely gotten over the shock of Mom being hospitalized and he drops that stunner."

"I'm sorry," Kelly said. "I can't imagine how awful you must feel."

"Thanks." She dabbed at her nose with the tissue again. "It's not just losing the ranch that hurts. It's knowing that the people I love most didn't trust me enough to include me when it came time to decide the fate of the only home I've ever known."

Kelly sped up and merged with freeway traffic. "Not to defend them shutting you out," she said. "But maybe your parents thought since the ranch belongs to them, it was their decision to make."

She swallowed another knot of tears and nodded. "You're right. Maybe that's another reason this hurts so much. Even though I'll always think of the ranch as my home, it really isn't mine."

"I'm sorry, hon," Kelly said. "This is terrible."

"Thanks for listening to me vent." She wadded up the tissue and stuffed it into her purse. "Back in that hospital room, it felt as if no one was on my side."

"What about Ryder?"

"He definitely wasn't siding with me." She'd never forget the guilty look on his face. "I'm sure he's thrilled he was able to talk my dad into selling out for his precious highway project. And thanks to my dad's insistence on secrecy, he was able to do it without any interference from me."

"If your dad decided to sell, it wasn't because Ryder strong-armed him," Kelly said. "Ryder's not like that."

"I know." She sighed, weariness winning out over the resentment she'd been holding onto. "I hate what he did to me, and I think he's insensitive and emotionally constipated, but he's not a crook or a liar."

"Emotionally constipated?" Kelly sounded as if she was trying not to laugh.

"You know—emotionally blocked. Keeping things inside. Not letting himself feel."

"Christa, you just described most of the men I know!"

"Ryder is worse. Because his family moved so much as a kid, he learned to never let himself warm to places or people."

"It sounds like you've gotten to know him pretty well."

"How well can you know a guy who thinks never getting involved is a good way to live?"

"Do you love him?"

The question startled her. She turned toward her friend. "Haven't you been paying attention?" she asked. "Ryder Oakes doesn't fall in love. That would mean getting close to someone. Being vulnerable."

"I'm not talking about Ryder's feelings. I want to know about you. Are *you* in love with Ryder?"

A physical pain gripped her as she thought of Ryder's arm around her shoulder, supporting and comforting her as she entered the MICU. She'd been expecting bad news, wondering how she'd bear up to the pain of seeing her mother helpless and sick, and his presence had given her strength. When the worst she could imagine had happened, Ryder had been the one person she had wanted to be with. Was that love?

"I think I could have fallen in love with him," she said. "Very easily."

"Then I hope things aren't as bad as they seem right now," Kelly said. "I hope you get another chance."

Christa sighed. What good was a second chance if Ryder wouldn't—or couldn't—change? She needed things from him that he couldn't give. "Right now, I have to concentrate on finding a job and a new place to live," she said.

"I thought your new marketing business was your job."

"A new business takes time to start bringing in income. I've got to start earning a paycheck right away if I'm going to pay rent. I doubt my parents plan on me moving with them."

"How long do you have before you have to move?"

"I don't know, but my parents talked as if they've had this planned for a while." Her throat tightened, pinching off the words. "For all I know, they've got a new home all picked out."

"I'd offer to let you move in with us, but there's nowhere for you to sleep."

Kelly and her mom shared a two-bedroom bungalow near the beauty salon. After her father had died, Kelly had moved back into her old room and the arrangement had worked out so well she had stayed on.

"Thanks," Christa said. "But I'll find a place." After all, she was twenty-six years old. Maybe she should quit dreaming and get on with her life. Maybe this latest setback was the universe's way of telling her that she really couldn't go home again.

CHAPTER FIFTEEN

IF ANYONE HAD asked Ryder to describe himself with one word, he might have chosen "dependable" or "easygoing." He was a man who faced every challenge with a level head, and completed every task without complaining. He could admit now, if only to himself, that he was so famously even tempered because he'd never really been tested by true crisis. For almost thirty years, he'd rocked along like a boat in calm waters, never really affected by storms around him.

Christa would probably say this was because he'd perfected the art of never getting involved. If you didn't let yourself get emotionally invested in anything, a bad turn of events didn't hurt you.

Except something was different now. Holding Christa as she struggled to cope with news of her mother's sudden hospitalization, he would have moved heaven and earth to make things right for her. The pain

on her face when she'd learned of the loss of
her home had made him want to lash out and
hit someone—maybe even Bud, who com-
pounded the hurt by not allowing Ryder to
tell what he knew about Bud's plans. Though
Ryder never could have gone back on his
word to his friend, he didn't blame Christa
for hating what he'd done. In her time of
greatest need, when she'd wanted him to be
a true friend, he hadn't been able to fulfill
that role.

She hadn't spoken to him since he'd confronted her in the hotel coffee shop, and he
didn't trust himself to go to her. Not yet.
His emotions were such a turmoil of hurt
and rage and desperation, he couldn't predict whether he'd scold her or beg her to
forgive him.

If this was what being in love did to a
man, he'd been smart not to venture into this
territory before. He threw himself into his
work, grateful for the distraction that would
keep him from examining his feelings for
Christa too closely. Maybe, with time, he'd
find his old even keel again.

But even work didn't offer the solace it
once had. Greg had ordered 'round-the-clock
crews on the highway, which meant Ryder

spent long hours on the job site, watching the pavement inch forward, all while enduring Greg's increasingly agitated phone calls about goings on in the state legislature. "They're going to come after us, I know," he said, as if he was predicting an attack by zombies, instead of legislation from a bunch of politicians.

So when his phone rang late one afternoon as he stood by his truck reviewing a line of concrete trucks waiting to fill forms crews had spent the previous night and morning building, Ryder almost didn't answer his phone. He wasn't in the mood to try to talk Greg off yet another ledge.

But a glance at the phone showed the number wasn't Greg's. Ryder brought the cell to his ear. "Dad? Is everything okay?"

"You act like the only time I call you is when something's wrong."

This wasn't far from the truth, but Ryder knew better than to argue. "How are you doing?" he asked.

"Very well. I'm in a terrific town house just off base, and I'm working with old friends. It's invigorating being so close to the policymakers and movers and shakers."

He chuckled. "I guess *I'm* one of those movers and shakers now."

"That's great, Dad."

"I've got some time off coming next week and I thought I'd fly down to Dallas, rent a car and drive out to see you."

"Oh, uh—" He wanted to say that now was not the best time. Not that he and Dad didn't get along, but the man couldn't stop being a father—or a colonel. Giving orders was as natural to him as breathing, even when the person he was ordering around was his son.

"How long has it been? Three years or so? Too long, in any case. I'm really anxious to see you."

"Sure, Dad. I look forward to seeing you, too."

"I've been looking at flights and I can be there Monday. Don't worry about putting me up at your place. I'll get a hotel room."

"Cedar Grove doesn't have a hotel or motel, Dad. But it's okay. I've got a spare bedroom." The futon stored there wasn't the most attractive in the world, but his dad probably wouldn't care.

"I'll text you my exact schedule when I have it."

They said good-bye and Ryder hung up, feeling as if he'd just been run over by one of his own road machines. What would Dad think of sleepy Cedar Grove? Ryder would take him to dinner at the Blue Bell and the Burger Barn, maybe spend a day fishing at the place Paul had shown him. They could head into Dallas for a day—though when Ryder would manage the time to do all this was anyone's guess. He might have to turn his dad loose on the town. Maybe Paul could help him find ways to entertain his father while he was here.

His phone rang again and he stifled a groan. "Hello, Mom," he said, forcing a cheer into his voice that he didn't feel.

"Your father tells me he's coming to Dallas. He says he's coming to see you, but he asked me to dinner."

"He is coming to see me. Are you going to have dinner with him?"

"I told him I'd think about it. Do you think I should?"

Ryder blinked. It wasn't like his mother to sound so indecisive. "That's up to you, Mom."

"I was married to the man thirty-five years. I suppose dinner wouldn't hurt."

"Do what you want, Mom."

"Maybe you could come and have dinner with us."

Ryder imagined sitting between his divorced parents while they made awkward conversation. "No. This is between you and Dad."

"I just thought the three of us…"

"I have to get back to work, Mom. You do what you think is right. Everything will be fine."

He ended the call and stared at the phone. He wanted to call Christa, to ask for advice on dealing with his dad, and laugh with her at the awkwardness of parents who suddenly turned to him for advice. Talking with her always sorted out his thoughts and helped him feel better.

But that wasn't an option right now. Maybe it never would be again. The thought sent a dull, throbbing pain up through his chest.

He pocketed the phone and pushed the pain away. He needed to buy sheets for the futon. The way to cope with all these changes was to not think of them. Do one thing at a time and eventually time passed and you woke up on the other side of whatever had hurt you, whether it was a move away from friends and home, your parents' divorce, or the loss of the one woman you might have loved.

"NO OPENINGS AT ALL? Do you know anyone else who might be hiring? Oh, all right. Well, thank you for your time." Christa disconnected the call and laid her phone beside her, then checked off another name on the list on the legal pad in front of her. She had spent the morning calling everyone she knew who was working in her field, asking about leads for jobs. So far she'd come up with a big, fat zero.

She had one more name she could call, though she didn't hold out much hope he'd be able to help her. As she'd predicted, she'd never received a call back from the marketing firm she'd interviewed with in Dallas, and Chad Bremer had never phoned to ask her out, either. But she still had his card, and the worst that could happen now was that he, like everyone else she'd spoken with this morning, wouldn't be able to help her. She had nothing to lose. She picked up the phone.

He answered on the third ring. "Hello?"

"Hello, Chad? This is Christa Montgomery. I interviewed with you a couple of weeks ago."

"Christa! Hey, good to hear from you."

"Have you filled the position I interviewed for?"

"Oh, yeah, sorry. We had so many good applicants and…"

"It's okay. I just wondered if you knew anyone else who might be hiring."

"No, I sure don't. But if I hear of anything, I'll be sure to let you know. How are you doing?"

He sounded genuinely concerned. "I'm doing okay. I was all set to start my own company, specializing in small business, and then some things came up and I decided I really needed to find a job with someone else."

"That's too bad. Sounds like you found a good niche to fill. We occasionally get calls from people whose projects are too small to warrant the fees we have to charge. I could have steered them to you."

"Maybe it will happen someday. For now, I'm calling everyone I know to put out the word I'm still looking."

"I'll keep my ears open for you."

"Thanks. How are you doing?"

"Great, actually. I just got engaged."

"Congratulations." Maybe she'd misread his previous interest in her.

"It's the funniest thing. The day after you interviewed with us, in fact, I had to go to a cousin's wedding out in Weatherford. I ran into the woman I'd dated all through college and it was as if we'd never been apart."

"I guess she was the one for you all along."

"To be honest, I don't think I ever really stopped loving her, but seeing her again after some time apart made me realize how truly special she is."

"That's great, Chad." She didn't even know this woman and she felt a small stab of jealousy. How wonderful it would be to look across the table at a man and know that he was the one you wanted to spend the rest of your life with.

"I'll be in touch if I hear of any job openings," he said. "And who knows—I may send you a small business client or two, just in case you change your mind about striking out on your own."

"Thanks, Chad."

She disconnected the call and made a note on her pad to send him a card. Would she ever want to get back together with any of the guys she'd dated in college? She shook her head. She'd never been serious about any of them; she'd never felt that special connection that made her want them to be a permanent part of her life.

The sudden voice warbling the familiar melody about life going on was a clear, high soprano. One Christa knew well from years of hearing it render children's songs, pop songs, church hymns and country ballads. But she hadn't heard it in so long it startled her now.

The song continued, and after a moment, Christa rose and followed it into the kitchen, where she found her mother perched on a step stool, pulling seldom-used soup tureens and casserole dishes off the top shelf of the cabinets. "Oh, hello, Christa. I thought I'd go ahead and pack up some of the dishes we don't use much. There's so much to do before we move."

Christa accepted the tureen Mom handed her. "I haven't heard you singing in a while," she said.

"I guess I didn't think I had much to sing about, but the doctor's report was so good, and I have the move to look forward to."

"You're looking forward to leaving the ranch?"

Mom climbed down from the ladder and went to the sink, where she began wiping down the outsides of the dishes she'd hauled down from the shelf. "I've loved living here, and I'm sure I'll miss it sometimes, but I'm looking forward to the change, too. We're thinking we'll find something a little smaller, but with a yard so I can still have flowers. All new appliances, within walking distance of stores and a library...I certainly won't miss having to drive miles to buy groceries or do our banking."

"I just never pictured you and Dad as city people."

"We haven't been, but having cancer has made me think about my priorities differently. There are a lot of things I've wanted to do with my life, and I want to do some of them now."

"What kinds of things?" She pulled a towel from the drawer and began drying the dishes her mother had washed.

"Travel, for one thing. That's hard to do when you have a bunch of cows and horses to look after. When I finish my treatments, your father and I are going to go to France.

I've always wanted to see Paris." She smiled, a dreamy look on her face.

"The hands would look after the place while you travel."

"You know your father—he never trusts anyone to do a job right except himself. And he'd never admit it, but he's getting too old to work so hard. After Paris, we're going to go to Vietnam, to visit where his mother is from. We might even find some family there he's never met. I know he's looking forward to that."

Christa tried to adjust to this picture of her parents as world travelers. How many other secret dreams did they have that she'd never realized? She'd never thought of them as anything other than her parents, static and unchanging. Silly, really. Of course they were active, interesting people with aspects of their lives that had nothing to do with her.

"I hope you have a wonderful time," she said. "I just wish you didn't have to sell the ranch to do it."

Mom dried her hands and turned to Christa. "I know this is hard for you, but you'll get used to the idea. After all, it isn't as if you were ever going to live here again.

You'll make a life for yourself somewhere else, and you can visit us wherever we are."

But that place wouldn't be the home where every corner was familiar, and every room held all the memories of her growing up. "Why didn't you warn me this was coming? If you'd mentioned it to me sooner, your final decision wouldn't have been such a complete surprise," she said.

Mom's smile faded. "I did tell your father he should talk to you about it. But you know your father, once he has an idea in his head. He didn't want to upset you."

He had upset her now; she'd been avoiding him since her mother's return from the hospital. "Finding out at the hospital, in front of Ryder, was such a shock," she said.

Mom patted her arm. "Have you spoken to Ryder since then?" she asked. "I know you were angry with him, but none of this is his fault. He never pressured us to sell, and he respected your father's wishes and didn't tell anyone we were considering the deal."

"No, I haven't spoken to him." She wasn't ready to forgive him for the way he'd hurt her.

"I know you're upset, but I think you're being too hard on him. He gave your father his word. You have to respect a man who keeps his word."

"I can respect him, but that doesn't mean I want to see him again."

Mom fixed Christa with the same sad, disappointed look she had used when she caught Christa hiding her uneaten peas in a flowerpot, or when Christa lied about breaking her grandmother's favorite vase. That look hurt worse than any harsh words. "You can't blame Ryder for a decision your father and I made. You can be angry with us if you like, but I won't let you take your feelings out on him when he did nothing wrong."

Maybe it wasn't right or even logical that she was angry with Ryder, but her feelings were real, and she couldn't do anything to change them—at least not until more time had passed. "If I see him, I promise to be civil," she said.

Mom's expression didn't change. "I was hoping the two of you would hit it off," she said. "You seem so well suited, and it would be nice to see you settled."

"I'd like to be settled, too, Mom, but maybe I should start with a job and a place to live. I have plenty of time in my life for romance." She'd keep repeating these words until she could believe them.

Mom grabbed a sheet of newspaper and began wrapping the dishes they'd washed and dried. "I think Ryder needs someone in his life."

"What makes you think that?"

"Call it a mother's intuition. The first time I met him, I thought, here is a young man who's searching for something."

Christa shook her head. "I don't think so, Mom. I think Ryder is happy with the life he has."

"No. Wandering from town to town like that, with no permanent home, is not what he truly wants. He may think he's doing well, but that's only because he's never known anything different. Given the right woman, I think he'd be happy to settle down."

"Seems like a big risk for the woman— maybe he'd be happy for a few months or a few years, then the next thing she knew, he'd be restless and wanting to uproot her and any children they had."

"Every marriage is a risk, if you look at it that way," Mom said. "But with the right two people, the gamble always pays off."

Tinny music from the other room signaled

a call coming in to Christa's phone. "I'd better get that," she said, and raced to answer it.

"Hello?"

"Hey, Christa! It's Paul, here at the bank."

"Oh, hi, Paul." Christa leaned against the dining table she'd been using as her desk. "What's up?"

"I was hoping I could hire you to do some marketing work for the bank. We want to put together some ads that play up our long history in the area. You know—'your grandfather trusted us and you can trust us, too' kind of thing. Something we can roll out in conjunction with opening our new branch out on the highway next spring."

"Um, I guess I could do that." Already, she could picture ads with black-and-white images of ranchers and cowboys, juxtaposed with color photos of modern businesses. "Did Kelly or Didi put you up to this?"

"They might have mentioned that you were taking some private clients. But what are friends for? So will you do it?"

"Sure. I'll need to meet with you to discuss your ideas."

"Do you have time this afternoon?"

She glanced at the papers spread across

the table. All she had planned for the afternoon was more cold calling. "Sure."

"Let's meet at one. I'll pull out some examples of what we've done before. I'm sure you can come up with something better."

"Thanks, Paul. I really appreciate it."

"Don't thank me yet until you see how little we pay. In case you didn't know it, banks are real cheapskates."

"I'm sure we can come to some kind of agreement." She wasn't going to sell herself short, but then again, she wasn't in a position to be overly picky.

She ended the call and returned to the kitchen. "That was Paul Raybourn at the bank," she said. "He wants to hire me to do an ad campaign for them."

"Oh, that's nice, dear." Mom fit a wrapped casserole dish into a packing box. "It's good to stay busy while you look for a full-time job."

Right. Something with benefits and a regular paycheck that could cover rent. "Anyway, I'm meeting with him this afternoon."

"You should look up Ryder while you're in town. Maybe he has contacts at the state who would have a job for you."

"What kind of work would I do for the state?"

"Oh, I don't know, dear. You're very talented. I think you could do almost anything."

Great. She'd put that on her résumé—that her mother thought she could do anything. She kissed Mom's cheek. "Don't work too hard and wear yourself out. I should be back in time to help with supper."

"Take your time."

Christa went to her room to change into something more business-like. As she closed the door, she heard her mom singing again, picking up where she'd left off earlier about life going on.

CHAPTER SIXTEEN

RYDER STARED OUT at the deserted construction site, the knot of tension in his stomach growing. At this time of day, the roar of graders and dump trucks should fill the air, and at least a dozen workers should be busy extending the short stretch of pavement toward town. Instead, the only sound was the sigh of wind in the trees bordering the road. A tumbleweed bounced across the scraped ground and came to rest against the wheel of an idle grader.

The jangle of his phone broke the eerie silence. He frowned at the number on the screen, then hit the button to answer the call. "Greg, what is going on?" Ryder asked, before his boss could even speak. "Why isn't anyone working on the site?"

"I tried to reach you earlier, but you weren't answering the phone." All the usual heartiness had fled from Greg's voice, replaced by a weariness that made him sound older.

"What's going on?" Ryder began to pace.

"The project's been cancelled. The legislature slashed the department's budget by fifty percent. As of this morning, we've had to halt every new construction project in the state."

"That's insane."

"They pledged not to raise taxes and this is their way of handling it," Greg said. "There's nothing I can do about it. I'm sorry."

"So all these people suddenly don't have jobs? And what about the work we've already done?"

"I was able to find places for some of the people but, yes, most of them are unemployed now. We'll get a crew out there to load up the equipment in the next day or two. We'll leave what we've done and hope the next election cycle we can pick it up again. I'm sorry, Ryder. I wish I had better news for you. And I wish I could keep you on. You're one of the best engineers I've had the pleasure to work with. But I don't have room in the budget for you."

Ryder watched another tumbleweed crash into the first, trying to absorb this news.

He'd been so focused on the impact this would have on his workers and the townspeople that he hadn't even considered what it would mean to him. "So I'm laid off, too," he said.

"I'm sorry. I'm really over a barrel here."

"It's not your fault, Greg."

"I'll let you know if anything changes. What are you going to do?"

"Right now I have a meeting with a banker in town. I'll have to break the news to him."

"I meant where will you go from here?"

"I don't know. I can't think that far ahead yet."

Greg said something about a separation package and unemployment benefits, but Ryder didn't really hear him. He was already focused on how he was going to explain this news to the people in town he'd come to care about.

He hung up the phone and started to punch in Christa's number. The line was ringing before he came to his senses and disconnected. He was the last person she'd want to speak to right now. And he needed more time to figure out what to say to her.

Twenty minutes later, he sank into the

client chair across from Paul's desk at the bank. "You look like you've been rode hard and put up wet," Paul said. "Is all the overtime getting to you, or is something else wrong?"

"Something's wrong all right."

"Oh?" Paul leaned toward him. "What is it?"

He glanced around the bank. This time of day, business was slow; only one other customer was at the teller window. Still, he kept his voice down. "I just got a call from my boss. The legislature is cancelling this project. They're defunding it, effective immediately. There's enough to pay for the work we've already done, but that's it."

Paul's eyes widened. "You're kidding."

"I wish I was."

"That's a lot of people out of work," Paul said.

"And I'm one of them." He rubbed his hand over his face, as if he could rub away some of the numbness. One moment he'd been doing a job he loved. The next moment—it was gone.

"What are you going to do?" Paul asked.

"I have no idea." He looked around the bank again. "I hope the people around here will understand this wasn't my decision and won't blame me for this fiasco. I got their hopes up about the new highway and now it's all gone. Just an ugly scar across the land—a few miles of pavement leading nowhere."

"We should organize a protest," Paul said. "A letter writing campaign or something. The state is wasting more money than they're saving by stopping the project."

"You can try, but I don't think it will do much good. They say the money isn't there, and the politicians have made a pledge not to raise taxes, no matter the cost."

"Then I guess we won't be building that new branch." Paul crumpled a sheet of paper and tossed it into the wastebasket beside his desk. "And all these loans we've written so other businesses can relocate won't be needed either."

"This is going to hurt a lot of people," Ryder said. "I wish I could do something to help."

"Hey, it's not your fault if things have gotten screwed up," Paul said. He looked toward the door. "Uh-oh."

"What is it?" Ryder turned to see Christa walking toward them. She wore a crisp summer shift, her hair loose around her face. She hesitated only a second when she recognized Ryder, then squared her shoulders and moved forward. He felt sick to his stomach. If she'd been upset with him before, she'd have no reason to change her opinion now.

He stood to greet her. "Hello, Christa."

"Hello, Ryder." She faced Paul. "Do you really want to talk about a marketing campaign, or was that an excuse to make me apologize to Ryder?"

"Hey, I had no idea he was going to be here this afternoon." Paul held up both hands. "Honest. I really did want to hire you to plan a marketing push for us, but now…"

Paul looked at Ryder, and Christa followed suit. "Now what? What's going on? Why do you both look so guilty?"

"The state cancelled the highway project," Ryder said.

She looked stunned, and lowered herself into the second client chair. "They're stopping it right where it is?"

"That's what I was told. They're loading up the equipment to head back to Austin sometime in the next day or two."

"That's crazy," she said.

"We are talking about politicians," Paul

said. He shuffled papers on his desk. "I'm sorry, Christa, but it looks like we won't be building that new branch, so I can't use your services."

She ignored him, focused on Ryder. "What about Mom and Dad?"

"With no highway, the state doesn't need the right-of-way through their ranch. Your home is safe."

"They were counting on that money for their retirement. I was talking to Mom just this morning. She was really looking forward to a new house, and traveling..."

"I'm sorry." He had a feeling he was going to be saying those words to a lot of people over the next few days, but he would never mean them more than he did right now. He'd come into town promising good things and a bright future to everyone. Now, none of that was coming true. Fairly or unfairly, people were going to blame him.

"Ryder's losing his job, too," Paul said.

"What will you do?" she asked.

"I don't know. I haven't thought about that yet."

She nodded. "Yeah. It's hard enough to absorb the news, much less think about what comes next."

"I'll call your folks as soon as I have more details from the state, but if they have any questions in the meantime, or just want to talk, tell them to call me." He had no idea what he'd say to Bud and Adele, but he wouldn't avoid them. They had every right to be upset and he wouldn't make excuses. This was all wrong. And completely out of his control.

"I'd better get home and tell them before they hear it from someone else." She stood and started to move away, then turned back. "I'm sorry about your job, Ryder. I know that isn't easy. None of this is."

Then she was gone, hurrying out the door, into the bright sunshine.

"She didn't sound like a woman who's holding a grudge," Paul said.

"She's still in shock," Ryder said. "Give her time and she'll probably be at the head of the lynch mob."

"You don't give people around here enough credit," Paul said. "They like you and they'll know you had nothing to do with this decision."

"Then why do I feel so responsible?"

"Because you're that kind of guy." Paul

flipped his pen onto his desk and sat back in his chair. "So what's next, chief?"

"I'll stick around long enough to answer people's questions. I owe everyone that. Plus, my dad's coming to town."

"Is that good or bad?"

"I haven't seen him in a while, but he has a tendency to try to take over. He'll have a lot of advice on how I should run my life. I really don't want to hear it."

"Then you'll have to distract him."

"Right. How can I do that?"

"Take him to the Blue Bell for banana chocolate-chip waffles and put him in a sugar coma. Then send him out to Little Creek with a fishing pole and no cell coverage."

"Or I could send him to my mom in Dallas. She has a lot of experience handling him."

"That would work, too. And give you time to focus on Christa."

"What about Christa?"

"You're not going to let her walk away from you, are you?"

"Paul, I don't have a job. I can't stay in town with no work to support myself. For that matter, Christa's unemployed and she doesn't know where she's going to end up living. Neither one of us is in a good position to start or continue a relationship."

"You idiot. When times are bad, you need your friends most. You two can help each other. And one thing's for sure—if you can get through this, your relationship can survive anything."

"I never knew bankers were such romantics." He stood. "Thanks for your concern, but I think I'd better leave Christa alone. We've both got enough to deal with right now."

"So you're not going to fight for her?"

He shook his head. "I know there are some battles a man can't win."

CHRISTA HAD GOTTEN what she wanted: the highway project cancelled and her family's ranch untouched, yet she found nothing to celebrate in this sudden turn of events. Dinner that evening had the air of a funeral, her mother long-faced and red-eyed, and her father withdrawn. "I can't believe this is happening," Mom said, staring at her untouched plate of meatloaf and mashed potatoes.

"I'm going to call my representative and give him a piece of my mind." Dad stabbed at a slice of meatloaf. "The government has done some harebrained things before, but this has to be their stupidest move yet."

"All those people out of work," Mom said. "Not to mention all the other income lost. Etta Mae said they've had enough extra business at the Blue Bell from the construction workers that she was planning to finally get a new roof on her house. When Janet called to tell me the news, she said Kelly had been crying all afternoon. With no highway coming in, the people building the new shopping center cancelled all the leases."

Christa's stomach hurt at the thought of her friend in such distress. She laid aside her fork. "That's terrible," she murmured.

"Ryder's out of a job, too," Dad said. "I don't know what he's going to do."

"What is this world coming to, when capable young people like you and Ryder can't get jobs?" Mom sipped iced tea and stared, dull-eyed, at Christa.

Christa shifted in her chair. She wanted to point out that Ryder was used to dealing with change, that he'd probably bounce back with no problem and move on to a new town and a new job with scarcely a ripple in his easygoing life. But she couldn't believe that anymore, not after seeing how devastated he'd been when she'd met him this afternoon. She hadn't realized how much this job meant to him until that instant. While she had family and home and lifelong friends close by to ease the pain of her job loss, his family was scattered, most of them far away. He'd defined himself by his job; without that, he had little left to cling to.

She pushed her plate away, unable to eat. "What will you do with the ranch now?" she asked. "Will you try to sell it to a private buyer?"

"Nobody wants to buy a ranch in the middle of a drought," Dad said. "Ben Simons, on the other side of the county, has had his place for sale for two years, without a single offer."

"I'm sorry," Christa said. "I really am."

What more could she say? She didn't have the power to give her parents back their dream of a comfortable retirement and travel to places they'd always wanted to see, anymore than she was able to restore Kelly's prospects for a new and expanded salon, or return Ryder to his job. All of that was out of her control, and yet she still felt guilty. Maybe because, if someone had asked her

even a few days ago what her preferred outcome of this project would be, having it cancelled would have been at the top of her list.

When had her perspective changed?
Maybe when she'd heard her mom singing,
and seen the happiness in her eyes when she
talked of going to Paris. Maybe when she'd
stood with Kelly in that half-finished store-
front and listened to her friend describe all
the new things she was going to try to grow
her business.

Or maybe she'd changed her mind during those tense moments with Ryder, when
she'd glimpsed the vulnerable, hurting man
beneath the brave, optimistic shell. She'd
spent so much time resisting all the changes
around her, without considering how much
keeping things the same could hurt the people she loved.

"Oh, Christa!"

She looked up at Mom's pained cry.
"What is it?"

"I just realized—without the highway
project and the new shopping center, you
won't have the marketing work you were
going to do for Kelly and the bank."

"I guess not." She hadn't even considered
this. "I'll find something else." It wasn't as

if those small jobs would have been enough to keep her going for very long.

Her father said nothing, shoveling in food with the automatic movements of someone who is eating out of habit than from any real hunger. Christa and her mother left their plates untouched. At last, Dad pushed back from the table. "I'm going out to the barn to check on the horses," he said.

Christa stood and began clearing the table. She carried the stack of plates into the kitchen and was running hot water into the sink when Mom brought in the remains of the meatloaf. "Let me get the dishes," Mom said. "You go and talk to your father."

"What am I supposed to say to him?" She added soap to the water and began sliding in the dirty plates.

"He thinks you're still upset with him about the decision to sell the ranch."

"I'm not upset with him. I understand why he did it."

"He needs to hear that from you."

"All right." She dried her hands on a towel. She couldn't do anything about most of the suffering those around her were experiencing, but at least she could make things easier between her father and her.

Dusk bathed the yard between the house and the barn in a heavy gray light. Christa walked the path she'd walked a thousand times, sometimes reluctantly—when she had to muck stalls or feed and water, or any other chores that interfered with her more important childhood or teenage plans—or eagerly—heading out for a ride, or to spend time with a new or favorite horse. Ryder had been right when he said those memories would never leave her, but without this place to invoke them, they would eventually fade and be less real.

The warmth of the barn closed around her as she stepped inside, the sweet aromas of hay and horse mingling in a scent she wished she could bottle. On evenings when city crowds and city traffic frayed her nerves, she'd open the bottle and inhale this reminder of a slower, simpler pace of life. "Dad?" she called.

"Back here."

She found him leaning over the stall of his favorite horse, Peanut. He held on to one end of a withered carrot while the gelding nibbled delicately at the other. "I guess I'll hang on to him a while longer," Dad said when Christa came to stand beside him. "Bob

Lytle had agreed to buy him from me. I didn't want to sell him, but we couldn't keep him in town, and Bob's son wanted him to ride, so I knew he'd have a good home."

"I'm sorry things didn't work out," she said. "I was upset about the sale at first, but I was getting used to the idea, and I could see the good in it."

"I used to say nothing the government did would surprise me, but I've got to say I never saw this coming."

"I guess no one did." She reached over the railing and rubbed the horse's nose.

Dad fed the last of the carrot to Peanut, then brushed off his hands. "I spent my whole life being my own boss, making my own decisions," he said. "It was one of the best things about ranching, for me. I succeeded or failed based on my willingness to work hard and follow through. But it's not like that anymore. Drought, falling prices— those are all things I've dealt with before, but not for this long and on this kind of scale. Everything's changing too fast and I'm tired of fighting it."

Christa wanted to cry out in protest. She didn't want to see him this way, looking old and spent. But she pressed her lips together and let him talk. He trusted her enough to reveal himself to her this way and she wouldn't cheapen the gift by making it about her and her feelings.

"The decision to sell wasn't easy." He glanced up and met her eyes briefly. "Part of me knew I was letting you down."

"Daddy, no!" She touched his arm. "I was wrong to object—you and Mom and your future are more important than any material possessions."

"Still, this is your heritage. Your home. I didn't want to give it up. But then your mom got sick and I saw that we'd already wasted so much time trying to hold on to a way of life that doesn't really exist anymore. If selling out meant an easier life for her, and more time for us to enjoy being together, then I knew I had to do it."

"I saw how happy she was with the prospect of a new place to live and new adventures," Christa said. "I wish I knew how to give that back to her—to give it back to both of you."

He turned to gaze at the horse, which was pulling hay from the rack in its stall. "I've spent my whole life believing I was in charge," he said. "That the choices I made shaped my life, and that it was that way for everyone else, too. I'm sorry if that made me too hard on you."

"You weren't hard on me, Dad."

"I wasn't very sympathetic when you lost your job. I figured if you put in the effort to look, you'd find the work. I know now it isn't that simple."

"It's all right, Dad. I was pretty paralyzed by the loss right after it happened. I needed that kick in the pants to get going."

"I should have talked to you more about the ranch," he said. "Even though the decision was mine to make, you had a right to know. Blame it on stubborn pride; selling out felt like surrender. I didn't like the idea of you seeing me defeated."

"Oh, Daddy." She hugged him close. His arms tightened around her, as solid and strong as ever. But for the first time, she felt he took as much comfort from her embrace as she took from his.

After a while, she pulled away. "We'll get through this together," she said. "No matter what happens, that's what counts most."

He nodded and cleared his throat. "The doctors say your mom is getting better;

that's more important than any piece of land or job or anything else."

"It is." Remembering that would help her keep her perspective.

"She doesn't know it, but I'm going to take her to Paris, if I have to sell everything on the place to do it."

She swallowed past the sudden lump in her throat. "Maybe it won't come to that," she said.

"You go on back to the house." He patted her shoulder. "I'll be along in a minute."

The moon had risen by the time she emerged from the barn, an almost full ivory disc shining overhead, bathing the yard in a silver light. Christa stopped and gazed up at it, and the stars beginning to pop out all around it. She never saw stars like this in the city. When she moved back there, she'd have to make it a point to get away from town regularly, to look at the stars and count her blessings.

Back in her room, she tried to read, but had trouble focusing on her book. She needed to do something—anything—to chip away at all the problems facing those she loved. But what could she do? Mounting a marketing campaign to convince the legislature to restore funding to the highway project seemed foolish, considering how proud the politicians were of meeting their budget-cutting pledge.

She'd headed up fund-raisers before, but the idea of Cedar Grove bringing in the kind of money needed to build a highway was ludicrous.

At this point, the highway seemed a lost cause. Maybe the solution lay in finding other ways to build up the town. She'd go back to her original plan of promoting Cedar Grove as the perfect place to live and vacation.

She pulled out her laptop and scrolled through her list of job contacts. Maybe someone she'd worked with in the past had connections that would help her. One of the first names on her list was Chad Bremer. She regretted now that she hadn't made more of an effort to secure the job with his company. She'd gone into the interview with the wrong attitude and she was sure it had showed. Her dad had been right when he'd diagnosed a lack of effort as one reason she'd been unable to find a job. She'd let grief over all she'd lost hang on too long.

She turned a page to the notes she'd made

during her interview with Chad and his co-workers. All those corporate clients she'd been reluctant to work with didn't seem so terrible now. She scanned the list of names familiar to almost every household—oil companies, major manufacturers and national chains. The list contained a few unfamiliar names too; she had to read the descriptions she'd jotted down to figure out what some of them did.

Her gaze fixed on one name in particular: Parsons and Miller. Her note read "private infrastructure—office parks, shopping centers, toll roads and bridges."

For a few seconds she was sure she stopped breathing. She stared at the words, zeroing in on toll roads and bridges. Then she switched to the internet and searched for the company name. The more she read, the more she was sure there was something here. Something really good.

"AH, THIS IS the life, isn't it?" Colonel Larry Oakes leaned back against a tree and looked out across the water at the red-and-white bobber floating on the surface. Heat-lakes shimmered on the dry pasture on the other side of the creek, but here in the deep shade of ancient cottonwoods the air was still and cool. "We should do this more often, son."

"Yeah, we should, Dad," Ryder said. So far, his visit with his father was going better than he'd expected. He'd debated not telling Dad about the project cancellation and Ryder's subsequent job loss, but with everyone he encountered wanting to know more about it, he'd known he wouldn't be able to keep the news a secret for long. To his surprise, his dad had been sympathetic and encouraging.

"You're smart and talented. You'll find something. Use this time to figure out what you really want to do."

What he really wanted to do right now was to sit here on this creek bank with his eyes closed, listening to the hum of cicadas in the trees and emptying his mind of the worries that had interfered with his sleep the past few nights.

"I think I could live in a place like this," Dad said. "Maybe I'll look around for a place and buy it."

"Are you thinking of leaving the military?" Ryder sat up straighter. This was definitely something new.

"Not right away. But I'm eligible for retirement now, and in a few more years it might be nice to step away from the rat race and think about what I want to do with the rest of my life. Owning a little place in the country might be the perfect thing."

Ryder had always thought of his father as a man of action, always moving, going, charging ahead. "You don't think you'd be bored?" he asked.

"I'd find things to do. Volunteer work. Hobbies. Maybe I'd ever start my own business."

"Doing what?"

"I have no idea. Anything I wanted. You can do a lot with the internet, and it's not as if Dallas is that far away."

Something about the casual manner with which he'd added this bit of information caught Ryder's attention. Was Dallas so interesting because it was the nearest big city—or because Ryder's mom—his dad's former wife—lived there? "Did you have dinner with Mom the other night?" he asked.

Dad remained focused on the bobber in the water. "We did. She looked very nice. I like her new hairstyle. She said she enjoys her teaching job."

"So you got along okay?"

Dad shifted the fishing pole from one hand to the other, then back. Finally, he looked at Ryder. "It was never about not getting along," he said. "She was tired of moving, everything always changing. I don't know why now, after all these years, she felt like that, but she did. And I didn't want to see her miserable."

"I'm sorry, Dad."

"You don't have anything to be sorry for."

Except that the two people he loved most hadn't been able to find a path to stay together after thirty-five years. Wasn't that worth mourning, just a little?

"Forget my sorry love life for a little bit and tell me about yours," Dad said. "Anybody special?"

His mind immediately conjured an image of Christa, making his chest feel heavy. "There's a woman I've been out with, but the timing is all wrong, for both of us."

"Then make it right."

"Ha. Sure, I'll get out my magic wand, watch out." He paused, hoping his dad would move on to another subject, but when he said nothing, Ryder had no choice but to go on. "We're both looking for work, not sure

where we'll live. And our personalities are
so different. It probably wouldn't work out."

"Excuses." Dad stabbed the end of the
fishing pole into the ground beside him and
twisted around to face Ryder. "Didn't I teach
you to go after what you really wanted? I
would have moved heaven and earth to be
with your mother when we met."

Ryder thought again of Christa, or rather,
of her grandparents, risking everything to
be together. That kind of courage and daring was something right out of the movies,
and just as foreign to him. "I can't make the
state pay for the highway so I can keep my
job," he said. "And I can't promise Christa
that I'll stay here forever in her hometown."

"Is that what she wants? A man who'll
never move or change?"

"She thinks that's what she wants, so it's
almost the same."

Dad shook his head and took up the fishing pole again. "Women!"

"Do you think you'll see Mom again?"

"I told her I'd stop by before I left town.
We're going to try something new—being
friends. We'll see how that works."

Ryder could be Christa's friend, but now
that she was out of reach, he realized how

much he wanted more. He just didn't know how to get what he wanted, or even where to start. Building highways was easy—he started with a survey and a plan, every step marked out. Building connections with people was a lot more difficult.

"WHAT HAS GOTTEN into you, Christa? You can hardly sit still." Kelly pressed down on Christa's shoulders, as if to seat her more firmly in the salon chair. "If you don't stop fidgeting, I'm going to cut your hair crooked."

"I'm sorry. I'll try to do better." Christa folded her hands primly in her lap and looked straight ahead into the mirror. "I'm just really excited."

"About what?" Kelly snipped away.

"I can't say yet. I might jinx it."

Kelly poked her. "Come on, tell me. I could use some good news. Ever since the state cancelled the highway project, this town has been the most depressing place on earth."

"It has to do with the highway," Christa said. "I may have found a solution to our problem."

"What?" Kelly almost dropped her scis-

sors. She recovered and stared at Christa, open-mouthed.

"I can't say anything more, but I've made some calls and I could be on to something good."

Frowning, Kelly resumed trimming Christa's hair. "Your definition of good and mine might be different. You never wanted the highway in the first place."

"I didn't. But I changed my mind."

"What changed it? Was it a certain handsome highway engineer?"

"Maybe Ryder had a little to do with it. But really, it was everyone here. My parents. You and your mom. I saw how the new highway was going to be good for all of you. Even though change is hard for me, I could see it was going to benefit everyone I loved. But I can't talk anymore about it. I said too much already."

"All right. We won't talk about the highway. So let's talk about you and Ryder. What's happening with you two?"

"Nothing's happening."

"You're not still holding a grudge about him keeping your dad's secret, are you?"

Christa sighed. "No. I'm over that. I don't like what he did, but I understand why he did it. And…and I respect him for it." She couldn't fault a man for keeping a promise.

"Then why aren't you two back together? I thought you were really falling for him."

"I was. But there's too much going on, for both of us. Life got in the way. I mean, we're two unemployed, practically homeless people. Neither of us has any business being in a relationship."

"Since when does emotion depend on how much money you have in your bank account or where you live? Because if those are criteria for a good love life, no wonder I can't get a date. I'm broke and I live with my mother."

"Maybe Ryder and I just weren't meant to be a couple." Christa shrugged. She'd worked hard not to let her pain over losing Ryder show on her face, and for the most part, she thought she'd succeeded. "One day, when the timing is right, I'll find the man for me. Someone like my grandfather, who'll move heaven and earth—."

"Girl, you have been watching too many romantic movies. Instead of waiting on a man who'll work miracles on your behalf, how about a man you'd risk anything to be with? Devotion is a two-way street, you know."

Kelly's words pinched at her. "Of course. I'm not asking for a guy who worships at my feet."

"You're not? Sure sounded like it to me." Kelly turned the chair around. "Let's get this color on, then I've got to comb out Mrs. Walker. Thank goodness my regular customers are still hanging in there with us."

"You'll be okay, Kelly. We'll all be okay."

"Keep saying that, Christa. Maybe soon I'll start to believe it."

RYDER TRANSFERRED THE last stack of T-shirts from the dresser to his suitcase, and then looked around the room for anything he'd missed. Two suitcases and a couple of boxes weren't a lot to show for three months in a town.

Always before, he'd been proud of his ability to travel light, but it seemed like a man of thirty ought to have more possessions than would fit in a pickup truck.

He moved from the bedroom to the kitchen. Emptying the refrigerator was next on his list. Not that there was much there— he'd eaten out most of the time. He pulled a trash bag from a box on the counter and opened the freezer door.

A memory flashed of his mother standing before the refrigerator in base housing in some western state—Nevada? Utah? She'd been tossing a pile of foil-wrapped leftovers into the open bag, tears running down her face. Ryder, who had been maybe ten or eleven at the time, had stared at her. "Mom, what's wrong?" he'd asked.

"Nothing." Thunk! Another frozen lump landed in the trash bag.

"Why are you crying?"

She stopped, and scrubbed at her eyes with the back of her hands. "People cry when they're sad," she said.

"Why are you sad?"

She sniffed. "Because I'm tired. I'm tired of always leaving friends. I'm tired of getting to know a place, of finally starting to feel at home, then having to leave."

"You aren't excited about going to a new place?" This was the speech Ryder's father always made—that they should all look forward to discovering a new place.

"I've seen enough new places." She turned back to the freezer. "I want to stay in a place long enough for it to feel old."

Ryder stared into the now-empty freezer. He hadn't thought of that memory for years.

Was this uneasiness he felt now because he, too, was ready to stay someplace long enough for it to feel old?

Cedar Grove might have been that place. But not now. Like his father, he had to go where the work was.

A knock on the door interrupted his thoughts. He closed the freezer and went to answer it.

"Christa!" He tamped down his elation at seeing her, and eyed her cautiously. "What can I do for you?"

"Can I come in?"

"Sure." He held the door open and she stepped into the living room. A hint of her perfume tickled his nose as she passed, stirring a deep longing. Was the longing for her, or for all the things he was leaving behind here—that sense of a deeper connection that he wanted, but could never have?

She glanced around the room, devoid now of his few photographs, books and personal items, though it still contained the furniture that had come with the place. Her gaze rested on the boxes by the door. "Are you packing to leave?"

"Without a job, I really can't stay."

"That's what I wanted to talk to you about."

"Have you found a job?" He shut the door and moved farther into the room.

"Not yet. But I've found you one—if you want it."

She looked as if she was trying very hard not to smile. He scratched his head. "I don't understand—you found me a job? Doing what?"

"Building a highway. The highway here in Cedar Grove."

"Why don't we sit down?" It felt awkward, standing in the middle of the room this way. He motioned to the sofa. She sat and he settled beside her. "Okay. Now explain yourself."

"I made some calls, and that eventually put me in touch with a company called Parsons and Miller. Have you heard of them?"

"No."

"They're a private company that specializes in constructing roads and bridges—toll roads and bridges, mostly. They fund the project, and earn the money back through tolls over a set number of years. When that time is up, they turn the roads over to the state or municipality. They're very interested in the highway project here."

He'd heard of this kind of thing—more popular in big cities, but apparently the idea was spreading. "What does this have to do with me?"

She opened her purse and took out a business card and handed it to him. "Call this man. He needs an engineer to oversee the project. I told him you might be interested."

He studied the card, though the words on it didn't really register. "You did this for me?"

"I did it for the town. Cedar Grove really wants this highway project. Even I'm starting to see the benefits of it." She leaned over and touched the back of his hand. "I'm sorry I blamed you when I found out my parents planned to sell the ranch. I was hurt and upset and I wasn't ready to listen when you tried to explain what happened. I know you couldn't break your promise to my dad."

He turned his hand over to grasp hers. "I wanted to tell you—or really, I wanted him to tell you. I knew you'd be upset. I hated seeing you hurt. I know how much your family home means to you."

She nodded. "Yes. But my parents are

really happy about the move—or they were, until the highway got cancelled and everything got put on hold. So starting up the project again helps them, too."

"You could have sat back and done nothing. The ranch would have stayed in the family and the town would have remained the same—exactly how you wanted it."

"How I used to want it." She squeezed his hand. "It's not all about me anymore."

He studied the business card again. "I never thought about working for a private company instead of the state."

"I don't know specifics, but I think they pay quite well. And you'd have a chance to complete a project you've already put so much time and effort into. You could stay in Cedar Grove."

"I'd like that."

"I'd like that, too."

His eyes met hers, trying to read the emotions in those brown depths. "Do you think we could try again, you and me?" he asked.

"I'd like that, too."

He pulled her close to kiss her. She tilted her head and brought her lips up to meet his, her arms reaching up to encircle him in a sweet embrace that confirmed what he'd known for weeks now, even if he hadn't been able to admit it to himself. "I love you, Christa," he said when their lips parted. "I should have told you before now."

"I love you, too, Ryder. It scares me to say it."

"You don't have to be scared." He tenderly smoothed the hair back from her forehead.

"I don't know if I'm strong enough for this kind of love. Love shouldn't have limits, but I don't know if I can follow you from town to town like a nomad."

"You don't have to. My nomad days are over. I'm staying right here. With you."

"You really mean that?"

"Yes. It wasn't even a tough decision to make. This feels like the place where I belong. And I think it's because of you. You showed me how to feel things I'd been afraid to feel before. I want to make my home here—and I want to make it with you. That is, if you're staying here in Cedar Grove. Or we could move to Dallas—wherever you need to be."

"I'm going to stay here," she said. "With the highway project a go again, I can help the local businesses advertise their services to commuters and new residents. And Chad

Bremer has promised to send me some clients. I think I can do this—and I have you to thank for the idea." She kissed him again.

"What about wanting a man who'd make a big, romantic gesture like your grandfather to prove his love?" he asked.

"I was being a little silly," she said. "Instead of idealizing my grandparents, I had a better example of love right in front of me, with my parents. They have the kind of equal, steady relationship I really want."

"I'll always do my best for you," Ryder said.

"I know that Ryder. And your best will always be enough for me."

"Have you told your parents the good news yet?"

"I thought maybe we could tell them together." She took his hand and pulled him toward the door. Yes, this was definitely where they belonged—hand in hand, facing whatever the future held, together.

* * * * *

REQUEST YOUR FREE BOOKS!

2 FREE INSPIRATIONAL NOVELS
PLUS 2
FREE
MYSTERY GIFTS

Love Inspired®

YES! Please send me 2 FREE Love Inspired® novels and my 2 FREE mystery gifts (gifts are worth about $10). After receiving them, if I don't wish to receive any more books, I can return the shipping statement marked "cancel." If I don't cancel, I will receive 6 brand-new novels every month and be billed just $4.74 per book in the U.S. or $5.24 per book in Canada. That's a savings of at least 21% off the cover price. It's quite a bargain! Shipping and handling is just 50¢ per book in the U.S. and 75¢ per book in Canada.* I understand that accepting the 2 free books and gifts places me under no obligation to buy anything. I can always return a shipment and cancel at any time. Even if I never buy another book, the two free books and gifts are mine to keep forever.   105/305 IDN F49N

Name _____ (PLEASE PRINT) _____

Address _____ Apt. # _____

City _____ State/Prov. _____ Zip/Postal Code _____

Signature (if under 18, a parent or guardian must sign) _____

Mail to the Harlequin® Reader Service:
IN U.S.A.: P.O. Box 1867, Buffalo, NY 14240-1867
IN CANADA: P.O. Box 609, Fort Erie, Ontario L2A 5X3

**Are you a subscriber to Love Inspired books
and want to receive the larger-print edition?
Call 1-800-873-8635 or visit www.ReaderService.com.**

* Terms and prices subject to change without notice. Prices do not include applicable taxes. Sales tax applicable in N.Y. Canadian residents will be charged applicable taxes. Offer not valid in Quebec. This offer is limited to one order per household. Not valid for current subscribers to Love Inspired books. All orders subject to credit approval. Credit or debit balances in a customer's account(s) may be offset by any other outstanding balance owed by or to the customer. Please allow 4 to 6 weeks for delivery. Offer available while quantities last.

Your Privacy—The Harlequin® Reader Service is committed to protecting your privacy. Our Privacy Policy is available online at www.ReaderService.com or upon request from the Harlequin Reader Service.
We make a portion of our mailing list available to reputable third parties that offer products we believe may interest you. If you prefer that we not exchange your name with third parties, or if you wish to clarify or modify your communication preferences, please visit us at www.ReaderService.com/consumerschoice or write to us at Harlequin Reader Service Preference Service, P.O. Box 9062, Buffalo, NY 14269. Include your complete name and address.

LIDIR13R

REQUEST YOUR FREE BOOKS!

2 FREE INSPIRATIONAL NOVELS
PLUS 2
FREE
MYSTERY GIFTS

Love Inspired.
HISTORICAL
INSPIRATIONAL HISTORICAL ROMANCE

YES! Please send me 2 FREE Love Inspired® Historical novels and my 2 FREE mystery gifts (gifts are worth about $10). After receiving them, if I don't wish to receive any more books, I can return the shipping statement marked "cancel." If I don't cancel, I will receive 4 brand-new novels every month and be billed just $4.74 per book in the U.S. or $5.24 per book in Canada. That's a savings of at least 21% off the cover price. It's quite a bargain! Shipping and handling is just 50¢ per book in the U.S. and 75¢ per book in Canada.* I understand that accepting the 2 free books and gifts places me under no obligation to buy anything. I can always return a shipment and cancel at any time. Even if I never buy another book, the two free books and gifts are mine to keep forever.

102/302 IDN F5CY

Name	(PLEASE PRINT)

Address	Apt. #

City	State/Prov.	Zip/Postal Code

Signature (if under 18, a parent or guardian must sign)

Mail to the Harlequin® Reader Service:
IN U.S.A.: P.O. Box 1867, Buffalo, NY 14240-1867
IN CANADA: P.O. Box 609, Fort Erie, Ontario L2A 5X3

Want to try two free books from another series?
Call 1-800-873-8635 or visit www.ReaderService.com.

* Terms and prices subject to change without notice. Prices do not include applicable taxes. Sales tax applicable in N.Y. Canadian residents will be charged applicable taxes. Offer not valid in Quebec. This offer is limited to one order per household. Not valid for current subscribers to Love Inspired Historical books. All orders subject to credit approval. Credit or debit balances in a customer's account(s) may be offset by any other outstanding balance owed by or to the customer. Please allow 4 to 6 weeks for delivery. Offer available while quantities last.

Your Privacy—The Harlequin® Reader Service is committed to protecting your privacy. Our Privacy Policy is available online at www.ReaderService.com or upon request from the Harlequin Reader Service.

We make a portion of our mailing list available to reputable third parties that offer products we believe may interest you. If you prefer that we not exchange your name with third parties, or if you wish to clarify or modify your communication preferences, please visit us at www.ReaderService.com/consumerschoice or write to us at Harlequin Reader Service Preference Service, P.O. Box 9062, Buffalo, NY 14269. Include your complete name and address.

LIHDIR13R